THE
HASIDIC
REBBE'S
SON

JOAN LIPINSKY COCHRAN

A Becks Ruchinsky Mystery

PERRICOT
PUBLISHING

The Hasidic Rebbe's Son
Copyright © 2021 Joan Lipinsky Cochran

This book is a work of fiction. All of the names, characters, organizations and events are either products of the author's imagination or are used fictitiously. Any resemblance to actual events or locations or persons, living or dead, is entirely coincidental.

Published by Perricot Publishing
Book cover design by PINTADO
Layout by www.formatting4U.com

All rights reserved
First printing
Print ISBN: 978-0-9998280-3-8
Digital ISBN: 978-0-999280-2-1
www.JoanLipinskyCochran.com

Printed in the United States of America

About the Author

Joan Lipinsky Cochran lives in Boca Raton, Florida, where she teaches writing and publishes food articles. Her novels and short stories have won numerous awards.

Other Books by
Joan Lipinsky Cochran

Still Missing Beulah:
Stories of Blacks and Jews in Mid-Century Miami

The Yiddish Gangster's Daughter
(A Becks Ruchinsky Mystery)

To access a Reader's Guide, go to the website

www.joanlipinskycochran.com

For Michael and David
My most treasured readers
And for those who have found the courage
to live the life they desire

1

Winter, New York

Menachem Tannenbaum slung his backpack over his shoulder and elbowed the bearded men in black hats out of his way as he raced down the stairs of Brooklyn's Kingston Avenue station. The high-pitched screech of steel on steel and the stench of urine hit him like a slap in the face as he sprinted through the turnstile toward the tracks. Chest burning, he leaped between the subway's closing doors. The car shuddered and jerked forward.

The rattle of wheel meeting track struck a percussive beat that echoed the drumming of Menachem's heart. He scanned the passengers' faces. The stranger who'd chased him was not in the car. His gaze swept the retreating platform. Not there either. He released his breath.

Though long accustomed to the stares of people who'd never seen men in the black coats and sideburns worn by Hasidic Jews, Menachem turned away from the thin Hispanic woman throwing surreptitious glances his way. He knew that, to such people, he was indistinguishable from the other black-hatted men on the train. He hoped the stranger pursuing him was equally blind. Even so, he sought the safety of obscurity and moved closer to the Hasidic men clustered at the front of the subway—a flock of crows dangling from a metal overhead bar.

Once the subway gained speed, he dropped into a bench and considered his options. He'd panicked—as usual. He should have slipped out of the deli the moment he spotted the stranger. He *thought* it was the man he'd seen with Levi two years earlier. The stranger had been thinner then and worn his black hair brushed back from his forehead like the old Italians in the neighborhood. Now his belly hung over his belt like a deflated basketball and his hair fell in a greasy tangle across his forehead.

But there was no mistaking the stranger's beady-eyed glare at Menachem in the deli. When the man rose from his chair and headed in his direction, Menachem threw a ten on the table and ran. From the pounding on the sidewalk behind him, he knew the stranger was on his tail. But the man had at least fifteen years and twenty-five pounds on Menachem and his footsteps soon faded.

Once his breathing was back to normal, Menachem's curiosity returned. What was the stranger doing in Crown Heights? This was the first time he'd seen the man since Levi's arrest two years earlier. He felt a stab of guilt at the thought of his friend. He'd visited Levi only once at the prison in upstate New York where he was sent for two years for drug trafficking. Menachem was devastated by the desperation in his best friend's eyes and didn't have the courage to return.

Levi was nothing like the easy-going young man with whom Menachem had spent countless hours studying Torah. The two had planned to attend college together after they graduated from Yeshiva High School. Then the matchmaker introduced Levi to Rivka and all he cared about was making enough money to get married.

Which is when the trouble began.

"What do you mean you're going to Amsterdam?"

Menachem asked in horror when Levi announced he was taking off after classes their junior year. "Why there?"

"I'm not leaving for good, you idiot. A man I met at shul says I can make a lot of money bringing medicine from Amsterdam into the United States."

"What kind of medicine?"

"I don't know. Medicine we don't have here. I'm not supposed to talk about it. In three trips, I'll have enough to marry Rivka and get an apartment."

Levi had an answer to every objection Menachem raised. Not that it mattered. He was so crazy about Rivka he'd do anything to marry her.

Menachem's cheeks flushed as he recalled his cowardice at running from the stranger in the deli. He should have called the police. But no, that wasn't an option. He shuddered as he considered what the man might do to his family.

Two months before Levi's arrest, Menachem had spotted his friend talking to the stranger in an alley near the yeshiva. Levi had pretended not to see Menachem. Concerned by the fear in his friend's eyes, though, Menachem had come close enough to overhear their conversation. The man was warning Levi he'd kill Rivka and Levi's parents if the young man revealed who'd sent him to Amsterdam.

A second later, Menachem stumbled over a brick in the alley and the stranger whipped around toward him. "You'd better keep your mouth shut too," he'd growled. "Ask your friend what happens to rats."

The subway jerked to a stop and the doors shot open, jolting Menachem back to the present. Two men in black hoodies brushed his knee as they left the car. He rose to join them but changed his mind. He'd be less conspicuous if he got off in Times Square with the other Hasidic men headed to jobs. He'd catch another subway there. To where, he didn't know.

Returning to his seat, Menachem saw a flash of movement on the platform. It was the stranger, his wool coat flapping as he ran toward the car. Heart racing, Menachem debated jumping off the subway and dodging the fat man. But the stranger might grab him or have an advantage chasing him in the unfamiliar neighborhood.

With seconds to act, he ran to the front of the subway and grabbed the cold metal handle of the door to the next car. It opened. He sprinted into the car and out to the platform as the door snapped shut. Glancing over his shoulder, he saw the stranger. He was inside the subway Menachem had abandoned, frantically looking around. When he spotted Menachem, he sneered and raised his hand, forming his fist and forefinger into a pistol. He jerked his hand as though firing at Menachem.

Menachem shivered as he raced across the platform and upstairs to the street. There was no question of returning home now.

2

Two Years Later, Boca Raton, Florida

Becks leaned over the staircase and called down to her son. "Is that you Gabe?" It was past midnight and the foyer below was dark. She'd been in bed reading but got up and threw on a house robe at the click of the front door. She'd moved silently to avoid awakening Daniel, her husband, who had fallen asleep hours earlier. Becks liked to stay awake to greet their son on his rare weekends home.

"I am in the kitchen with a friend," he yelled from downstairs.

A friend? She leaned farther over the stairwell, hoping for a glimpse of the visitor. Gabe *never* brought friends home. Her greatest fear when sending him off to college was that he wouldn't make friends—that students in his dorm and classes would be put off by his lack of emotion and strange way of speaking. In the year and a half he'd attended the university, Gabe had never even mentioned a friend.

"Okay if I join you?" she asked.

Becks made a practice of remaining upstairs until Gabe finished his obsessive coming home routine: set his backpack, straps up, on the bottom step of the stairwell, go into the kitchen for a glass of lemonade, then eat a single slice of Swiss cheese. Only then was he ready to see her. But tonight she was anxious to meet his friend.

"Of course." Gabe's words floated up the stairs. She listened for a hint of tension but heard none. Tying the belt of her too-snug robe and running a hand through long unkempt curls, she descended the staircase.

Gabe stood in front of the open refrigerator, its light throwing a bluish cast over his fine features. Warmth filled Becks' chest. He was so handsome. His square, dimpled jaw, broad cheekbones and well-shaped skull gave no hint of the Asperger's that had caused Gabe—and his parents—such pain.

"I made chili tonight," Becks said, stepping between the kitchen island and Gabe to peer inside the refrigerator. The kitchen was large and modern, its floor-to-ceiling white cabinets topped with shiny black granite counters. Though delighted by her six-burner gas stove and state-of-the-art double oven, Becks' most cherished piece was the oversized table she'd bought the day before she'd moved into the house twenty-five years earlier. Its broad pine surface was scratched and dented from thousands of family meals, homework sessions with Gabe and her other son Josh and conversations with friends and neighbors.

"There's enough chili for both of you," Becks said as she took a heavy ceramic pot out of the refrigerator and placed it on the counter.

When she turned to say hello to the boy behind the kitchen table, her jaw dropped. The pale young man stood at least six and a half feet tall and was as thin as a tomato stake, with a long nose and close-set eyes—Ichabod Crane in a yarmulke. Thin threads of cotton escaped beneath his button-down white shirt and Becks realized with a start that the boy wore tzitzit, the ritual vest donned by *frum* or ultra-religious Jews. She struggled to regain her composure.

"This is Menachem Tannenbaum. You can call him Menny. You said I should bring friends to the house,"

Gabe said. He looked at her, expressionless, before opening the silverware drawer. "He moved into my dorm this semester. You do not mind, do you?"

"Of course not," Becks said, smiling. She hoped the boy hadn't noticed her rudeness. Gabe laid out two place settings, following the routine he always adhered to—fork an inch to the left of the plate, knife and spoon an inch to the right. That done, he turned to the pot of chili, putting it on a burner and turning the flame to low. The pungent aroma of peppery stew filled the kitchen.

Becks bit her tongue as he stirred three times to the right, then three times to the left, making identical circular motions with a wooden spoon. She looked at Menny to see if he'd noticed. Hating herself as she thought it, Becks wondered what Menny hoped to get out of his friendship with Gabe. And why her son had befriended the ultra-religious young man.

Then she remembered: Gabe's obsession with Talmud. It had grown out of his bar mitzvah training but, as with everything that interested him, became a fixation. By the time Gabe was fourteen, he was reading everything he could find on the topic and lining the walls of his bedroom with hand-made posters containing Talmudic quotations. He also greeted strangers with a litany of arcane facts about Jewish law. Becks hoped he'd drop that fixation for something more practical in college. Of course he hadn't. And now he'd found a companion who was, presumably, as obsessed with the subject as he was.

"Nice to meet you," she said, then added, "Where are you from?" figuring Jewish geography—a game of identifying Jewish people both parties knew—was a safe topic.

"New York. Crown Heights." The boy blushed and raised a hand to his head before dropping it to his side. His thick chestnut bangs fell across his eyes. "That is, I was. I left to finish school." Becks was surprised to hear the young man speak with a Yiddish accent, a guttural sound from the back of his throat. Her grandparents had spoken with the same inflection and it sounded odd, as if feigned, from such a young man. "I transferred from City College to the University of Miami this summer." He bit his thumbnail and directed an imploring gaze at Gabe, who adjusted the burner beneath the chili.

"Menny's in economics with me this semester," Gabe said. "We sit in the third row. I am in the seat near the window. He sits five chairs over. Did you know that economics is the study of human behavior in the face of a scarcity of resources? Economists classify resources into labor, capital, natural resources and entrepreneurship." He blushed and turned back to the stove, again stirring three circles to the right, three circles to the left.

"How are you and Dad?"

Becks hesitated. It was one of Gabe's trigger points. She and Daniel had reunited six months earlier after a yearlong separation she demanded when she learned of her husband's affair. Gabe resented Becks for making his father move out and wouldn't talk to her for a month.

"Dad had a hard week but everything's fine. How about you?"

"All is good." Gabe reached into the overhead cabinet for a soup bowl. After setting it squarely in the middle of the counter, he glanced at Menny and took out a second.

"Unless you kids want anything, I'll head back up," she said, sensing the boys' need for privacy. Gabe said good night. She smiled at Menny, who looked down without responding.

Ten minutes later, lying in her dark bedroom and listening to Daniel's gentle snoring, Becks wondered why Gabe brought the boy home. She couldn't deny her son was odd. Still, Menny was downright peculiar. It was more than the yarmulke and tzitzit, although those were strange enough. The boy looked pale and sickly and seemed frightened. Was he afraid of her? She didn't mean to be intimidating. She considered waking Daniel. But it was late. There'd be time to discuss Gabe's new friend in the morning. And find out why their son had brought the strange young man home.

3

"You okay with this?" Gabe said, placing a steaming bowl of chili on the table before Menny. "We have peanut butter and wheat bread if you would like a sandwich."

Menny raised his head—Gabe realized he had been praying—and picked up his spoon. "This looks great." He smiled crookedly. "Thanks for asking."

Gabe never knew what Menny would eat. When they first met, Menny would not touch most of the food in the dorm cafeteria. He assumed Menny was like him—picky. But Menny explained he was kosher. Lately, though, he was not so careful about what he ate.

Gabe had debated a while before bringing Menny home. They were friends and his mother had encouraged him to bring friends to Boca Raton for the weekend. Even so what he wanted to ask his parents went beyond a brief visit. His mother was always lecturing him about helping others so he was pretty sure she would agree. His father might be another story.

Once the boys were through eating, Gabe led Menny upstairs and showed him into his older brother's room. Josh was a junior at Emory and rarely came home but insisted the room remain unchanged—a shrine to his athletic abilities. Every shelf held a collection of trophies and ribbons and the walls were crowded with group shots of Josh's baseball and soccer teams. Josh worshipped sports and treated his trophies like religious icons. It wasn't all that different, Gabe thought, from the leather bands and boxes Menny kept on his desk for praying.

"Shower's there." Gabe pointed to the door opposite the twin bed. "You need anything else?"

"What did you have in mind?" Menny said, sinking onto the navy spread at the foot of the bed. "Dancing girls?"

Gabe laughed. "In your dreams." He pulled the door shut behind him.

Menny remained at the foot of the bed, hands dangling between his knees. A wave of sadness washed over him as he sank into his usual Friday night funk. He missed his family. Badly. A few hours earlier, they'd have gathered at the dining room table for the Sabbath meal. He wiped his eyes as he pictured his mother bowed over flickering candles, chanting prayers. A lacy white tablecloth would be laid out with his mother's best crystal and china. Before fleeing Crown Heights two years earlier, he'd looked forward to Shabbat all week—his family, cousins and neighbors singing and praying and chattering much as they had the week before. His father came home early from shul to say the blessings as the aromas of roast chicken and baked challah wafted in from the kitchen.

Would he ever know such peace again?

Friday night was always special but his last Sabbath at home had been more elaborate than usual. His Aunt Deborah and Uncle Chaim had come to Brooklyn for a wedding and his mother had prepared her famous brisket and prunes along with roast chicken. Dessert was an apple pie.

"So tell me, Hannah, any prospects for our Menny?" his aunt asked once the platters of roast chicken, brisket, and vegetables had made their way around the table. "What is he, eighteen now? All the pretty girls will be taken."

Menny avoided his mother's eyes. He was in his final year at the yeshiva. Most of his classmates were engaged and the neighbors were starting to talk. The matchmaker, a widow named Bashri, had sent him to the homes of five girls. All were pious, attractive young women. Even so Menny wasn't interested in marriage. Not yet. Once married, he'd be expected to start a family. There'd be no chance of attending university or medical school then. Instead, he'd be sent to rabbinic school and follow in his father's footsteps.

"No one yet," his mother said, refilling Aunt Deborah's glass with the sweet red wine she served on Shabbat. "Menny is picky. It's got to be just the right girl. Not everyone is fit to become a rebbetzin." She used the Yiddish term for a rabbi's wife. "He'll find someone soon."

Menny didn't bother to correct her. There was no point. She knew he dreamed of becoming a doctor and opening a medical clinic near their home. But, as with his father, she'd have no part of it. It was fate, bashert, that he become a rabbi like his father and grandfather before him.

Menny rose from the bed, his chest heavy. He'd never become a doctor or rabbi now. His life was collapsing like a house being bulldozed. He ached to confide in someone, to ask for help. Gabe's mother seemed so kind. Still she'd never let him stay if she knew the truth.

If the man looking for him at school was the one who'd chased him in New York, his life might be in danger. The one time he'd visited Levi in prison, Menny had offered to tell the police about the man who'd convinced his friend to sell drugs. But Levi, his face drawn and his body so thin his uniform floated around him like a spacesuit, had turned even paler.

"No. You don't know what that monster's capable of doing. He'll kill Rivka and my parents. Your family, too, if he finds out you ratted on him."

Levi's hands trembled as he spoke and Menny held his tongue. He sensed his friend had witnessed the man's cruelty and believed the stranger's threats.

Shivering at the thought, Menny rose, then showered and got into bed. The cool sheets felt like silken clouds after the rough fabric he'd grown accustomed to in the dorm. He hadn't slept in days and was desperate for rest. Each time he closed his eyes, the stranger from the deli chased him into the subway or down an alley. On really bad nights, the man crouched in the bushes across from his family's home and Menny awakened struggling for air.

He was sick of running and hiding and knew he shouldn't impose on Gabe or his parents. But when the stranger showed up on campus and Gabe offered to bring Menny to Boca Raton, he jumped at the chance. It would provide a modicum of safety, a chance to catch his breath and figure out what to do next.

Because, if the stranger found him, he was as good as dead.

4

Sunlight streamed in through the French doors that led to the patio as Becks placed two cups of coffee on the kitchen table. She'd risen early to brew Daniel's favorite, Kona, and the heady aroma of ground beans filled the kitchen.

Daniel yawned and stretched in his chair before wrapping a warm arm around her waist. "How'd I get so lucky?"

Becks hesitated before returning his hug. Since Daniel's return, she'd vacillated between relief at saving her marriage and resentment toward her husband. Everything seemed fine on the surface and she went through the motions of being a good wife. Shopped. Cooked. Brewed coffee.

But she'd made sacrifices for her family. She'd been happy with her career as an investigative reporter until Gabe came home from kindergarten crying because his classmates made fun of him. Reasoning she'd return to work in a few months, she took a leave of absence to help him adjust. That never happened. Instead, Gabe was diagnosed with Asperger's Syndrome and Becks spent the next ten years driving him from the speech therapist, to the child psychologist, to his special education classes. She'd found freelance work as a food writer and still missed the camaraderie and challenge of newspaper work.

Daniel made no sacrifices. He claimed his busy patient schedule prevented him from meeting with Gabe's teachers or specialists. Yet he had found time for an affair with his nurse!

She loved Daniel. At least, she had before his affair. Now she wasn't so sure. She didn't know if she'd ever trust him enough to offer the unconditional love she'd given years earlier. The truth was her decision to take Daniel back had more to do with concern for her sons than affection for her husband.

"Sweetheart?" Daniel's voice broke through her reverie. "You okay?"

"Fine." She forced a smile.

It was mid-October but temperatures in Boca Raton were still in the eighties. The kitchen faced onto the pool and bright splashes of sunlight sparkled on the water. It rippled under a faint breeze and threw a watery pattern of undulating light onto the kitchen walls.

"Did you hear the kids come in last night?" Becks dropped into the chair opposite Daniel. "Gabe brought a friend."

"I didn't hear a thing. I was out the minute my head . . ." He stopped speaking as the doorbell rang.

Becks checked her watch. It was just before seven. "That's my dad."

Her father—everyone called him Tootsie, his childhood nickname—had gotten into the habit of driving up from Miami to visit Becks and Daniel on Saturday mornings. She loved her dad and appreciated his desire to be with family. The problem was he showed up earlier and earlier each week.

She rose and padded to the front door.

"Everything okay?" Becks said, stepping back to let her father in. "I didn't expect you until later."

"Later schmater. What am I supposed to do? Sleep all day like the codgers at the old folks' home." He leaned down—at six foot, three inches, he was a head taller than Becks—to kiss the top of her head. "I'll have time to sleep when I'm dead."

Becks groaned at the old joke. Her father, at eighty-six, was in good health. Two years earlier, he'd moved into an independent living building at the Schmuel Bernstein Jewish Home for the Aged in Miami. Three of his buddies already lived there and the four played poker every day. Tootsie loved to complain about the place. The food was "crap," the residents were demented and the walls were built of cardboard. But he was happy. And, as Becks told Daniel when he got sick of Tootsie's complaints, who were they to deprive the old man of one of his greatest pleasures?

"We'll probably go out late this morning," she said, leading her father into the kitchen. "Gabe got in after midnight."

"That's fine, Doll. I can wait. Meanwhile, get me a cup of coffee?" Her father greeted Daniel with a smack to the back of his head and plopped into Becks' recently-vacated chair. "Make sure it's hot."

Daniel shot Becks a crooked smile. Her father demanded, rather than requested.

"Coming right up." She emptied the carafe into a mug and zapped it in the microwave before placing it in front of her father.

"So what's going on?" She leaned against the counter, ready for his next order.

"Some broad from down the hall started banging on my door about four this morning. I had to call security."

"What did she want?"

"Damned if I know. A lot of these women, they get

lonely. And when they find out there's a handsome guy a few doors down . . . Well, you know what happens."

Daniel looked up from the newspaper. "No. Tell me."

Tootsie shot him a dirty look. "When you grow up."

Becks slid into the chair next to her father and turned to her husband. "Has Gabriel said anything to you about a boy named Menny?"

"Is that who he brought home last night?" Daniel said.

"Yeah. An orthodox kid. Menachem."

"Doesn't ring any bells."

"He's got the whole look—white shirt, black pants, tzitzit."

"Sounds like one of those curlies." This from Tootsie.

Becks and Daniel stared at her father, who twirled a finger next to his ear. "Hasids. You know. The Yids with the peyos."

"You think Menny's Hasidic?" Becks knew little of the Hasidic community, only that they were ultra-religious Jews who lived apart from the world, like the Amish. She'd seen men in black coats and women in long skirts pushing strollers and shepherding children along Collins Avenue in Miami Beach and assumed they were Hasidic. But she'd never met one.

"Menny didn't have the curls. Or the big hat."

"Wait a sec." Daniel cocked his head to the left. "Gabe told me about him. The two went to services at the school's Chabad."

"What was that all about?"

"I think Gabe's lonely. And you remember Shoshanna."

Becks nodded. Their older son Josh met Shoshanna, his first college girlfriend, at a Friday night dinner at Emory University. It was held at the school's Chabad, a religious center led by a rabbi from the Chabad-Lubavitch sect of Hasidism. That relationship had lasted almost a year, ending when Josh realized he wasn't as comfortable with the traditions surrounding orthodox Judaism as he thought.

"Maybe Gabe thinks he'll meet girls," Daniel said.

"About time." Tootsie snorted. "I was beginning to think he was gay."

"Dad!" Becks said. "Why would you say something like that?"

"He never dates." Then, turning to his son-in-law, "Didn't it occur to you?"

Daniel shook his head. It was too early to deal with the old man's crazy ideas.

Becks was getting milk from the refrigerator when she heard footsteps in the kitchen. She turned to find Daniel standing, his eyes wide, staring at Menny. She stifled a laugh. He was doing an even poorer job than she had at hiding his reaction.

"Good morning," Daniel's voice was heartier than usual. "Everyone sleep well?"

Tootsie didn't pretend to play it cool. "Jeeze Louise, Gabe. What's wrong with your friend?"

"Grandpa!" Gabe glared at Tootsie. Then, to Menny, "My grandfather has no social skills."

The old man laughed, then rose and shook Menny's hand. "Sorry about that. You feeling all right, son?"

"Yes sir," the boy said, backing away from the table. "I think I'll just—"

"Sit over there," Gabe said, "I will get our coffee."

Becks never knew whether to blush or laugh at what came out of her father's mouth. Half the time she was too shocked to react. She tried to remember if he'd always been that way—or just as he got older.

"We thought we'd go to Golden's Deli for brunch," she told the boys, changing the subject. Then, smiling at Menny, "It's become our Saturday morning tradition."

Menny froze in the act of pulling a chair away from the table. "I don't . . ." he murmured. "That is, I'm not . . . hungry." He threw Gabe a frightened glance.

"Don't worry about hungry," Daniel said, his head in the paper. "Your appetite will return the minute you smell their bagels. Drink your coffee and get dressed. I'm starving."

Menny stepped away from the table as the color drained from his face. "Please. Go without me. I don't feel well." He hurried from the kitchen. No one spoke as his steps echoed down the hall.

"Where are you going?" Gabe called after him. Then, to his parents, "Thanks a lot. You scared him."

"What are you talking about?" Tootsie said.

Gabe rolled his eyes and ran upstairs.

"What did we do?" Becks asked once Gabe was out of earshot.

"Damned if I know," Daniel said.

"Would it be so bad if we had breakfast here?"

"Fine, but I'd like to know what's going on." Daniel rose from the table. "We're not a dumping ground for Gabriel's lost souls. I don't mind his bringing friends home. Still I deserve to know what the kid's worked up about."

"Daniel can't you . . ."

He threw his paper on the table and followed the boys. Becks hoped he wouldn't yell at Gabe. Daniel meant well but he tended to make things worse. More often than not, she was the one who spent hours calming her son afterward. The last time that happened, she'd been forced to cancel a meeting with her editor.

Becks looked at her father, who shrugged. "The

curlie's probably a mental case. A lot of them are. Praying all the time. You'd go nuts too."

"Daaad." Becks dragged out the word.

"And the women? They're so ugly they have to wear wigs and scarves."

"Honest to God. Where do you come up with this stuff? "She opened the refrigerator and debated lecturing her father about the impropriety of his comments. At eighty-six, though, he wasn't about to change. She looked across the kitchen island to the wooden table, where he was glancing at a section of the newspaper. "Omelets or pancakes?"

By the time Daniel returned downstairs, Tootsie was halfway through his breakfast and the aroma of pancakes and maple syrup filled the room. Another plate of hotcakes sat atop a pile of newspaper inches from the elderly man.

"I told the boys they could come down and eat later," Daniel said, shaking his head. "Gabe yelled at me to go away."

"Probably are fagilas." Tootsie waved his hand in a limp-wristed gesture. "They don't want you to know."

"Will you drop it, Dad?" Becks added more pancakes to her father's plate and shoved the syrup in front of him. Turning to Daniel, "Should I try?"

"Let it go for now." He nodded toward Tootsie and raised an eyebrow. Her dad was hunched over his pancakes, chewing with his mouth open. "We can talk to the boys after they cool off."

But Tootsie didn't miss much. "Don't let me stop you," he said, bits of pancake flying from his mouth. "You want to talk to the homos, I can stay here." He forked two more pancakes from the serving platter. "You can tell me what they say later."

5

Becks was standing in the driveway waving at her father's retreating car when Daniel stuck his head out the front door. "The kids are downstairs."

She went inside and followed her husband to the kitchen. The boys were waiting at the table, Menny biting his thumbnail and Gabe rocking back in his chair, a habit that had landed him on the floor more times than she cared to remember. Becks eyed them. Was Tootsie right? Gabe had only been on one date in his life. She told herself that had more to do with his social ineptness than anything else, didn't it? Still, if he was gay, couldn't he find someone more attractive? She shook her head. Now she was listening to Tootsie? That was crazy.

Gabe rose, his hands beating loosely against his sides. "I am sorry we got mad." His voice trailed off as he looked at his friend. "I brought Menny home to get away from the dorm. But there is more to it."

Daniel arched an eyebrow and glanced at Becks. The two seated themselves across from the boys.

"Dr. and Mrs. Ruchinsky," Menny broke in, "I probably shouldn't have come here. My life is complicated. I never meant to upset you. If you want me to leave, I'll go."

"It's okay, Men," Gabe spoke gently, as though addressing a child. "You can tell my parents."

Becks and Daniel exchanged glances. Gabe's compassion—an emotion he'd never shown before—seemed genuine.

Menny grimaced and palmed a lock of hair off his forehead. "I don't know. It's hard to trust anyone." He stared down at his clasped hands. "I grew up in a Hasidic community in Brooklyn. You've heard of the Lubavitch?"

Becks nodded. She'd heard they were the most open of Hasidim's insular sects.

"Two years ago, I had to leave. It's a long story. I can tell you some other time." His eyes shifted from Becks to Daniel as though gauging their response. "People were angry at me for abandoning the community. My father's an important rabbi and I was supposed to become one too. It's a family tradition."

"Did you want to be a rabbi?" Becks asked.

"I didn't but that's not why I left. I had to leave for, well, personal reasons. I can't talk about it. Just the same, my brother told me that members of our community talked about kidnapping me and bringing me back."

"Why would they do that?" Daniel asked. "Don't other youngsters leave?"

Menny rubbed his chin and raised a hand to his head. Becks realized, with a start, that he was reaching for the hat and beard he'd abandoned when he left his community.

"Most of the kids who take off aren't that bright and don't do well in yeshiva. Nobody minds except their parents. I was the first smart student to leave and people were afraid others would follow."

"So that's what you're worried about?" Daniel, as always, cut to the chase. "Being abducted?"

"I don't know what to think." Menny spoke slowly and quietly as though weighing every word. "A man came to the dorm looking for me. I don't know who he is, but

I'm afraid he's here to drag me home." His gaze fell on Becks before returning to his hands, now balled into fists on the table. "I thought I was safe at school. Then . . ." He swallowed. "Gabe met him."

"I was leaving for class when I saw the man." Their son took up the story. "He had greasy hair and wore a yarmulke. I did not like him. He stood real close to me and kept touching my shoulder. He had a bulge under his jacket. It looked like a gun."

"A gun?" Becks gasped.

"He went room to room, looking inside open doors and asking if anyone knew Menachem. I said I had not heard of anyone with that name." Then, to Menny. "That is a weird name."

Menny responded with a bleak smile.

"The guy said he was a family friend who stopped by to say hello and that he would come back another time," Gabe continued. "That was yesterday. Menny wanted to get out of the dorm before he came back."

"I'm glad you did," Becks said. Her palms grew damp as she pictured Gabe face to face with an armed stranger. She made a mental note to call the university's security service then rose and retrieved a carton of orange juice from the refrigerator.

"Why didn't you go to the police or campus security?" Daniel said.

"What would I tell them?" Menny raised his shoulders in an exaggerated shrug. "That I'm afraid because someone's looking for me? I have no proof he wants to kidnap me."

Becks began to fill the glasses she'd set out earlier. "Do you have any idea who he was?"

"He might have been sent to scare me. My brother said members of our shul are afraid I'll start my own religious group and get other young people from the community to join. I'd never do that."

"Have you called your father to find out what he knows about the visitor?" Daniel said. "Can't he assure the others you're not a threat?"

"I tried. He won't talk to me."

Becks' stopped in the process of returning the juice to the refrigerator. "Why not?"

"He's angry at me for leaving. He says I brought shame to the family and ruined my sisters' and brothers' chances of making good matches."

Becks wanted to reach out to the boy, whose eyes had grown alarmingly sorrowful.

"Mom and Dad, I need to ask you something." Gabe broke in. He'd tilted his chair back and balanced precariously on its rear legs. "Can Menny stay with us a few days? Until that bad man goes away?"

Becks and Daniel exchanged glances.

"That's an awful lot—"

"We'll discuss it," Daniel interrupted, "and let you know."

"What do you think?" Daniel asked once he'd closed the door to the master bedroom. Becks had turned it into a sophisticated, peaceful retreat, draping the bed with a cream linen duvet and installing wooden plantation shutters a shade lighter than the oak floor. Daniel seated himself at the foot of the bed and Becks took the silk parson's chair opposite. "We'd be asking for trouble if we took the kid in."

"You think someone's after Menny?" Becks said.

"No. It's just that I'm not sure the boy's all there. Or telling the truth. His story seems a bit far-fetched."

"I don't know. I'm inclined to believe him. Not the whole thing, of course. The dorm visitor may have been a family friend and the boys may be letting their imaginations run wild. Menny seems upset about something. A few days of rest couldn't hurt."

Daniel tilted his head. "You want to keep him here?"

"Not really. If we refuse, we have to tell Gabe we think his friend's lying or taking advantage of him. Do you want to do that?" Becks said. "Menny will be bored by the end of the week and Gabe can bring him back to the dorm."

"So you don't mind . . ."

"Sure I mind." She snapped out the words. "But it's for our son." She rose and walked to the door. "Agreed?" she asked over her shoulder.

Daniel shrugged. "We need to let him know it's just this once."

"Fine. I'll tell Gabe."

Gabe returned to Miami after dinner Sunday night, leaving Becks and Daniel alone with their visitor. The boys had spent most of the weekend in Gabe's room and Menny seemed uncomfortable at the table, pushing food around his plate and biting his nails.

Returning to the kitchen after seeing Gabe off, Menny asked Becks if she'd mind his going to his room. She was relieved at not having to make conversation with the boy but hurt by his eagerness to avoid her and Daniel. Tomorrow, she'd make an effort to talk to Menny. She had no intention of letting him hover around the house like a phantom, retreating to his room the minute she or Daniel approached.

"So what's your plan for tomorrow?" Daniel asked once Menny's footsteps sounded on the stairwell.

She was washing dishes while Daniel dried. "I'll get on with my work and leave him to study or watch television."

Her husband laughed.

"What?"

"I saw you eyeing Menny during dinner. You'll have his family history by the time I get home."

"I don't know." She checked a glass serving bowl for grease spots and handed it to Daniel. "He seems pretty close-mouthed."

"He's a troubled kid and it sounds like this visitor has gotten to him. Maybe you can help him figure out who the man is and what he wants. Then Menny can return to school."

"Sure, why not?" Becks said. "I've got nothing better to do." She shot her husband a dirty look.

She hadn't spoken more than five words to the boy since the morning after his arrival and doubted he'd open up to her. He seemed like a lost soul and she wanted to help him. But what could she do? She struggled to get Gabe to talk to her and doubted she'd have any more luck with the strange young man.

Daniel looked up from the cabinet where he was squatting to put away serving platters. "What do you say we head upstairs? We can watch television and spy on Gabe's friend."

Becks punched his shoulder. "You are so mean. And you accuse me of being nosy."

Truth be told, Becks was anxious to find out what had frightened Menny. And to make sure Gabe was safe.

6

"Are you up yet?" Becks knocked lightly on Menny's door the next morning. "It's almost ten."

She heard shuffling. A moment later, Menny opened the door. His eyes were puffy and he rubbed them with his fists, much the way Josh had as a toddler. The clean odor of fresh linen rose from his body and Becks felt a flush of warmth remembering the times she'd awakened her sons and noticed the same scent. As much as she resented Menny's visit, she liked the idea of having a young person in the house as company. She'd be grateful if a friend's mother protected her sons from danger.

"I've got to leave in an hour and wanted to know if you'd like eggs," she said.

Menny gave a quick nod and smiled. "That'd be great. If you don't mind."

"Not at all. Come down and I'll have them waiting."

Ten minutes later, Becks was at the sink scouring out a frying pan when Menny came into the kitchen dressed in the same outfit he'd worn all weekend—a white shirt and black pants beneath which dingy white socks emerged. Becks reminded herself to teach him how to use the washing machine and to go through Josh and Gabe's old clothes for something he could wear. She spooned scrambled eggs onto a plate and placed it on the table. He took a bite and groaned softly. "These are just like my mom's. I wish I'd learned to make them."

Becks turned around "She wouldn't show you?

"I guess she would but I'd have felt funny asking"

Becks raised an eyebrow and leaned against the sink.

"Boys in our community don't cook. Our mothers do." He laughed, then his eyes grew sad.

"You miss her, don't you?" Becks asked, coming around the kitchen island and seating herself across from Menny. "How often do you see your mother?"

"Never. My father won't let me visit. And everyone in Crown Heights knows everyone else's business so he'd hear about it if I snuck home."

"Can you meet her somewhere else?"

"She won't leave the community."

Becks watched as he took the last few bites of egg, pushing them onto his fork with a scrap of toast. She felt sorry for him and his mother. She'd be devastated if she couldn't see Josh or Gabe. It was hard enough when they left for college and she knew she'd see them during school breaks. "How long has it been?"

He shrugged. "Two years."

"Does she know where you are?"

"Not exactly. I wrote her a letter two weeks after I left and gave it to my brother to deliver. I couldn't tell her why I left Crown Heights but told her I was fine, that I had a place to stay and planned to attend high school instead of yeshiva. My brother said that she went into her room and cried after she read it. When my father found the letter, he tore it up and forbade her to contact me."

"And since then?"

Menny shrugged and wiped his nose with the back of his hand. "I've sent her letters through a neighbor. But I'm afraid to give an address to write back. My father might find out where I live and come after me. I called the house once and my father answered."

"What did he say?"

"He yelled at me and insisted I was depressed and should see a psychiatrist. When I refused, he threatened to sit shiva for me."

Becks was horrified. Menny's father would, essentially, be declaring him dead. The man sounded heartless. "So that's it?"

"I guess so. I'm trying to make a new life. It's hard." He stared out the window then returned his gaze to Becks. "I appreciate your taking me in. It's nice to have time to think."

"Can I help?"

He smiled, the first genuine grin she'd seen since he arrived. "I wish you could. But I've got to work things out for myself. You've done enough already."

Becks glanced at her watch and rose, regretting the lost opportunity to get to know Menny. Who knew when he'd open up again? "I've got to go. I promised a friend we'd meet at eleven for coffee. Make yourself at home." She grabbed her purse off the counter. "We'll talk when I get back."

7

Becks backed out of the driveway, careful to avoid the BMW parked on the street across from her home. It had been three days since Gabe's return to school and she needed to get out of the house. Menny was driving her nuts.

Not that he wasn't a good kid. He was and she'd learned a lot about the Hasidic community from him. But he was so awkward and helpless. He managed to make himself breakfast and lunch now—cereal and a sandwich. It never occurred to him to pour leftover milk down the drain or rinse his dishes. And his room was a mess, the bed unmade and what little clothing he owned draped on every surface. It was a bit of a shock after Gabe, whose Asperger's was compounded by obsessive-compulsive behaviors. He couldn't stop neatening.

That morning after breakfast, when Menny came upstairs to find Becks making his bed, he smiled sheepishly. "I'm sorry," he said. "I never had to clean up at home."

Becks looked up from the sheet she was smoothing. "Why not?"

"My mother and sisters did it for me. If they caught me or my brothers helping, they told us to run back to the yeshiva. It was our job to study."

She started to laugh but realized he wasn't joking. "How many brothers and sisters do you have?"

"Three of each."

"Almost enough for a baseball lineup," she said.

Menny looked confused and she smiled. "You need nine. Did you mind studying so much?"

"I didn't think about it. That's the way things were. Up at seven, prayers at seven-thirty, then breakfast and studying until lunch. It went on like that until late at night. That's one reason it's been so hard."

"What do you mean?"

"Getting used to the world outside Crown Heights. It's so different. I knew where I was supposed to be every minute of the day and night. We had hundreds of rules about what we could and couldn't do. I never thought about them until I left. It was good and bad. We couldn't watch television or read English-language newspapers, which makes life a lot harder for me now. Sometimes I feel like I'm on a foreign planet. The kids in the dorm couldn't believe I'd never heard of the Beatles or Curt Cobain."

Becks looked up from fluffing the pillows. "What's wrong with television?"

"It distracts from prayer. I watched TV a lot after I left, though. It helped me learn to speak English."

"You didn't speak English?"

He laughed. "Everyone's shocked by that. I knew a few words but I grew up speaking Yiddish."

Becks sat at the foot of the bed and looked at the young man slouched against the closet door. So that's where his accent and odd phraseology came from. She'd gotten to know Menny a little better in the past few days. He told her about working with a tutor to earn his General Equivalency Diploma. He'd also found a job in an upstate New York religious community to earn money to enroll at City College. A math professor there helped him get a full scholarship to the University of Miami. Although Menny was open about his past and spoke fondly of his family, he steered clear of one subject—his departure from Crown Heights.

"Why did you decide to leave home?" Becks blurted. She hadn't meant to be so blunt. The question had been gnawing at her for days.

Menny walked to the desk and picked up a book. "I can't talk about it."

Becks waited.

"I'm sorry." He returned the book, his eyes downcast. "It might get my family in trouble. I didn't want to leave. I don't belong here." He swept his arm across his body in a gesture that seemed to encompass the room, the house, his new world. "And it's not safe for me to return to Crown Heights."

Becks waited for him to continue but Menny stared at his shoes and kneaded his hands. She felt a sudden tenderness toward the boy and fought an urge to hug him. She'd read that Hasidic custom prohibited men from touching women other than their wives, even to shake hands. "What will you do? Has your time here helped you decide?"

Menny leaned against the desk and crossed his arms. "I'd like to become a doctor." He glanced up as though expecting her to protest. "People from my community rarely do that. I've thought about returning to Crown Heights and opening a clinic. If they let me."

Becks didn't ask who he meant. One thing she'd learned from Menny was that the Hasidic community lived by its own set of rules. For all she knew, deserters weren't welcome back.

Resigned to accepting Menny's explanation, she rose and gathered the pants and shirts he'd draped over his chair. The sweatpants and tee shirts she'd found in Gabe's room sat folded and unused on the dresser. Menny didn't offer to help as she stood, arms full, and headed for the door.

"I wish I could go home," he whispered, taking her place at the foot of the bed.

She turned in the doorway as he wiped a hand across his eyes.

"I wish I could help you." She meant it. Her heart ached at the sorrow in his voice. The poor kid had been walking a lonely path for some time and there was nothing she could do.

When he didn't respond, she left the room.

Five minutes later, Becks was in her car, heading to the market to pick up ingredients for the stuffed cabbage she was testing for her monthly food column. It wasn't the investigative reporting she'd done years earlier but it kept her in the writing game. She was trying a recipe she'd adapted from one her friend Aviva gave her and planned to pick up kosher ground beef. Menny, who'd subsisted on eggs, cereal, peanut butter sandwiches and pasta since moving in, would appreciate a real dinner with kosher meat. And, if all went well, she'd use the recipe in a forthcoming cookbook. Her first, on Jewish cooking, was due out in six months and she was considering what to write about next.

Checking the rearview mirror as she backed out of her driveway, Becks saw a man get out of the black BMW parked across the street in her neighbor's swale. She expected to see Helmut. This fellow was shorter and, though it was hard to tell from a distance, heavier. A friend of Helmut, she thought? His son-in-law?

She looked at the grocery list on the passenger seat. What had she forgotten? Oh yeah, lemons. She'd pick up two.

She flipped on the blinker and took a left onto Jog Road.

8

Returning from a meeting with her editor two days later, Becks pulled to the side of the road as a fire truck, its siren piercing the low hum of traffic, sped past. She was five minutes from home and couldn't wait to celebrate the front-page story he'd assigned. She'd pour a glass of Cabernet and go upstairs to begin research. Driving slowly, she entered her neighborhood and turned off the main drive into her street.

"Oh. My. God." She gasped as she stared down the street at the flashing lights. The fire truck was parked in her driveway. A rescue vehicle emblazoned with red and yellow lettering sat behind it.

Her mouth went dry and she gunned the engine. Was Menny hurt?

Becks pulled into a neighbor's driveway, leaving the car door open as she raced across the road to her house. Clouds of smoke billowed out of the front door. Two firemen wearing heavy black jackets, boots and helmets dragged a hose from the truck to the front porch and went inside. As she tried to follow, another fireman, older than the others, took her arm.

"That's my house. I need to know if my visitor's okay," she said, tugging to get away.

Everyone's fine, ma'am but we can't let you inside.

The boy," he nodded toward the rescue van, "inhaled some smoke. They're seeing to him now."

"The boy . . ." She spotted Menny on the grass in front of the vehicle. A paramedic held a plastic oxygen mask on his face.

"Menny," she cried out, striding over. Her hands shook as she reached down to him. "What happened? Are you okay?"

Eyes wide above the mask, the boy tried to stand and the paramedic put a restraining hand to his shoulder. "Mrs. Ruchinsky. I'm sorry. I made eggs. I didn't know." Menny coughed and pulled the mask from his face but the paramedic replaced it.

"Don't be silly. I—."

"Why don't you give us a few minutes?" The paramedic interrupted her. "We need to make sure he's okay." The man's voice was firm.

After a pause, Becks nodded and turned toward her house. The two firefighters she'd seen entering came out the front door and spoke with the older man. He motioned her over. After a glance at Menny, who sat on the grass breathing oxygen, she complied.

"Doesn't look too bad. Still it's going to be awhile before we can let you in. It was a small stovetop fire and the boy put it out with an extinguisher."

"We saw one cat. Is that all?" the taller of the two firefighters asked.

Becks' stomach sank. "Mulligan. Is he okay?"

"He raced out the minute the boy opened the front door. Almost knocked me over." He motioned toward the house. "We're still checking around. We need to ventilate the house and double check the oven and breakers. The fire was confined to the stove. Still, there's smoke damage throughout the first floor."

Her shoulders slumped. She was grateful Menny was fine but suspected the smoke and fire had done severe damage. It would take days to deal with repairs. Yet another burden on top of taking care of the boy. She hated herself for the thought but there it was.

Realizing there was nothing she could do, Becks stood in front of her house, chatting with neighbors as the firemen set up giant fans in her front door. Helmut, the elderly neighbor from across the street, kneeled on the grass near Menny and spoke to him in a calming tone. Helmut and his late wife, Olga, had become the community's self-appointed grandparents. Helmut had a gentleness about him that was exactly what Menny needed.

An hour later, the fans were dismantled and the older officer—his badge read Capt. Jim Stevens—escorted Becks and Menny inside. The house reeked of smoke and Becks' heart sank at the sight of the gray residue that clung to her floors and walls. Smoky filaments of ash-covered cobwebs formed geometric patterns at the intersection of the walls and ceiling and would take days to clean.

When they reached the kitchen, Becks jerked back and brought a hand to her face. The top of her range was black and the front burner grates had warped into freeform sculptural configurations. Behind them sat a metal pot, its bottom scorched. A powdery coating—she assumed it came from the fire extinguisher—covered the stovetop and a vee of soot climbed the rear wall and extended across the ceiling.

Menny stood by the sink, breathing heavily as she surveyed the room.

"My God, Menny. What have you done?" Becks said, her voice sharper than she'd intended. "Can't you boil an egg without starting a fire?"

She immediately regretted her words.

Menny stared at her like a fox cornered by hounds and

stumbled back. "I'm sorry, Mrs. Ruchinsky. I wanted to cook but . . ." His eyes fixed on the scorched stovetop and his body froze. A moment later, he sprang into action, grabbing a handful of paper towels and dampening them under the faucet.

"Don't worry. I'll clean up." Menny scrubbed the range, creating a greasy smear. "I'll go to the market and get tonight's dinner. What would you like?"

"Let's worry about taking care of this mess first," Becks said, struggling for a reassuring tone. She reached under the sink and handed him a bottle of kitchen degreaser. "Try this."

Walking to the front door with Becks, Capt. Stevens suggested she call her insurance company and have an electrician check the breaker box. "And take it easy on the boy," he added. "This happens all the time." He boarded the fire truck and left.

Menny apologized repeatedly as he and Becks scrubbed counters, walls, appliances and floors. As they worked, Becks tried to comfort Menny with funny stories about Josh and Gabe's escapades in the kitchen. The time Josh blew up a hard-boiled egg in the microwave. Gabe's attempts at making grilled cheese sandwiches, which always turned black. She hoped his laughter meant he was over the shock of the fire and her angry reaction. Capt. Stevens was right. It could happen to anyone.

She was relieved to find most of the damage was superficial. Two burners needed replacement and her insurer promised to send a service to clean and paint the walls the next day. Once the kitchen was restored, she sent Menny upstairs for a shower.

Emotionally and physically drained, she went to her bedroom and showered before collapsing on the bed. In seconds, Becks fell asleep.

It would be her last peaceful nap for weeks.

9

Becks stared through the living room window to the empty driveway below. Sheets of rain swept across the road, turning her neighbors' homes into hazy watercolor blurs. She edged closer to the glass to see down the darkened street. The palm trees in Helmut's yard swayed in the wind. A large puddle obscured her driveway. But no sign of Menny.

When she came downstairs three hours earlier, Menny announced he was going to the kosher market for dinner. He seemed to be in good humor, excited at the prospect of getting out of the house. The sky was growing darker but he'd refused her offer to drive or lend him a bike and insisted on walking the two miles to pick up the meal. Now it was six and the market had been closed for an hour. She reassured herself he'd run into a store or bus shelter to wait out the rain. He had a cell phone. Why hadn't he called?

It wasn't the first time that week she'd questioned her wisdom in agreeing to take Menny into her home. Most nights, he stifled dinner conversation with his inability to meet Daniel's gaze and she felt uncomfortable leaving him alone—which meant rushing through errands and avoiding chats with neighbors. That, obviously, hadn't been enough. But there was something about the boy—his vulnerability and lack of guile, perhaps—that endeared him to her. On the rare occasions their eyes met, he gave her a genuine smile that promised friendship.

One of the advantages of sending her sons off to college was that, as long as they were away, she didn't worry about whether they were staying out late or hanging with the wrong crowd. She couldn't do that with Menny. And, as hard as she tried to drive it out of her mind, she knew he'd come to Boca Raton to avoid being kidnapped. A frightening thought clawed at her conscience. Had his pursuers found him?

"Becks. Are you all right?"

She whipped around. It was Daniel. She hadn't heard him come in. He greeted her with an inquisitive smile. "You look frightened."

"Menny's gone," she said, clasping her hands in front of her body. "He left for the kosher market to get dinner three hours ago. He started a fire in the kitchen today and I lost my temper. The fire engines were here, the whole deal. I assumed we'd worked things out. Now I'm afraid he's taken off for good."

"I doubt that," Daniel said, his eyes narrowing. "He probably needs time to himself. He'll be back soon enough."

"You didn't see the look on his face when I yelled." She stepped forward and Daniel took her in his arms.

"You can be pretty scary. But Menny's not stupid. He'll realize you lost patience and return home. That's what Gabe would do."

Becks felt the tension leave her shoulders as she pressed her cheek into his chest. She inhaled the familiar scent of starched cotton and leather. Daniel wasn't perfect. Still it was comforting to have him home again. Six months earlier, after he moved back, she felt awkward and ill at ease. But as they resumed their life together her world returned to normal. Or almost normal. She still grew jittery when he didn't call to say when he'd show up for dinner. Then again, neither did Gabe or Josh when they lived at home.

At the thought of Gabe, her shoulders tensed. "What'll I tell Gabe? I promised to keep Menny safe." Gabe had trusted her to protect Menny and she'd let him down. How would he react to his friend's disappearance? Lose control and scream? Withdraw and refuse to speak?

"We'll cross that bridge when we have to. Meantime, I'm ready for dinner." Daniel sniffed and wrinkled his nose. "Must have been some fire. Let's order Chinese. By the time it gets here, Menny will be home."

But the food came and no Menny. Becks pushed the fried rice around her plate and rose every few minutes to stare through the living room window. It reminded her of the nights she lay awake, anxious for the scratch of Josh or Gabe's key in the front door lock. Tonight, as then, her imagination ran wild and she pictured Menny's body sprawled next to Jog Road, the victim of a hit and run.

Daniel eyed her wearily each time she left the table. After her third trip to the living room, he smacked his hand on the table. "Enough already." He rose and grabbed his keys off the hook by the garage. "Come on. We'll look for him."

Earlier that week, the heat had broken, giving way to the balmy breezes and cool weather that drew visitors to South Florida. But the temperature had dropped since lunch and the leather seats in Daniel's car felt icy and unyielding. She shivered, whether out of fear or cold she couldn't tell. She raised the car's thermostat, releasing a blast of warm air that engulfed her like a cashmere blanket.

After weaving through the narrow streets inside their community, Daniel pulled onto Jog Road. Although it had stopped raining, the black, water-slicked asphalt reflected the lights of oncoming cars like an airstrip in a forties-era film.

"Where to first?" he asked.

"The kosher market. We can look for Menny on the way."

Becks' gaze flickered from one side of the street to the other as they passed the landscaped entrances of gated communities. High walls partially hidden behind deep hedges and mature palms separated each neighborhood, interrupted here and there by Mediterranean-style gatehouses and marble-tiled fountains. Once they'd crossed Glades Road, the private neighborhoods gave way to multi-story office buildings and strip malls. All were dark and deserted.

"Take a right here," Becks called as they approached the narrow street that snaked between mid-rise office buildings to Shapiro's Kosher Market. A minute later, Daniel pulled up to the store.

At nine o'clock, Shapiro's lights were off and the parking lot deserted except for the shadows of acacias swaying in the moonlight like skeletons in a graveyard dance. Daniel and Becks got out and walked to the back of the building. Nothing there except a stack of yellow crates and a green dumpster. Becks jumped at the sound of a scratch behind the dumpster. But it wasn't Menny. Just a rat. Returning to the car, they spent the next hour cruising through nearby neighborhoods. Becks slumped in her seat, her eyes gritty with exhaustion. Still no Menny. She wrapped her arms around her body as dread filled her chest.

Where was Menny? Had the kidnapper he feared— and that she and Daniel had refused to believe in— abducted the boy?

10

"What do you mean there's nothing you can do?"

Becks had been on the phone for fifteen minutes, explaining that Menny was missing and needed immediate help. She'd called the police the minute she got home but the officer seemed immune to her rising panic. Her voice had grown shrill and she was beyond caring. "The boy's been gone for six hours. Can't you put out an all-points bulletin or something?"

Daniel glared at her from across the kitchen table, where he'd brought the two of them cups of tea. When she ignored him, he brought his hand across his throat in a slicing motion. She turned away.

"Yes, he's twenty." She listened for a moment and winced. "Who said anything about forced entry? I told you he was worried about being kidnapped."

She looked at Daniel and rolled her eyes.

"I understand. But won't it be harder to find him if you delay? After all, this is Boca. Are you so busy chasing criminals you can't look for a kid?"

Daniel dropped his head in his hands.

"All right. I'll come down tomorrow." She slammed the phone into its cradle and turned to Daniel. "Our tax dollars at work."

"Becks, be reasonable."

"Don't talk to me about reasonable. Where do you think he is?"

"I've told you a million times. He's cooling off. Probably called a friend to get him. Or took a cab to Miami."

"That doesn't sound like Menny." She stood and stretched to release the tension between her shoulders. "You'd think he'd call to tell us he's safe."

"He might not think of it."

Becks tilted her head.

"Boys can be self-involved at that age. Josh never called and forget about Gabe. When's the last time he called? And remember, Menny grew up around meek little hausfraus who obeyed their husbands and kept their mouths shut. Unlike you." Daniel laughed. "He needs a break."

She looked at Daniel, her gaze unfocused. "You think so?" She wanted to believe him even though it didn't sound like something Menny would do. He was awkward, no denying that. But to disappear without a word?

"It's been a long day. Let's hit the sack. Things will fall together tomorrow. I'm sure he'll call and apologize. Then you can work things out and bring Menny home if that's what he wants." Daniel rose. "You coming up?"

She stood and walked to the light switch. "I guess so." She flipped off the lights. "I wish I had your confidence."

That night, Becks lay in bed, eyes wide open. Her heart sank as she pictured Menny walking down a dimly lit street or sleeping on the ground beneath roadside vegetation. Was she wrong in thinking she and the boy had developed an understanding? He'd opened up to her on a few occasions, telling her stories about his younger siblings. The possibility that he'd left without a goodbye left a hollow ache in the pit of her stomach. It was, she realized, a lot like the sense of abandonment that haunted her when Daniel left. She'd dealt with that. And Daniel had returned. But Becks didn't know how she'd cope if Menny was kidnapped . . . or worse. It was hours before she fell into a fitful sleep.

11

Becks choked on the pungent odor of ammonia as she entered Shapiro's Kosher Market the next morning. The conditioned air felt brittle and cold and she put a hand to her forehead to block the irritating blink as fluorescent lights flickered to life.

Too jittery to remain in bed, she'd risen at six and tiptoed into the bathroom to avoid waking Daniel. The police officer she'd spoken with the night before said to come to the station at nine. That left three hours to look for Menny. The kosher market still seemed like the best place to start. Someone might remember him from the night before. By six-thirty she was dressed and by seven she had her car keys in hand. Daniel, finishing his coffee and newspaper at the kitchen table, waved off her apologies for leaving so early. He had a patient at eight and would leave soon.

When she arrived at the market, Becks saw lights toward the back of the store and shadows moving behind the colorful posters advertising the week's specials. Potato chips. Fuji apples. Kosher chicken. The sliding glass doors to the market whooshed open and she went inside.

"Sorry, ma'am, you'll have to come back at eight," a balding man in a white cotton apron said as he placed his mop in a yellow pail near the entrance. "We don't open the registers for another half hour."

"I'm not shopping. I'm looking for someone," Becks said. "A young man who walked here from my house last night. He never returned."

The janitor crossed his arms. "You need to talk to someone who was here last night." He looked over his shoulder, toward the meat counter. A woman in a white uniform was arranging gleaming cuts of steak in the glass case with the care a jeweler might take to arrange diamond necklaces and emerald rings. "Malcolm, our butcher, was here. I'll see if he's in." He left for the back of the market.

As she waited, Becks wandered up and down the aisles. She was surprised to find the same products she'd see in any small market. Pickles. Potato chips. Oatmeal cookies. Everything seemed to be available in a kosher form.

"Can I help you?" A bass voice sounded behind her.

Becks turned to find a portly black man in a white butcher coat.

"I understand you're looking for someone." He spoke with a heavy island accent. He glanced over his shoulder at the woman arranging steaks. "Hilda, make sure to put out the tray of briskets."

"A young man staying with me walked here to pick up dinner last night. He never came home. I thought someone might have seen him." Becks stepped back to make way for a man pushing a cart of muffins.

"What did he look like?"

"Skinny and extremely tall with longish brown hair. He was pale."

"Kind of shy, right?"

"You saw him?"

"Just for a minute. He came in, wandered up and down the aisles and left with his father."

"His father?"

"I assumed so. Short, heavy guy with a thick black beard. Looked like a Hasid."

Becks stared at the man as much for the bomb he dropped as his pronunciation of Hasid. He used the hard, guttural "ch" sound few but fluent Hebrew and Yiddish speakers could articulate.

"Did Menny seem okay?"

"Is that the kid's name?"

"Menachem Tannenbaum."

"I saw the two talking but couldn't hear them. The boy looked upset. Still he seemed willing enough to go with the older man. I had a line of customers and didn't pay much attention."

"Damn. He should have called me." Becks didn't realize she'd spoken until the butcher responded.

"You know kids. He probably decided to take off with his father and that was it." He took a step toward the back of the store. "If there's nothing else, I need to get to work."

She hesitated. "Just one more thing."

"Sure."

"Do you have cameras here?"

"Sorry." He shook his head. "We're not that high tech."

Becks thanked the butcher and glanced around the market. There was nothing more to learn here. She returned to her car and started the engine.

It was just before eight and, with time to kill before her meeting at the police station, Becks returned home determined to contact Menny's family. She ran upstairs to her office and sat at her desk, staring out at the road. An SUV drove by, its double row of seats crammed with elementary school-aged children. She shifted a manila file with her recipes to the back of her desk and pulled a pen and yellow legal pad from the top drawer.

Efforts to phone and text Gabe for Menny's family's phone number proved futile. He was probably sleeping. All she had to go on was the boy's last name and the fact that he lived in Crown Heights. After searching the internet for twenty minutes, she narrowed the possibilities to twenty names. This was her tenth call and the third in which a person picked up. She heard a man's voice.

"Hello. Is this Rabbi Tannenbaum?"

"Yes, what is it?" The man spoke with a heavy Yiddish accent.

She explained why she was calling and asked, for what felt like the hundredth time, "do you have a son named Menachem who goes to school in Miami?'

Silence.

"Sir?"

What do you want?" It came out as a barked, "Vat do you vant?"

"Menachem is a friend of my son's. He's been staying at my home for a few days."

"So what's the problem?"

"He went to a grocery store yesterday and never came home. I was told he left with his father." She pulled a pencil from the Mason jar on her desk and tapped it against her keyboard.

The man grunted. "It wasn't me. I no longer have a son named Menachem. And, now, if you don't mind, I need to get back to work."

"But don't you . . ."

The line went dead. Becks sat a moment, slack-jawed. What kind of man speaks that way of his son? She returned the phone to its cradle and broke the pencil between her fists.

No wonder Menny left.

Menny said he'd been in touch with his mother on rare occasions. This might be one of them. There was no point in calling her now, though. Mr. Tannenbaum would hardly let his wife talk to Becks.

So where did that leave her? Becks leaned back in her chair and tossed the broken pencil into the wicker trash can under her desk. Gabe? He might have seen Menny at the dorm or know of a friend the boy trusted enough to go home with.

She picked up the phone, paused and set it back down. What would she say? She'd promised to protect Menny. And failed. It would be easier if she called on the drive to Miami and told him over lunch.

Becks' relief at delaying the difficult conversation faded as she remembered she still had to stop by the police station. She hoped the officer she'd spoken with the night before was not on duty. Enfield? He'd been condescending and rude. Not that she'd been such a prize. Taking a quick look around her office and pulling down the roll top to hide her mess, she grabbed her purse and went downstairs.

12

Becks felt her blood pressure rise as the uniformed officer led her from the police department's sterile gray waiting area through a long corridor to the squad room. The large linoleum-tiled space was crammed with back to back metal desks, most piled high with papers, catalogs and overstuffed accordion files. Well-worn paperback directories sat atop the black file cabinets that lined three walls and an ancient floor fan turned sluggishly, providing little relief from the muggy heat.

Although Becks watched her share of police dramas, she was unprepared for the clamor in the crowded room. A few officers stood around chatting with one another while a handful mumbled into phones at their desks. Toward the back of the room, a scantily clad woman struggled to get away from the plain clothes officer pulling her along by the elbow.

The knot in her stomach twisted a half turn when Becks' escort steered her to a desk near the door and introduced her to Enfield. Just her luck! The officer barely glanced up before motioning Becks to a metal chair next to his desk and returned to his computer. Enfield was in his early thirties and looked more like a personal trainer than a cop, with dark hair combed back into a slick ponytail and outsized biceps that strained at the arms of his uniform. A spit-sized goatee sprouted at the base of his chin.

Enfield seemed as interested in Menny's disappearance as he had been the night before. Even so, Becks was stunned when he refused to act. When he finally turned toward her, she gave him the basic information—Menny's name and age, a physical description of the boy, what he wore when last seen and what the butcher said about his leaving the kosher market with an older man.

"Frankly, Mrs. Ruchinsky, it's early to worry," Enfield insisted. "He's not a child. People that age come and go when it suits them."

"Not Menny." She struggled to hide her frustration. "This was a frightened young man. And he wouldn't take off without telling me."

"He could be anywhere," Enfield continued, ignoring her comment. "Back at school. Camping with friends. Have you contacted his parents?"

"His father. He said he hasn't seen or talked to Menny in years."

"Was he worried?"

"No."

"Then there isn't much we can do."

Becks felt like slamming her hand on the desk. "Menny said he was worried about being kidnapped."

Enfield looked up from his computer. "Why would someone kidnap him?"

"I told you last night." She raised her voice, drawing a sharp glare from an older policeman rifling through a file drawer behind Enfield. "Don't you listen?" Then, regaining her composure, "He heard rumors that members of his religious community wanted to bring him back to New York. They're afraid other young people will follow his lead. Then, last Thursday, someone got into his dorm and tried to find him. The man claimed to be a friend of his family, but Menny said the visitor didn't sound like anyone he knew."

"The kid sounds paranoid."

"No." She drew out the word. "Menny's father is an important Hasidic rabbi and members of his father's community are afraid Menny will start his own sect. He was well-liked. Hasidic Jews pass the rabbinic title from father to son. It's unheard of to abandon that legacy."

Officer Enfield, who'd gazed blankly at Becks throughout her explanation, twisted his lips and stood. Feeling defeated and angry, she rose.

"I'll alert our officers to keep an eye out for the boy," Enfield said. "And call me if he returns or you hear from him. Most of these kids show up in two or three days so I wouldn't worry. If he's not back soon, let me know and we'll get word out."

Becks struggled to find words that would convince the officer Menny was in danger. She had a feeling—intuition sounded so trite—that he was hurt. She gritted her teeth in frustration and shoved her chair against Enfield's desk.

The officer snapped his laptop shut and escorted her down the hall to the waiting room, his footsteps echoing in the narrow corridor. Looking over her shoulder as she left, Becks saw him scowl and turn away.

13

"What do you mean Menny is gone?" Gabriel said as he slipped into the passenger seat of Becks' car. She'd called from the road and arranged to pick him up after class in front of the university's engineering building.

"We argued yesterday and he took off."

"Jeeze, Mom." He slammed the door.

"Now wait a minute. He nearly burned down the kitchen. Of course I was upset."

"What did you say to scare him off?"

"I don't remember." She took a deep breath to control her exasperation at Gabe's inability to understand her anger. "Something about most people being able to use an oven. It doesn't matter now."

She pulled around the circular drive that fronted the building and, after a few blocks, took a right on to Ponce de Leon Boulevard, which ran the length of the college. An elevated train rumbled along its tracks to their left across from the university's sleek buildings and lush green lawns.

"The point is I'm doing everything I can to find him." She told Gabe about her call to Menny's father and visit to Shapiro's and the police station. "Did Menny say anything about friends or relatives here? Someone older he trusted enough to go off with."

"The only person I can think of is the rabbi at Chabad. Menny trusts him. He is bald and fat but he does not look old. Menny never left the dorm except to go to classes and Chabad. He studied a lot. It took him longer than most people to do his work."

"He must have told you something about his past, maybe someone he didn't get along with?" Becks fought to mask her impatience.

Gabe was silent as Becks pulled on to Dixie Highway and edged her aging Mercedes into the left lane. After waiting what felt like an eternity for the light to change, she took a left onto Sunset Drive. Passing art galleries, restaurants and upscale boutiques, Becks parked in front of the French bistro where she'd reserved a sidewalk table. It was a quarter to one and the shopping district was crowded with well-dressed businessmen and women on their way to and from lunch.

"Menny mentioned living in a small town in upstate New York," Becks said after a young woman in pigtails seated them and handed out menus. "Did he tell you anything about that?

"Not much. The place had a funny name. I can't remember what it was."

"Did he have any friends there?"

Gabe lifted his shoulders and quickly dropped them. "I think he worked as a bookkeeper. He wanted to make money to go to college. Everyone in the town was Hasidic but Menny said he left after a few months. He didn't like it."

They stopped speaking as the waitress approached to take their orders.

"Is that why he moved here?" Becks asked when the server was out of earshot.

"No. He came to Miami for the same reason everyone else does. Lots of sun. Lots of Jews." Gabriel glanced at his mother out of the corner of his eye; she could see he was checking her reaction. She laughed and he smiled. She treasured the rare occasions when he made a joke.

"There is one other thing," Gabe said. "You know that man who came to see Menny the day we left. Menny said he did not know the man. I believe Menny because he does not lie. But the man acted like he knew Menny."

Gabe stopped speaking and turned to watch two girls in short dresses stroll by. Then, smiling sheepishly at his mother, he continued "Was the man Menny left the grocery with tall and fat? The guy looking for him was a big, fat man."

"The butcher at Shapiro's said he was short. He didn't mention his weight. What did Menny say after you told him about the visitor?"

"At first he looked scared. Then he acted like he was not worried." Gabe frowned. "He agreed to come up to Boca Raton to hide. So he was scared. Right?"

Becks nodded.

A minute later, the waitress slid their orders on to the small cast iron table—Caesar salad for her, a hamburger for Gabe.

"Since when do you eat hamburgers without cheese?" Becks asked as the server retreated.

"What do you mean?"

"You used to be king of the cheeseburger." Cheeseburgers were on the short list of foods Gabe *would* eat. "You trying to get rid of the freshman fifteen?" She laughed. Despite a marked lack of coordination which prevented him from playing team sports, Gabe looked as lean as ever.

He glared at her. "I did not gain fifteen pounds. Menny never ate cheese with a hamburger. It is not kosher. Did you know that the Jewish dietary laws were received by Moses at Mount Sinai at the same time he received the Ten Commandments?"

Becks sighed. "No Gabe. I didn't know. Let's talk about that some other time. Right now, I need ideas about how to find Menny."

"I will ask around. Maybe another kid in the dorm saw something. Mom, you will find him?" His voice took on a plaintive tone, much as it had when he was younger and wanted her to solve a problem—stop a bully, get other kids to play with him. It was a long time since he'd asked for a favor and her shoulders slumped at the prospect of failing him.

"I'll do my best," she said, not bothering to add there wasn't much she could do. She wasn't having any luck convincing the police to investigate. "He'll show up in a few days. Dad says he's upset and will be back when he's ready."

"You think so?" Gabriel said. He took a bite of his hamburger.

Becks raised her palms. She had doubts and couldn't lie. Gabe would sense it. "Darling, I just don't know."

Tired and cranky from the sludge-like traffic on I-95, Becks walked into a house filled with the aroma of spicy sausage and found pepperoni pizza and Daniel waiting at the kitchen table. He was peeling mozzarella off his tee shirt.

"How'd it go with Gabe?" he said, handing her a slice after he'd cleaned himself up.

"He took it pretty well but the police were useless. They're sure Menny will come home eventually." She took a bite. The pizza sizzled against the top of her palate and she gulped the iced tea from Daniel's glass. .

"They're probably right." He slid another slice onto

his plate. "Why don't you give Menny the weekend to cool off? You can call the police if he isn't home Monday. By then, he'll have recovered from your outburst."

"You think so?" She watched Daniel eat a third slice of pizza. He seemed so unconcerned about their guest's disappearance. Did he not care? Or was she making herself crazy for no reason?

He looked up and smiled. "I do. Come on. Eat up before it gets cold."

Becks wasn't convinced but she hadn't learned anything that day that would help her find Menny. And with a deadline on her Sabbath dinner article looming, she needed to get back to work. She took a second slice of pizza. Monday would come soon enough.

14

Daniel was working at the hospital so Becks spent the weekend testing apricot chicken recipes she planned to feature in her article on traditional Sabbath dinners. Fortunately, she'd found replacement grates for her stovetop at an appliance store near her home and could brown the pieces before putting them in the oven. As she cut up chicken and heated oil early Sunday morning, she recalled Menny's reaction to her outburst—his eyes wide and face pale as he backed away from her. She felt so sure he'd calmed down by the time they finished cleaning the kitchen. So why did he leave? Embarrassment? Shame? Fear of her temper? She was so preoccupied with the reasons for his departure she nicked her thumb chopping onions.

By noon, she was at her computer finishing up the article—two thousand words, three recipes—when the doorbell rang. She jumped from her chair and ran downstairs.

It had to be Menny.

"Just a minute," she called out. Her pulse raced as she opened the door. "Honey, what . . ."

She brought a hand to her throat.

Officer Enfield waited on the front porch, his gaze glued to his feet. A middle-aged man in a blue blazer stood next to him.

"May we come in?" the older of the two asked. Becks

recognized him as Detective Cole, the officer she'd dealt with a year earlier while investigating her father's criminal past. Things hadn't gone well between them. If he remembered, he hid it well.

Becks stared over Enfield's shoulder into the police cruiser. Menny wasn't there. Her knees grew weak and she grasped the door jamb.

"Is Menny . .?" She swallowed to clear the lump in her throat. "Did you find him?"

"Why don't we talk inside?" Cole's voice deepened in command.

Turning, Becks led the officers to her family room and motioned them to the sofa before dropping into a wingback chair. The men sat ramrod straight, knees forward, feet flat on the floor. She struggled to control her foot, which was jiggling involuntarily against the chair leg.

"I'm sorry," Cole said. He seemed genuinely concerned. "We think we found Menny's body."

"Menny's body?" The words didn't seem real. "You mean he's . . ." Becks clutched the arms of her chair and half rose as bile filled her throat. She grew light-headed and dropped back into the seat.

Cole stood and walked toward her, but she waved him off. It felt like hours before her nausea and fogginess passed enough to speak. "How did you . . . that is when . . ."

"A jogger found a young man's body near Potomac Road around seven this morning." Becks stared at the antique clock on the end table. It was half past noon. "Officer Enfield was the first to respond. When I arrived, he mentioned your report of a missing boy. We found his wallet."

"Do you know when . . ?"

It's too early to tell. He seems to have fallen off his bike into the canal."

"His bike?"

The detective nodded. "We found it a few feet from the water."

Becks frowned. "He didn't have a bike."

Cole raised an eyebrow. "He could've stolen one."

"Menny? A kid like that doesn't steal."

The policemen exchanged uneasy glances.

Gazing past the officers, Becks watched as a blue jay winged its way across the yard and alit on her birdhouse. Menny dead? Impossible. Was she really sitting here listening to these officers talk about his "body?"

"Ma'am." Detective Cole broke in.

Her neck grew warm. "I'm sorry.

"We'll need you to identify him."

"Of course." She tried to swallow the lump in her throat. "When?"

"Now if you can."

"I . . . I guess so. Where is . . . he?"

"By the E-3 canal. On Potomac Road near St. Andrews. The medical examiner's office is still on the scene. It looks as if he slipped and went in. His head hit the culvert so he may have been unconscious when he fell in the water." Becks winced. "It appears to have been an unfortunate accident."

"An accident?" Her voice rose.

"There's no reason to suspect otherwise. As I said, we're still investigating. We'll know more after the autopsy."

"I don't understand. What was he doing on Potomac? It's not on the way to Shapiro's Market. That's where he was headed."

"Maybe he got lost or decided to explore," Cole said.

"Not Menny." She stared at the officers, her palms clasped as though in prayer over her mouth. She took a deep breath and tried to process what Cole said. Menny dead? That was hard enough to accept. But the detective was wrong. Menny's death was not an accident. There were too many coincidences. His fear of being kidnapped. The stranger at the dorm. She'd run through this with Officer Enfield. Now she told Detective Cole. He listened and took notes without commenting.

Becks rose and put her hands on her hips. "Menny did not get lost. I made him a map before he left. And I offered him a bike, which he refused. It doesn't make sense."

"It seldom does," Officer Enfield said. It was the first he'd spoken and Becks glared at him. Then she caught herself. It was the best he could do. Though she wanted to blame him, she doubted the officer could've prevented what happened.

The detective rose and buttoned his coat. Enfield stood.

"Do you want to come with us now? Or would you prefer to meet us at the canal?" Cole's brow furrowed. "Can I call someone to be with you?"

"I'm fine," Becks said as she walked the men to the door. It was a lie. She was devastated by Menny's death and furious at the ease with which they'd written it off as an accident. She felt as though her head would split with anger. "I'll be there soon."

Once the police were gone, Becks returned to the family room and stared into the backyard. Her chest felt heavy but she couldn't cry. She was too angry at the police, at herself, at the world. How could this innocent young man be dead? Guilt ate at the edges of her consciousness like a reel of burning film, melting and fading slowly to the interior. How could she have yelled at Menny after all he'd been through? What kind of monster let a lost soul like that wander off on a rainy night? And why had she dismissed his claim that a strange man was pursuing him?

Detective Cole said he was still investigating Menny's death. But it sounded as though he'd made up his mind: Menny had slipped off a bike and knocked his head on a culvert before falling into the canal! That may have happened—Becks had doubts. The police *had* to look into the possibility he was murdered. Menny deserved that much.

Becks knew she was delaying the inevitable but made herself a cup of tea and called Daniel. He offered to join her at the crime scene and Becks said she'd be fine. Daniel, who sounded busy and stressed, didn't press the issue. They decided to drive to Miami after Daniel got home that afternoon to tell Gabe.

First, though, Becks had to identify Menny's body. She grabbed her purse and got in the car, steeling herself for what she knew would be one of the grimmest moments of her life.

15

The City of Boca Raton is a network of canals and even the most expensive communities are islands bordered by a grid of weed-choked ditches. Built to create farmable land out of Everglades muck, the drainage canals carry runoff from South Florida's torrential rains to the ocean. Without these channels, the city would be a pestilence-ridden swamp.

When Becks pulled off Potomac Road, the banks of the E-3 canal were teeming with investigators. Yellow crime scene tape bordered the area, blocking curious bystanders from crossing the sandy soil and brush that led down a steep embankment to the water. Behind the tape, technicians in black cargo pants buzzed around the canal, measuring and photographing the scene, making charts and sliding samples of sand and plants into bags. Becks stopped a moment to watch a technician brush gray powder on the handgrips of a rusty bike near a stand of saw palmetto.

Spotting Becks, Detective Cole waved her over. She pulled back her shoulders to brace herself before slipping under the tape and joining him and a diminutive middle-aged man kneeling near a black body bag. As she drew near, the sickly-sweet smell of rotting flesh assaulted her. She held a hand over her nose to block out the revolting odor.

"Are you sure you want to do this?" Cole said as he crouched and reached toward the bag. The outline of a long, narrow body showed through the fabric.

Becks swallowed. "Yes."

Although she expected to see Menny, Becks gasped as Cole unzipped the bag and confirmed her fears. The boy's face was swollen and blotchy and bits of flesh hung loosely from his cheeks like a creature from the swamp. But the nose—or what was left of it—was unmistakable.

She turned away. "It's him." Her voice caught.

"Thank you," Cole said. He nodded and two men waiting nearby shifted the bag onto a stretcher. They carried it toward a white van parked on the swale.

Becks took a step back to leave but the detective cleared his throat. "One more favor. Could you take a look at this?" He removed a small plastic bag from his pocket and held it out to Becks. Inside was a large gold charm in the shape of a six-pointed star. "Do you recognize it? We found it near the road and thought it might belong to the boy."

"It's a Star of David. I never saw it on Menny."

"Thank you." The detective turned and handed the bag to a technician. Looking back toward the street, Becks watched the men slide Menny's body into the van. A minute later, the vehicle pulled off the swale and drove west.

Becks blinked and wiped her eyes. She felt oddly disappointed at the absence of sirens and flashing lights. It seemed something significant should mark the body's removal. A bugler playing taps? An a cappella dirge? She gave herself a shake. All of that noise and light was for the living. The dead got nothing. Just a lonely ride to the morgue. The van's rear lights flashed as it took a left onto Military Trail.

Not yet ready to go home and face the ugly reality of Menny's death, Becks turned to face the crime scene. A small woman in a black uniform knelt near the canal and swabbed a rust-colored spot on the cement culvert that spanned the water. Was that where Menny hit his head?

She chewed her lower lip. No. Menny did not hit his head on the pipe. At least, not after slipping in the sand. And he didn't steal a bike. Most telling, he wouldn't stop by the canal to explore the embankment. He was too upset to do anything but visit the market and return home with dinner.

Menny was murdered, pure and simple. It was up to her to convince the police to investigate. No matter what it took.

16

"That's crazy," Daniel said as he pulled out of the driveway before heading to Miami. It had been five hours since Becks identified Menny's body and they were on their way south to tell Gabe about Menny's death. They'd been arguing since Daniel walked into the house. "This is none of your business. The police will handle it. If they say it was an accident, it was an accident."

"But they won't consider murder." Becks jammed the buckle into her seat belt. "When I went to the station to report him missing, the police blew me off. Today, I tried to convince the detective that Menny might've been murdered and he ignored me. All they care about is getting the case off their books."

Daniel was quiet as they pulled onto Jog Road and then took a left on Glades. "Do you have proof he was murdered?"

"Of course not." They'd stopped at a light and Becks looked to her right, where an elderly woman in leopard skin pants pushed a stroller along the sidewalk. Becks turned back to Daniel. "We knew Menny was afraid of being kidnapped."

"Based on what? A rumor that people in his community were upset he left? A dorm visit from a man who may or may not have been a threat? It's not much to go on."

Becks was about to respond when the woman with the stroller drew alongside the car. Spotting a fluffy white dog in a rhinestone collar where a child should've sat, she nudged Daniel. He glanced over and smiled.

As much as she hated to admit it, Daniel was right. She didn't have much to go on. Even so, she didn't believe Menny's death was an accident. How'd that bike reach the canal bank if Menny hadn't brought it? She'd mentioned that to Daniel, who pointed out she had no proof Menny couldn't ride a bike. She'd check with the boy's mother—if she could reach her. At the thought of Mrs. Tannenbaum, Becks' throat grew tight. This could've happened to one of their boys.

"Have you talked to Menny's parents?" Daniel asked as though reading her mind.

"The police informed them today. If there is a funeral, I'd like to go."

"Of course." He reached across the seat and rubbed her arm. His hand was rough but warm and comforting. "I know you feel responsible, sweetheart. It isn't your fault. What happened to Menny is terrible, a horrible accident. But it wasn't because of anything you did."

"I'd like to believe that." She bit her lip, struggling to hang on to her anger at the police. It was a lot easier to deal with than the guilt she'd been battling all day. At least twice that afternoon, it had blanketed her like a layer of ash, leaving her nearly paralyzed. "I promised to protect him."

"I did too."

"That's different"

Daniel glanced at Becks, eyebrows drawn in a deep frown. She stared ahead at the road. The traffic on I-95 moved at a snail's crawl.

"What do you mean?" he asked.

Becks searched for the words to explain how Menny's death had forced her to face the reality that she couldn't shield the people she loved. She'd always seen that as her role. The mother. The protector. She was frightened by the realization that what happened to Menny could've happened to their sons, especially Gabe, who was so innocent and vulnerable.

"I'm the one who was at home with Menny most of the day," she said, "and I got to know him pretty well. I knew how sensitive he was and should've controlled my temper." Her stomach roiled as she recalled the frightened look on his face when she'd yelled at him.

"You couldn't have anticipated his death." Daniel shifted into the left lane, edging his VW between a Buick and Audi.

Daniel was right. And his words assuaged some of her guilt. Even so, she'd let Menny and her son down. The prospect of breaking the news to Gabe left her cold and queasy.

Becks and Daniel parked behind Gabe's dorm and walked around to the entrance, where they found their son watching a soccer game on the field that fronted the building. Becks sensed from the slump of his shoulders that he yearned to be on the field, yelling and laughing and kicking the ball. But Gabe was clumsy and had never done well with team sports. Or anything else that involved youngsters. She couldn't keep track of the number of times he'd hit other toddlers for touching his toys or refusing to play by his rules. His awkwardness and weak social skills still prevented his making friends or fitting in with new groups of people.

Today, he looked so young and handsome and—there was no other way to describe it—innocent as he waved and ran toward his parents. Her heart ached as she realized Menny's death would end that. Gabe had few friends and the loss of even one might send him into a tailspin. She sighed deeply, anticipating a tantrum or, at the other end of the spectrum, complete withdrawal and silence. It could go either way and take days to recover.

As he walked toward them, Gabe glanced at the watch that never left his wrist. "You made it in record time. Forty-seven minutes. That's fifteen less than last time. How fast were you going?"

"Seventy-five. Eighty," Daniel said. Gabe, who'd never outgrown his obsession with numbers, would turn it into a math problem.

He looked around. "Where's Menny? Didn't you bring him?"

"He couldn't make it," Becks said, anxious not to lie. "Why don't we go for a ride and talk?"

Daniel led the way to the rear of the building and got in the car. When Gabe stood at the back door without entering, his father reached back and opened it. "Get in. We'll fill you in on what happened with your friend."

Gabe hopped into the back seat and bombarded them with questions. "Why didn't Menny come? Is he mad at me? Why did he stay home?" His voice rose in frustration. After a five-minute drive past shops and homes along Red Road, Daniel pulled into the parking lot of a tennis complex and switched off the engine.

He pivoted to face Gabe in the back seat. "I'm afraid we have bad news, Gabe. The Boca Raton police found Menny's body this morning." He waited a few seconds. "He drowned in a canal near Potomac Road."

Becks glared at her husband. Did he have to be so blunt? Gabe sat up straight and his eyes grew wide. "His . . . his body? What do you mean his body?"

"I'm sorry sweetheart," Becks said. "A jogger found Menny this morning. The police think he slipped and hit his head on a concrete pipe. They said he was probably unconscious when he went in the water."

Gabe's lips trembled. "He is dead! Menny is dead? I do not believe you." He stared at Becks, then at Daniel. "You told me he went out to pick up dinner? Why was he at the canal? It is not on the way home." He rubbed the crease in his pants between his thumb and index finger.

"Becks." Daniel's voice held a warning.

She hesitated, concerned about Gabe's reaction. He was upset but he wasn't having a meltdown—yet. She didn't know if he could handle her suspicion Menny was murdered.

"I asked the police about that." She glared at Daniel as though daring him to interrupt. "They said he might've gotten lost or gone there to delay his return home. They found a bike where he went in and thought he fell off."

"Menny could not ride a bike."

Becks stared at Gabe. "How do you know?"

"I said he could borrow mine a few weeks ago when he was late to class. He said he didn't know how to ride it."

Gabe stared blindly ahead for a few minutes before splitting the air with a loud moan. He dropped his head in his hands and continued to moan, rocking back and forth, back and forth, a movement he'd long relied upon to relieve stress. Becks had witnessed it hundreds of times and still fought a strong urge to comfort Gabe with a touch to the shoulder, a pat to the head. That would make it worse. Daniel—who had a habit of leaving the room during Gabe's meltdowns—scowled and stared out the window.

After five minutes, Gabe raised his head. His eyes were red. "I can't believe Menny's gone." He sobbed and looked at Becks, anger and confusion playing across his face. "He was my friend. You were supposed to protect him. You promised." He slammed his fists into the seat.

Becks swallowed to relieve the ache in her throat. "I'm sorry." She reached over the seat for his hand but he jerked it away. "We can't bring Menny back. Maybe we can convince the police to investigate. I saw where he went in."

Gabe stared at her. "You went to the canal?"

"The police were still on the scene. I wanted to find out why he slipped. I'm trying to convince the detective to look into it." She decided it would be best not to describe the crime scene.

"Why?" Gabe spoke in a monotone. "You think someone pushed him?"

Becks held her breath, afraid he'd withdraw. But he kept talking.

"What did the police say?"

"They hemmed and hawed," she said and added "refused to listen" so Gabe would understand. "Said they'd consider it. I don't think they will. It was probably a horrible accident but I want to be sure." She got a tissue from her purse and handed it to Gabe. "I mentioned Menny's fear of being kidnapped and told them about the stranger who came to the dorm. Is there anything you haven't told us . . . do you know someone we could talk to about Menny's past?"

Her son's face, which had grown pale at the news of his friend's death, regained color. "I could contact his brother. Menny emailed me a Torah commentary a few weeks ago and copied it to Moshe. If I haven't deleted it . . . ." His voice trailed off as he sank back in his seat.

"That would be great. Did you see anything in his room that might help us?"

"No."

"Does he lock his door?" Becks asked.

"Yes."

"I'd like to take a look."

"Me too."

"Would your residence advisor let us in?"

"She might. Or we could use my key."

Daniel shook his head as Becks sighed. The obvious was often less than obvious to Gabe.

"Is that legal?" Daniel started the engine and fastened his seat belt.

Becks secured hers. "Why not? He gave Gabe the key. It's not like the police are running down here to investigate. And I don't see his parents flying to Miami to retrieve his belongings."

Daniel shook his head. "It sounds an awful lot like breaking and entering. I should call and let Tootsie know he may have to bail us out."

"Don't you dare," Becks said as Daniel put the car in reverse. "He'll come running over to help."

17

The administrator of Gabe's dorm had been sympathetic when Becks explained he had Asperger's and suggested he move into a single room so he could retreat when overwhelmed. Menny had a single too. But the difference between the rooms couldn't have been greater. Gabe was obsessively tidy, each book organized by color and size, with the spines aligned a perfect half-inch from the edge of the bookcase. His desk was clear of objects and his sheets were so tautly drawn a drill sergeant could bounce a quarter on the bed. Except for the Torah quotations hung in a neat row on the wall above the bed, the room looked like a scene from a military recruiting film.

When they returned to the dorm, Gabe removed Menny's key from his desk drawer and handed it to Becks. She hesitated before taking it. She'd want to be the first to enter her son's room if, God forbid . . . Given Rabbi Tannenbaum's reaction, though, the odds seemed slim he'd come to Miami for Menny's possessions. She followed Gabe and Daniel across the hall and unlocked the door.

"Pathetic isn't it," Gabe said, flipping on the light.

Becks couldn't argue with her son's assessment. She'd expected the room to hold a sense of Menny, for the objects he owned and pictures he hung to shed light on the boy's life the way a museum's collection provided insight into a culture. But the room felt abandoned, as though whoever lived there had deserted it years earlier. A faint odor of mold and unwashed laundry hung in the air. A knot of yellowing sheets lay atop the narrow mattress and crumpled tissues and dust bunnies littered the floor. A dozen textbooks were scattered across the desk next to the one unique object in the room; a nest of leather straps and boxes Becks recognized as tefillin. She blinked away a tear as she imagined Menny at his desk, wrapping them around his arm and forehead as he prayed in the airless room.

The only other sign that someone had occupied the room were two unframed photos Menny had taped to the wall above the desk. In the smaller of the two, he smiled at the camera, his arm draping the shoulders of a teenager who, like himself, wore a traditional Hasidic frock coat. Becks recognized the pockmarked stone background as Jerusalem's Wailing Wall. In the other photo, three tousle-haired girls in purple dresses and silver cardboard "tiaras" grinned at the camera. Behind them, a plump, rosy-cheeked woman held up her hand as though to block the lens. Becks slipped the photos into her purse. She'd see that his parents received them.

"Mom, Dad, look at this," Gabe called from the closet, a sheaf of papers in his hand. "I found it in a shoebox on the floor."

Becks took the papers and sat on the bed to read as Daniel and Gabe continued to scour Menny's meager belongings. The first page was a copy of a two-column article—no source—about government funding for a yeshiva in Kleynshtot, New York. According to the writer, town leaders had stolen thousands of dollars in federal funding intended for the school. Two of the conspirators had disappeared. The next page was an editorial that read, in part:

Of all the acts the governor granted as he left office,

*few strike as close to illegal as his decision to reduce the
prison terms of three New York Hasidic Jews convicted in
2009 for bilking millions of dollars from the government.
The funds, intended for the construction of a yeshiva, went
toward community housing and into the pockets of the
convicted men.*

Why had Menny held on to these articles? Then Becks
remembered. Menny had mentioned living in a small town
in upstate New York? Kleynshtot sounded familiar, but the
crimes took place before Menny got there. Maybe he was
doing a paper on the topic. She asked Gabe.

"I do not know. He was taking biology, chemistry,
economics and some kind of math. Game theory, I think."

Becks searched the room, rifling through Menny's desk
and closet once more. She found several three-ring binders
crammed with what looked like algebraic proofs but nothing
more on Kleynshtot. She slipped the papers Gabe had found
into her purse. When Daniel frowned, she whispered, "for
the police." Detective Cole might toss the articles. Still, she'd
feel better knowing she brought them to his attention.

Satisfied they'd learned all the room had to offer, Becks
and Daniel said their goodbyes and returned to the car. Gabe
went back to his room, promising to give Menny's key to the
residence advisor that evening. As they drove north, Becks
watched the sun slip behind the warehouses and gas stations
along I-95 before wobbling like an egg yolk and seeping
below the horizon. The concrete buildings glowed orange in
the fading light. Becks was tired. But she needed to make
one more stop before going home.

Daniel slammed the driver's side door and stomped across
the parking lot toward Tootsie's building. "I don't know
why you can't phone your father," he called over his
shoulder. "It's late and I need to get up early tomorrow."

"We won't be long," Becks said, running to catch up. It was dark and damp and humidity hung over the black-tarred lot like a sodden blanket, releasing a sweet odor of damp bitumen. Even so, a dozen elderly residents sat in neatly aligned rows of chairs on the front porch of her father's building. Becks waved at two elderly ladies who'd wiggled their fingers at her. Old friends of her mother? She couldn't tell in the sickly yellow light.

She'd spent the entire drive to her father's trying to convince Daniel that Tootsie might be able to help her look into Menny's death.

"You've got to be kidding." He gunned the engine. "Menny fell in a canal and drowned. That's all we need to know. Don't stir things up. It'll only make Gabe feel worse."

When Becks didn't respond, he continued, "How do you think Gabe would take the news Menny was murdered? It's tough enough losing a friend at his age. But discovering he was killed? That would send Gabe over the edge."

Becks shrugged. Nothing she said would convince Daniel she owed it to Menny and his parents to look into the boy's death. Her husband could be right about Gabe's reaction but she doubted it. He'd come around quickly enough after learning of the boy's death. As for stopping at Tootsie's, she hadn't seen her father in a while. He'd owned a restaurant supply business before retiring and was still in touch with all sorts of characters—some of them not so kosher. Who knew what connections he had in the Hasidic world?

When Becks called from the car to say they were coming, Tootsie announced that he'd just left his regular poker game and was feeling flush. She and Daniel should come upstairs for a drink. Becks smiled. The last "cocktail" he'd offered her had been Manischewitz on ice.

Becks and Daniel crossed the lobby in an uncomfortable silence that persisted as they rode the elevator and walked down the hall to Tootsie's apartment.

"So, what brings you to Miami?" Tootsie greeted them at the door and led them into the combination living and dining room. The one-bedroom apartment he rented in the Sadie Sackowitz Independent Living Facility was a fraction the size of the house in which Becks grew up. Tootsie made it feel like home, though, filling its walls with colorful modernist paintings her mother had purchased at estate sales. A small kitchen with a pass through opened to the common area. On the far side of the room, a tiny table with two chairs faced sliding glass doors that framed a tiny cement patio and the narrow, sparsely planted walkway that served as Sadie Sackowitz's excuse for a garden,

"We came to see Gabe and thought we'd stop by," she said as the three took seats. "Are you feeling all right?"

"I can't complain. Speaking of which, you ever get rid of the curlie Gabe brought home? That was one strange kid."

Becks bit her lower lip.

"He died," Daniel said.

"What?" The old man's chair creaked as he jolted forward.

"The police found his body this morning. He left our house to go to the grocery store but never returned. The police found him in a canal."

"Jesus Christ," Tootsie said. "What happened?"

Becks glared at Daniel, then told her dad about Menny's fear of being abducted and the stranger's visit to his dorm. She also filled him in on the kitchen fire and losing her temper with Menny.

When she finished, her father leaned back and folded his arms. "Just goes to show. You don't want to mess with those black hats."

Daniel, opening a beer in the kitchen, snorted.

"What're you talking about?" Becks said.

"The Hasids. They're a bunch of gangsters."

"How can you say such a thing?"

Daniel held up a second beer. She shook her head.

"I been around. They could have drowned the kid. You think the long coats and sideburns mean they're better than us? Ha." He barked out a laugh. "Those Yids know how to work the system. They're all on welfare, you know."

Becks considered the Hasidic families she'd seen in Miami Beach. They seemed comfortable and well-dressed, pushing what looked like new strollers. The children, though heavily bundled for Florida's warm weather, seemed healthy.

"How do they manage that?" Daniel asked, coming around the kitchen to join them in the living room.

"Political donations." Tootsie gave a brisk nod.

"Come on, Dad," Becks said. "You can't be serious?" Her father was a wealth of information, much of it made up.

"There's a lot you don't know, Doll. Tell you the truth, I'm not sure how much of that goes on down here but it's routine in New York. You deliver the votes and you get the tax breaks, housing funds, you name it." He paused and stared at Becks as though waiting for her to object. When she didn't, he leaned forward, hands on his knees. "A lot of these guys are in the jewelry business. Cash only. Then you've got these towns full of deadbeats who think taxpayers should support them so they can spend their time praying."

"How do you know this?" Becks asked. Her father hadn't lived in New York in fifty years. And he'd never mentioned ultraorthodox friends. Then again, there was a lot she didn't know about him. A year earlier, he let slip that he'd worked with members of the Jewish syndicate as a young man.

"Hasids have to eat too." He smirked. "You haven't seen the fancy kosher restaurants in Miami Beach? They had to buy their pots and pans somewhere. Some of my best customers were curlies."

"Your customers told you?" Daniel asked.

"They're not ashamed. Figure they're God's chosen people so they have a right to game the system. Some of the restaurant owners who moved to Florida asked me to fake sales receipts so they could avoid taxes. Acted like it was business as usual."

Becks groaned inwardly but decided not to argue. For all she knew, her father was right, though she doubted it. Instead, she reached for her purse and pulled out the papers from Menny's dorm. "You hear of this place, Kleynshtot? A Hasidic community near the city." She leaned across the table to hand him the pages.

He grasped a corner between his thumb and index finger and held the sheaf away from his body as though handling a dead rodent. "What is this?"

"I found these articles in Menny's dorm. They're about Hasids from Kleynshtot who got caught defrauding the government."

"So?"

"So your grandson's only friend died. I thought maybe you knew someone who could shed light on who Menny was, or how he might be connected to this Kleynshtot business?

Tootsie rolled his eyes and gave Daniel a look that read "Dames." "I'll ask around." He glanced at the first page. "Weird name for a town." He handed the papers back.

Daniel cleared his throat. Becks took the hint and stood. "Good to see you, Dad. We'd better be going."

"Do me a favor, will you, Doll," Tootsie said as he walked them to the door. "Stay out of this. The police know what they're doing. If the curlie was murdered, they'll find out. You," he waited a beat before continuing, "need to mind your own damn business."

"Fine," Becks said, opening the door to his apartment.

Riding downstairs in the elevator, Becks wracked her brain, trying to figure out why Menny held on to the articles. Was the man who asked about him at the dorm involved in the scheme to defraud the government? If so, and Menny knew, that might provide a motive for killing him. But how would Menny have learned of the scheme or the man's involvement? Becks was so lost in thought that she didn't notice the elevator open until Daniel took her arm and led her out.

Tootsie had an uncanny talent for digging up info through his friends. Maybe he'd open a door or two to Menny's past, Becks thought, sliding into the passenger seat and pulling her door shut.

18

"Is anyone there?" Becks shouted into the phone the next day after lunch. "Can you hear me? Should I call back?"

She'd been at her desk all morning, phoning Menny's parents. Detective Cole had called at nine to tell her the medical examiner had released Menny's body. It was being flown to New York that afternoon. This was the fifth time Becks had dialed the Tannenbaum's and the first time she'd heard the line pick up. She'd spaced the calls an hour apart, hoping the family would return home and answer the phone.

"Vat do you want?" It was Menny's father.

"This is Becks Ruchinsky. I called a few days ago about Menny."

Silence.

"I wanted to tell you and Mrs. Tannenbaum how sorry my family and I are about your loss. I thought maybe if I told you . . . well, we were very fond of Menny."

She didn't know what to say. And Rabbi Tannenbaum wasn't making it easy.

"Listen, Miss, I appreciate your call. We'll deal with this ourselves. I have to go."

"Will there be a funeral?"

No answer.

"I'd like to . . ."

She heard a faint click. He'd hung up on her!

"Damn," she said, slamming the phone into its cradle. The man was a hard SOB. Granted, he'd lost his son and was grieving. She'd be devastated, too. But to hang up on someone calling to offer sympathy?

Menny's father was a rude, boorish man. That wasn't her problem. Just the same, she knew Menny's mother would find solace in hearing about her son's last days. Becks would want the same if, God forbid, one of her boys died. And Becks liked Menny, wanted to do what she could for his family.

A trickle of guilt clawed at her conscience. What if they learned that she'd yelled at their son? She'd have to explain what happened. Becks pushed the thought from her mind. Her mission now was getting Mrs. Tannenbaum on the phone without the rabbi running interference. She wasn't having much luck. Which left one solution. She'd fly to New York and meet her.

It was a crazy idea and she didn't know if Mrs. Tannenbaum would talk to her. Daniel and Tootsie were right. It wasn't any of her business. Even so, above and beyond any moral obligation, Becks was curious about the Hasidic life Menny had left. And she might learn something that would convince the police the boy was murdered.

She opened her laptop and booked her flight.

19

Sushi Joe's was busier than usual for a weeknight and steel knife blades flashed under pinpoint lights as the chefs behind the sushi counter carved ahi tuna and salmon into paper-thin slices. After greeting the hostess, Becks and Daniel made their way past the fifty-gallon fish tank and seated themselves at the counter. Daniel was unwrapping his chopsticks when Becks spoke.

"I'm planning to go to New York this week." She held her breath, waiting for his reaction. She knew he'd be upset. .

He set the chopsticks down. "Why?"

"I want to meet Menny's mother and tell her about his time with us."

"Wouldn't she call if she wanted to talk to you?"

"I don't think she knows I exist. I told you how controlling his father was."

"That was when Menny was alive." Daniel picked up the menu. "Wouldn't he tell his wife that Menny stayed with us? That he wasn't alone at the end? "

"I doubt it. I called him today."

"How'd that go?"

"He hung up." Taking the black linen napkin from the counter and placing it across her lap, Becks wondered how Daniel would've reacted to a condolence call from a stranger after his mother's death. He hadn't spoken to anyone for days, leaving it to Becks to contact relatives about the date and time of the funeral.

"You're probably wasting your time," Daniel said

Becks shrugged and waited as the waiter served steaming cups of green tea. She took a sip, then flinched as it burned her tongue. "At worst, it'll be a chance to visit your dad. I thought I'd stay with him."

Daniel said nothing for a moment, then set his napkin on the table. She'd forgotten that he hadn't mentioned their earlier separation to his father. "Are you going to tell him about us?"

"Only if he asks."

Daniel scowled. "Let me go on record as saying I don't want you poking around in police business. I know you, though. Once a reporter, always a reporter." He took her hand and massaged her fingers. "Do what you need and come home. If you learn anything, let the police know. If not, I hope you'll let this go."

Becks smiled and gave a vague nod. She was relieved he hadn't objected. She might learn something useful in New York. It would have to be rock solid, though, to get the police to investigate Menny's death as a murder.

20

Two days later, Becks ascended the stairs of the Kingston Avenue subway station in Crown Heights. She was grateful to be leaving the dank moldy underground even though it meant stepping into the icy wind of an unseasonably cold October morning. She rarely traveled to New York in winter and no matter how many layers of clothing she piled on, she shivered from the cold. She stopped at the top of the stairs to catch her breath. The subway station reeked of unwashed bodies and she'd run up two flights of steps to avoid being trampled by the crowd of men in black coats.

It had taken forty-five minutes to reach Crown Heights from her father-in-law's apartment on the Upper West Side and the contrast between the two communities couldn't have been more dramatic. As the subway drew closer to Brooklyn, the expensively coiffed women in designer suits abandoning the car were replaced by young men with peyos and beards. They stood and leaned into one another, whispering in soft cadences that echoed the Yiddish intonations of the Old World.

Now, shivering on the corner of Kingston and Eastern Parkway, Becks was taken aback by the drab conformity of the men and women on the sidewalk. Except for two black teenagers leaving the station, the men were virtually identical in their nondescript black coats, loose pants and broad-brimmed hats. Where a coat hung open, it revealed fringes of tzitzit extending below a long-sleeved white shirt.

The women looked equally dreary. Even the most attractive of them wore shapeless coats, black stockings and ill-fitting wigs and pushed double strollers with infants and toddlers in snowsuits. Many trailed strings of children like broods of chicks, the older girls clasping younger brothers' and sisters' hands. Several women stared at Becks, their eyes hooded and wary. She hesitated before crossing the street, surprised at sensing herself a foreigner in this intensely Jewish community. If it weren't for the grimy three- and four-story brick buildings along the street, she could've been back in eighteenth-century Warsaw.

Becks had found Menny's parents' address through the internet before leaving home. The hard part would be following the convoluted map her father-in-law, who'd grown up in Brooklyn, had drawn for her.

Stepping around icy patches along the sidewalk, Becks made her way down Kingston, past small storefronts marked by elaborately serifed signs in what she recognized as Hebrew and Yiddish lettering. The occasional English-language sign revealed most were kosher markets and butcher shops or Judaica stores. Halfway down the block, she stopped to peer in a glass window that sparkled with crystal and silver candlesticks, colorful menorahs and a collection of dreidels. The prices seemed reasonable so she made a note to stop by later. As she was about to leave, an elderly woman with a large headscarf and even larger smiled hobbled to the window and beckoned for her to enter. Embarrassed to ignore her and tempted by the warmth of the tiny shop, Becks complied.

"So darling, what brings you out on this nasty

morning?" the woman said, taking Becks' elbow and leading her into the shop. Without waiting for an answer, she continued, "We have lovely dreidels for the kinder, candlesticks if you're making a shidduch." Becks had learned enough Yiddish from her father to recognize kinder as children and shidduch as a match. The shop smelled of mildew and silver polish. Specks of dust floated in the weak rays of sunlight that penetrated the glass storefront.

"I was window shopping. I thought I might stop in later to pick up a few gifts."

"You're not from around here, are you?" The woman's voice rose and her sidelong glance suggested she would love nothing more than to know who Becks was visiting. Though uncomfortable under the woman's less-than-subtle scrutiny, she suspected the elderly yenta knew everybody in the neighborhood. Crown Heights struck her as the kind of neighborhood where *everyone* knew their neighbors' business. The woman might be able to direct her to the Tannenbaum home.

Misreading Becks' hesitation, the woman brought a hand to her chest. "I don't mean to pry." She smiled and patted Becks' shoulder. "I'm Faigy Mendehlson." Becks shook the woman's outstretched hand. It was tiny and gnarled. "Tell me what you want and I'll look around. You can stop in when you're through with your business."

The shopkeeper seemed kind. And word of a strange woman's visit was, no doubt, already circulating around the community. "That's nice of you. I'm Becks Ruchinsky. I'm trying to find Menachem Tannenbaum's home."

"Menachem?" Faigy whispered. "You knew him? Such a good boy. And smart." She shook her head. "He broke the rebbe and Hannah's hearts when he left. And then this . . ." Her voice faded as her hand drifted to her cheek. "His father is one of our most important rebbes."

"I've heard." Becks left it at that.

"How'd you meet Menachem? Had you seen him recently?" The tiny woman drew close to Becks, releasing a dry, sweet odor of faded violets.

"He was my son's friend. I promised him I'd visit Menny's mother the next time I was in New York." The woman's concern for Menny seemed genuine but Becks felt uncomfortable revealing information the family might not want to share.

Faigy nodded and compressed her lips. "I understand." She glanced at the clock over the entrance door. "I'll take you."

"I couldn't ask . . ."

"Not to worry. Business won't pick up until later this afternoon. The men are in shul now and the women are home from taking the children to school."

Becks felt the tension leave her shoulders and realized she was more apprehensive than she'd anticipated about encountering Menny's father. She imagined him as a tall cadaverous man in black who'd swoop down on her like a vulture when she showed her face at his door. Faigy's presence might make things easier and force her to control her temper.

"Wait here. I'll get my wraps."

When Faigy emerged from the curtained opening at the back of the shop, she was barely recognizable as the fragile, birdlike woman who'd greeted Becks. Her head was swathed in a fringed paisley scarf that hid everything except her shiny black eyes and her body was encased in a black coat over which she wore a red down vest. The coat reached her ankles, revealing a pair of white sneakers and black stockings.

After switching off the lights at the back of the store and securing the deadbolt, Faigy grasped Becks' elbow and they made their way down Kingston Street. "It's not far but my balance isn't what it used to be."

Faigy stepped gingerly, cautious to avoid snowdrifts and ice patches, and it took fifteen minutes to go two blocks. The women turned right onto a tree-lined street of well-kept brick homes. The oaks along the sidewalk looked bare and desolate under the slate winter sky and Becks could picture them green and leafy and alive with birds on a summer day. Another ten minutes down the road and Faigy stopped in front of a narrow, four-story house. Though a tree grew in the tiny swale of grass opposite, the house filled its lot so completely it couldn't accommodate another blade of grass. After waiting a moment for Faigy to catch her breath, Becks helped her up a short flight of stairs to the porch.

Heart pounding, Becks pressed the buzzer and stepped back so Faigy would be visible through the peep hole. If Rabbi Tannenbaum was home, she didn't want her face to be the first thing he saw that morning.

21

The woman who opened the door was not the mousy rebbetzin—rabbi's wife—Becks had expected. Instead, a petite, full-bosomed woman with milk-white skin, pink cheeks and hair the same rich chestnut as Menny's greeted them. It looked disheveled, as though she had not brushed it in days, and the tight set of her lips suggested she was struggling to control her overwhelming grief.

"Faigy. How are you?" Hannah Tannenbaum said, throwing a questioning glance toward Becks. She grasped a red and white checked apron, its strings trailing as though she'd pulled it off while running to the door. "Come in. You must be freezing." She stepped back, holding the door as Becks and Faigy came inside. "We'll go to the kitchen where it's warmer."

After hanging her coat in a narrow closet, Becks followed Faigy and Hannah down a narrow, dimly lit hall, passing a framed mirror draped with a sheet—a mourning tradition her parents had observed after Grandma Yentl's death. Becks remembered, with a jolt, that the Tannenbaums hadn't yet buried Menny and would sit shiva for several days after. They reached a kitchen where two toddlers sat on the floor building a tower of wooden blocks. The older wore peyos and his short hair was capped by a Mickey Mouse kipa. The younger child's wispy blond hair reached his shoulders.

The kitchen, though large, was modestly furnished with white metal cabinets and an ancient gas stove. Hannah invited the women to sit at a large wooden table before reaching into a stainless refrigerator, the room's only nod to modernity, for a carton of milk.

Faigy and Becks pulled out chairs and sat.

"So, tell me Faigy, who is your friend?" Hannah said. She set the milk on the table and lit the flame beneath a metal tea kettle. The room had grown quiet and Becks looked up to find the toddlers staring at her. Hannah—who fussed about, setting out mugs, tea bags, sugar and milk—shook her head at the children.

"This is Becks Ruchinsky, Hannah. She's come from Florida to talk about . . ." Faigy hesitated then nodded toward the toddlers, "a relative." Hannah raised an eyebrow and finished arranging the tea things.

Once Hannah poured the tea, Faigy leaned forward and placed her hand on their host's wrist. "She knew Menachem." She barely breathed the words.

Hannah froze and the color drained from her cheeks. Her chest rose and fell in what appeared to be a tremendous effort to restrain tears. She pulled her wrist from Faigy's hand and turned to the children.

"Asher, Schmulie, you want to watch *Aristocats*?

The youngsters scrambled up from the floor and followed their mother into the adjacent room. In a few minutes, Becks heard the sound of cartoons.

When Hannah returned, her color was back.

"My son. Menachem. You knew him?"

"He was my son, Gabe's, friend and stayed at our house for a few days before his death." She waited for Hannah's reaction before continuing. The woman blinked and brought a hand to her mouth. "Gabe asked us to take him in because he was concerned someone from your community wanted to kidnap him. He disappeared last Friday after going to a kosher market to pick up dinner. When he didn't return a few hours later, my husband and I looked for him and called the police. Then, three days later . . ." She took a deep breath. "I'm so sorry. That's why I'm here. I wanted you to know how fond I was of your son."

Hannah, who'd been standing at the head of the table, nodded and pulled out a chair. She sank into it with a heavy thud and put her head in her hands. "I should have known." Her voice broke. Faigy put a hand on Hannah's shoulder as the woman sobbed. After a few moments, she wiped her eyes and glanced toward the room in which the children watched their movie.

"My husband doesn't know and," Hannah turned to Faigy, "he mustn't find out. I've been in touch with Menachem. He mails my letters to Mrs. Selznick next door who brings them to me when the rebbe's out. Menachem didn't provide a return address because he was afraid his father would find him. I hadn't heard from my son in a week. I hoped it meant he was busy with his classes." She stared at Becks. "Why was he staying with you?" Her voice had grown hostile. "He could have called me if he was in trouble."

Becks straightened up in her chair. Was this how police felt when they brought bad news to anxious families? Her throat felt as raw as the pain etched in Hannah's face and she swallowed before speaking. "I hoped . . . that is, I called Mr. Tannenbaum after Menny disappeared from our house. I thought he'd returned home."

"I heard nothing of this." Hannah spoke quickly.

Becks debated a moment about sharing the rabbi's reaction but continued. "This might seem an odd question. I'd like to know if Menachem could ride a bike."

Hannah raised an eyebrow. "A bike? What kind of question is that?"

"I don't know if the police mentioned this. They found a bicycle where he slipped into the water. I didn't lend him one and my son says he didn't know how to ride."

"That's right. My husband didn't feel it was safe for the children to ride bikes in this neighborhood." Hannah's brow furrowed. "Why? Is that important?"

Faigy placed a hand on the woman's arm. "Let her speak."

"I'm not sure what it means." No point in airing her suspicions at this point. Becks glanced toward the front door, anxious Rabbi Tannenbaum might return early. "Why did Menachem leave?"

"He wouldn't tell me. I think he might have been ashamed of himself . . . embarrassed after his best friend went to jail."

Becks set down her mug and leaned in toward Hannah. Finally, she was getting somewhere. "What happened?"

"Levi got mixed up with drugs and got caught bringing them back from Amsterdam. Menachem was devastated. A year later, he took off. He never said why." She looked at her hands, then up at Becks. "Menny was not involved with drugs." She spoke rapidly. "Maybe he knew something . . . Levi could have . . . I just don't know."

Becks let that thread of conversation drop. As she knew from friends, the mother was often the last to know.

"Menny told me members of your community were afraid he left to start his own group of followers. He heard they might kidnap him and force him to return."

"God forbid." Hannah spit over her shoulder. "I heard the rumors. My husband says they're not true." She wouldn't meet Becks' gaze. "Most of the young people who leave are . . . lost souls, misfits. Menachem was brilliant, a leader. Naturally people were upset when he left. No one would kidnap him though."

Faigy, whom Becks had forgotten in her interchange with Hannah, broke in. "Hannah, darling, you don't know anything for sure. Ask the rebbe. Tell him what you've learned. Then we can ask this lady to help us." Turning to Becks, "Nu? You can find out what happened to the boy?"

"Me?" Becks was stunned by the question. She was here to offer her condolences and see if his family knew anything she could share with the police. But find the murderer?

"Faigy. Hannah. You don't understand. I'm not a policewoman or a detective. I'm a writer. A housewife. You should call the Boca Raton police or hire a private detective."

Hannah waved her hands in front of her face as if to ward off the evil eye. "My husband would never have it. Call in strangers? We couldn't. You're a sophisticated lady. You know the world out there." She gestured helplessly toward the front door. "You could ask around, couldn't you? At least see what you can find out?"

"I'd love to help but . . ."

Faigy stood. "Then you will." It was a command. "We need to let Hannah look after the children. She'll talk to the rebbe tonight and we'll stop by Friday." She took Becks' arm and led her to the front door. Hannah joined them but stood mute, dabbing at her eyes with a tissue as the women pulled on their wraps.

"Darling, we'll get to the bottom of this," Faigy said. "Talk to the rebbe, see what he says. This nice lady will help us."

Becks shot a quizzical glance at Faigy. When she'd wandered into the Judaica shop that morning, she had no intention of signing on as a detective. She'd have to straighten Faigy out. She buttoned her coat and helped the elderly woman down the porch steps.

Returning up Kingston toward the shop, Faigy chirped hello to the young mothers with strollers and the elderly couples scurrying along with grocery bags. She seemed to know everyone in the neighborhood. Becks waited until Faigy unlocked the deadbolt and switched on the lights before speaking. "I don't think you understand. I'd like to help Hannah. There isn't much I can do. She needs the police or someone who knows how to investigate a murder."

"But we don't know that Menachem was killed, do we?"

Becks, surprised by this line of reasoning, admitted they did not. She followed Faigy into the back of the store, where the woman shrugged off her vest and coat.

"The funeral is tomorrow. It would be best if you didn't attend. You'll come back Friday, pay a shiva call. If the rebbe has nothing to add, you visit with Hannah and go home. If he does, you bring it to your policeman friends." Becks smiled at the irony of her description. "It'll take a few minutes of your time. No big deal."

They'd been together two hours and the shopkeeper had her pegged. If Becks learned anything from Rabbi Tannenbaum, she'd feel compelled to follow up.

"Tell you what," Becks said. "I'll meet you here Friday after lunch. You make the shiva call first and find out what Hannah learns from her husband."

After slipping a pink and black apron with dancing cats over her dress, Faigy led Becks to the front of the store, stopping to pull a silver necklace with a hamsa, an open-palmed good luck charm, from the counter near the window. She wiped it off with the front of her apron, keeping her eyes down. Becks suspected she hid a smile.

"You're a strong woman. Like your biblical namesake," Faigy said. "What you're doing is a *mitzvah*. A good deed. Take this and think of the boy." She handed

Becks the necklace. "Do your best to find out what happened to him."

Becks hesitated before accepting the gift. But it was given in such a spirit of kindness and generosity, she couldn't refuse.

Thanking Faigy, Becks slipped the necklace into her purse and followed the shopkeeper to the door. "Thank you, dear," the elderly woman said. "I can't ask anything more."

22

The *bibimbap* Becks picked up in Koreatown was lukewarm by the time she ascended the subway stairs near her father-in-law's apartment an hour later. Even so, Milt was grateful for dinner and she was grateful not to venture out in the cold again. They ate at the kitchen table and watched wisps of snow fall on Columbus Circle. Milt's apartment, though small, was comfortable, the bookshelves that lined most walls filled with texts and books from his thirty-year career as an English teacher. Photos of his late wife, Sylvia, and of Becks' and Daniel's boys sat atop an upright piano that had been squeezed in behind the living room couch.

Becks dug into the spicy rice and beef dish but Milt picked at his food.

"Are you feeling all right?" Becks asked. It had been a year since his heart attack.

"I'm fine. Just not that hungry."

As Becks piled their empty takeout containers into the trash, Milt patted her chair. "Sit a minute. We need to talk."

"Don't you want coffee?"

"It can wait."

Becks' chest grew tight at Milt's tone. He'd seen his cardiologist that afternoon. She returned to the table. "Is everything okay?"

"The doctor says I'm fine," he said, apparently sensing her concern. "I want to get something out in the open and I need you to be honest with me."

She knew what was coming and took a deep breath.

"My sister—I know she promised to keep it secret— let slip that you and Daniel lived apart for a while. She wouldn't say why."

Becks hesitated. She saw no point in keeping the separation a secret but felt disloyal telling Milt she'd thrown his son out for cheating. "We were growing apart. Anyway, it's not important," she said. "What *is* important is that we're together again and love each other."

"Becks." Milt crossed his arms over his chest. Then, more gently, "I'd like to know what happened."

"I don't want you to be angry with Daniel. I've managed to get over it . . ." She let the sentence die.

"I respect that. Still, he is my son. And it pains me that neither of you came to me with your problems. You know how much I treasure you both."

"Your heart attack . . . we didn't want to add to your troubles."

"Yes, but afterward?"

"Did you ask Daniel?"

"Never mind Daniel. I want to hear it from you."

She stared out the window. The snow had ended and the puddles along the curb reflected the streetlights on Amsterdam Avenue. Milt needed to know *she* was not at fault.

She chose her words carefully. "My best guess is Daniel went through a mid-life crisis. He was depressed after his mother died and overwhelmed by Gabe's constant demands. I think he dealt with it by having an affair with one of his nurses." She took a deep breath. "When I learned about the affair, I threw him out." She was surprised by how hoarse her voice had become.

"For how long?"

"A year."

Milt pursed his lips. "How are things between you now?"

"We're fine. You don't need to worry." It was a lie. She didn't know if she'd trust Daniel again. She still had moments of deep sadness, remembering her shock at his betrayal and the intolerable loneliness of the months that followed. The back of her throat grew tight.

She rose and circled the table to hug Milt. "And even if we weren't, you'd still be my favorite father-in-law."

Milt laughed. Then, mimicking a New Jersey gangster, "I bettah be. If not, I got dis goon, Tootsie, I can send to convince youse."

Becks disentangled her arms from Milt's shoulders and kissed the top of his head. "He'd do it, too."

23

"Why can't you tell me what Hannah said?" Becks asked as she helped Faigy negotiate the frozen sidewalk along Kingston Avenue. The streets were buzzing with shoppers and Becks tried not to stare at the brigade of young women with what appeared to be identical wigs waiting with matching strollers in front of a kosher bakery. Becks' mouth watered as the aroma of freshly-baked challah emerged from the shop. She had taken the subway to Crown Heights early Friday, as promised, expecting the shopkeeper to share what the rabbi said about plans to abduct Menny. Instead, Faigy insisted Becks join her in paying a shiva call.

"You were one of the last people to see Menachem alive," Faigy said. "Maybe you have a few kind words to share."

"I already spoke with Hannah."

"This is different. The funeral was yesterday. Every Jew has an obligation to comfort the grieving."

After a few minutes of argument—the woman *was* convincing—Becks agreed to accompany her.

When they reached the Tannenbaum's, Faigy clasped Becks' arm. "Please don't be angry with me, dear. The rebbe wants to meet privately with you."

Becks jerked her arm away. "I'm not talking to the old …" she caught herself, "man. I don't need more of his insults." She knew she was being thin-skinned and didn't care. Becks turned to leave. Faigy grabbed her elbow.

"You mustn't be so quick to judge, darling. The rebbe can be stubborn and impatient. That's because he carries a heavy weight for our community. If a man wants to divorce his wife, he talks to the rebbe first. If a woman can't conceive, she prays with the rebbe. He's a wise man and no decision is made without him. Listen to what he says. If you're unhappy, leave." She stared into Becks' face, her eyes red and phlegmy. "Do it for Hannah."

It had snowed on Thursday—the day of Menny's funeral—and the house looked shabby and foreboding. Patches of mud lined the cement walkway and grimy droplets of water beaded the metal stair rail. A red pail, apparently abandoned by a child months earlier, lay at the bottom of the stairs rusting in the chill air. A plastic pitcher of water and bowl sat on a small table alongside a pile of washcloths and Becks remembered that her grandparents had observed the custom of washing their hands before entering a house of mourning.

Becks took Faigy's elbow and helped her up the stairs. "All right. I'll talk to him."

Hannah looked pale and fragile as she bade Faigy and Becks enter. After hanging up their coats and hugging Faigy, she led them down a narrow hallway, at the end of which loomed large mahogany double doors with shiny brass knobs. The pink of her cheeks had faded and the house, absent the voices of children, felt oppressive and bleak. Hannah knocked.

"Come in." A deep voice resonated from within.

Opening both doors, Hannah stepped aside and swept her hand toward the rabbi as if ushering Becks into a royal chamber. Rabbi Tannenbaum's study appeared to be one of the few rooms in the house where children were *not* welcome. Cavernous and dark, it emitted the musty odor of aged books. The rabbi, wearing a black suit and white shirt, sat in shadow on a low backless stool. A determined ray of sunlight penetrated a small window at the back of the study, throwing light across the polished mahogany desk behind the rabbi and offering the only spot of cheer. A wooden chair overflowing with books sat to the rabbi's left.

Becks felt as though she'd intruded into the rabbi's sacred sanctum—which did nothing to ease her annoyance at being tricked into meeting him. He was tall and broad-chested with a long black beard and thick fly-away eyebrows that canopied deep-set eyes. A broad-brimmed fedora sat atop a pugnacious forehead, concealing his eyes and leaving Becks unsure as to whether he'd welcome or snub her.

The rabbi rose and bowed toward Becks. Her back twitched as he stared at her, lips drawn together, and examined her face. After a moment, he nodded. "I owe you an apology."

He nodded at Hannah and Faigy and motioned, palms down, for them to sit. They perched on folding chairs lined up along a wall. The rabbi returned to his stool and indicated a wingback next to his desk, "Please make yourself comfortable."

Becks complied. She felt uncomfortable staring down at her host, who'd returned to his stool, and suspected the rabbi's choice of seating was deliberate.

"I was devastated when Menachem left," he said, "especially since he refused to explain why. I didn't sit shiva for him but I prohibited his brothers and sisters from having contact. It may sound cruel; it was one of the most painful things I've done." He dropped his hands to his lap and stared at them. His eyes were damp when he looked up. "Menachem, may his memory be a blessing, was a brilliant

Torah scholar and a good man. My father started our community for the few Jews from our village in Poland who survived the war and found their way to America. He led it for thirty years. I've been the rebbe for almost as long. I assumed Menachem, as my oldest son, would take my place."

The rabbi took a book off the stool and leafed through it. Becks felt a pang of sympathy as his shoulders rose and fell in silent sobs. "I'm sorry for my rudeness," he said once he regained his composure. "It felt like an affront when a woman, a stranger, called to ask about the son I'd almost disowned. Then when you called again, I was shamed by the fact a stranger knew more about his death than I did." He paused and looked at Becks.

"I see."

The rabbi leaned forward. "I am asking your forgiveness. You don't have to grant it but the Talmud says we must ask an injured party to forgive us. I'd be grateful if you'd confer yours."

Becks weighed her response. She was outraged by the man's treatment of Menny but sensed his pain and the sincerity of his request. Who was she to deny forgiveness? She couldn't judge the man. She'd never known what it was like to lose a son—first to the world outside one's own and then to death. Forgiving the man wouldn't bring the boy back. Still, it might ease his guilt.

"I forgive you." Her words sounded stilted.

"Thank you." He nodded twice. "My wife told me you took Menachem into your home. We're grateful for your kindness. She also mentioned your suspicions and I assure you that no one in our community would kidnap or harm my son. A few men were afraid he'd start a separate group. I ended that talk. Most of the discontents who raised that issue have left our community."

He stood. "What happened to Menachem, may he rest in

peace, was God's will. Nothing can bring him back but we can honor his memory. I understand you are looking into his death, that you don't believe it was an accident. I hope you're wrong. Even so, you have my permission to continue."

Becks pressed her fists into her thighs. *His* permission?

"If there's nothing else . . ." The rabbi reached for a book on the adjacent stool.

At the sound of metal against wood, Becks glanced over her shoulder to find Faigy and Hannah rising and smiling expectantly. They seemed impressed with the rabbi's words.

Becks was not.

"There *is* one more thing," she said, turning back to the rabbi. "Menny told me he was happy here, that he didn't want to leave. Do you have any idea why he felt compelled to abandon his community?"

The man's eyebrows merged into a deep frown. "I wish I did."

"He told me returning here would endanger his family. Did someone threaten him? Did he argue with you?"

The rabbi's visage darkened. "Certainly not."

"All right then." Becks fought to mask her satisfaction at wiping the self-righteous look off the man's face. "I'll leave you now."

She strode through the double doors, Faigy and Hannah trailing close behind.

Returning to the front of the house, Becks heard the murmur of voices—friends had evidently arrived to sit shiva with the family—and turned down Hannah's invitation to lunch. Instead, she and Faigy wrapped up against the cold and retraced their steps to Kingston Street, ducking into the first delicatessen they encountered. Inside, posters of kosher hot dogs, corned beef sandwiches, knishes and matzo ball soup lined the walls. Hungry and relieved to be free of the rabbi, Becks slid into a worn leather booth opposite the older woman.

"A glass of tea for me, darling," Faigy told a young waitress with pierced eyebrows and purple hair. Becks ordered a pastrami sandwich.

As she waited for her meal, Becks watched waiters race past with plates of knishes and noodle pudding, thick corned beef sandwiches and bowls of chicken and cabbage soup—the foods of her youth. When a waiter walked by with a dish that smelled *exactly* like her grandmother's Sabbath brisket, Becks reflected that, from a culinary perspective at least, these *were* her people.

A minute later, the waitress arrived with Becks' pastrami and a glass of hot tea for Faigy. She was surprised to see the shopkeeper place a lump of sugar between her teeth and sip the tea through it as Grandma Yentl had done.

"So nu, you got the rebbe's blessing. That's quite something," Faigy said, setting her glass of tea on the table. "You'll find out what happened to Menachem?"

"You heard the rabbi," Becks said. "His death was God's will. Why look further?"

Seeing the hurt in Faigy's eyes, she apologized. "Even if I was in a position to look into this, which I'm not, I don't have much to go on. So far, no one's told me anything useful. At least, nothing I can bring to the police."

"I understand. But it's *bashert*, fate. Something will come to you." She raised her hands toward the ceiling as though in supplication. "A bit of knowledge. An intuition. A dream." She tapped Becks' hand. "You'll know what to do."

Becks smiled at the woman's faith in her detecting skills. "I'll do what I can."

If she learned anything useful, she'd pass it on to the police. If not, at least she'd be able to tell Gabe, Faigy and the Tannenbaums she'd done her best.

24

Driving home from the airport Sunday night in Daniel's tiny Volkswagen, Becks filled her husband in on the meetings with Menny's parents. "Rabbi Tannenbaum was a pompous ass. I almost fell off my chair when he said that Menny's death was God's will." She shook her head. "Why should *I* knock myself out when he's so sure Menny's death was fate?"

"That's a valid question." Daniel merged onto I-95. "I admire your tenacity, sweetheart. If Menny's parents don't question his death, why should you?"

Becks had no more reason to suspect Menny was killed than she had before visiting New York but she couldn't share that with Daniel. He'd pressure her even further to stop asking around. "You're probably right."

For the next two days, she focused on the knish article she'd promised her editor. As she fried onions and mashed potatoes to create the doughy pucks, she felt a nagging suspicion she'd missed something—or knew something she hadn't recognized as important. She considered what she'd learned in New York. Menny's parents didn't know why he left, which was disappointing. And, although Rabbi Tannenbaum dismissed her concerns about Menny's kidnapping, she wasn't ready to rule it out. The only proof she had that his death wasn't an accident was Menny's inability to ride a bike. That and his fear of being kidnapped.

Becks was emptying the dishwasher Wednesday morning when it came to her. She hadn't thought to ask if anyone at the kosher market had seen Menny with a bike. She couldn't imagine why they would have but it was worth finding out. She tossed the still-warm plates on the counter, pulled off her apron and got in the car. If nothing panned out, she'd at least let Malcolm, the butcher who'd helped her, know what became of Menny.

The parking lot at Shapiro's Kosher Market was packed with SUVs and Becks waited for a half dozen stroller-wielding mommies to cross the street before pulling into a spot. She hated to bother Malcolm while the market was busy but knew the bike question would plague her until she found out. Throwing her purse strap over her shoulder, she marched through Shapiro's glass doors.

Malcolm, his portly figure wrapped in a clean white apron, was packaging a brisket in white butcher paper when Becks reached the meat counter. She waited until he'd handed it to an elderly woman before speaking.

"I don't know if you remember me. I was in here asking about a missing boy."

"Oh yes. Did he show up?"

"Not exactly. He had an accident." She chose her words carefully. "He fell into a canal and hit his head."

Malcolm spoke over his shoulder as he washed his hands in the sink behind the counter. "That's a shame. Is he all right?"

"No. He drowned."

He spun around. "Drowned! How?"

"The police said it was an accident, that he slipped off his bike." She hesitated, unsure of how much to share.

"The problem is he didn't leave our house with a bike. Do you know if anyone here saw him with one or if a bike went missing that night? I want to find out what happened after he walked out with the man you mentioned."

Malcolm rubbed his chin. "Tommy might be able to help. He was working the register that night. I told him about your visit and asked if he noticed anything. He did but I can't remember what." The butcher came out from behind the counter and motioned Becks to follow.

"Hey, Tommy," he called as they neared the registers. "This is the lady I told you about. She was looking for that Hasidic kid who left with his father." Then, to Becks, "Was it his dad?"

She shook her head.

"You said something about noticing, what was it, the car?" Malcolm said to a teenager with severe acne. A cardboard "closed" sign sat at the entrance to his station.

The boy tossed wispy blond bangs off his forehead as he looked up from the rubber belt he was scrubbing. "Yeah, it was a black BMW, a 5-series."

"You didn't happen to get the . . ."

"License plate?" Tommy finished. "No. Sorry about that. It was a word, though, I remember that much. A short word."

Black BMW? An alarm went off in Becks' head. Hadn't she seen a black BMW in front of Helmut's house a day or two after Menny arrived? Come to think of it, she'd seen a black BMW driving slowly past her house the day before he disappeared. It *had* to be the same car.

"My God." She grabbed Tommy by the shoulders and kissed his cheek, then laughed as she remembered you didn't do that to a teenage boy. He turned bright red but grinned good-naturedly.

She told Tommy and Malcolm about seeing what

might have been the same car in front of her neighbor's house. "It may be related or it may not. At least it's a start. I'll let you know what happens."

Nearly tripping over the rubber welcome mat in her rush to leave, Becks raced to her Mercedes and headed home. She was willing to bet Helmut, her neighbor, had seen the car. A retired engineer, he fancied himself the neighborhood warden and noticed everything. And with his eye for detail, he probably remembered the license plate.

She drove slowly, contemplating what she'd learned. Tommy's disclosure wasn't substantial. Still, it supported her gut feeling that Menny's death was not an accident. After her visit to New York, she'd considered moving on, satisfied the police were right about his slipping on the canal bank. But Menny's departure in a BMW similar to the one she'd seen on Helmut's swale? That was too great a coincidence.

Becks wasn't sure if she was cheered or disappointed by this new information. It meant she couldn't stop looking, which was turning into a time-consuming chore. She knew, though, that she'd be haunted by the young man's death until she learned everything she could about how Menny's life had ended. And convinced the police to investigate.

25

The problem, Becks realized as she settled into Helmut's plaid sofa a half-hour later, was that her neighbor had become a hoarder. He'd saved every magazine that arrived in the mail since his wife's death seven years earlier. On the rare occasions Becks ventured inside his house, she had to step carefully to circumnavigate the stacks of *National Geographic* and *Smithsonian* that lined both sides of the hall that led to the family room. The entire house was a claustrophobe's nightmare, every table and shelf chock-a-block full of the porcelain swans, Hummel figurines and decorative Christmas plates Lydia had collected.

Now eighty, Helmut Schmidt had owned his home longer than anyone else in Becks' neighborhood and felt personally responsible for everything that happened there. He'd been on the homeowner's board for more than thirty years, retiring after a heart attack prevented him from taking daily strolls to identify problems. An overgrown lawn. A mildewed driveway. He still reported problems to the new board and was a pain in the neck if your house wasn't kept up. Still, Becks liked him. He truly cared about the neighborhood and the people who lived there.

"No coffee for me," Becks called into the kitchen where Helmut fussed over a drip brewer. Her nose itched from the dust.

Once the coffee was made, Helmut brought his mug into the family room and sank into his recliner. "You're running around so much these days, I never see you. I miss our sidewalk chats."

"Me too. I've been busy with work and we had Gabe's friend with us." She recalled Helmut's kindness toward Menny after the kitchen fire. "Did Daniel tell you what happened to him?"

Helmut sipped his coffee and nodded. "What a shame. Daniel told me you ran up to New York to see his parents. That was kind."

Becks shrugged, then startled as something thumped against her calves. She looked down and laughed. Orpheus, Helmut's gargantuan calico, had bumped against her.

"What do you feed this creature?"

"Anything he damn well wants."

Despite its heft, the cat jumped gracefully onto the edge of Helmut's recliner before settling on his owner's lap. He stroked the cat's ears.

Seeing her neighbor relax, Becks decided to broach the subject of Menny. "Did Daniel mention that I had questions about Menny's death?"

Helmut raised his eyebrows. "What kind of questions?"

"It's not much to go on but Menny seemed frightened by something when he stayed with us. And he had no reason to go near the canal where he drowned. The police say he fell off his bike." She paused. "The problem is he didn't have a bike. He didn't even know how to ride one."

Helmut nodded and continued stroking the cat.

"A day or two after Menny moved in, I saw a black BMW in front of your house. It showed up again the next day. Did you notice it?"

"I assumed it was someone visiting you."

"It wasn't. And now it turns out the last time anyone

saw Menny, he was in the passenger seat of a similar car. Did you see what was written on the plate?"

"As a matter of fact, I did."

She smiled and raised a victorious fist. "I knew you would."

Helmut chuckled at her enthusiasm. "I wouldn't have noticed but it seemed an odd choice for a license plate. S. H. I. N. A few numbers followed. I can't remember them. Does that mean anything?"

"Not yet." Becks stayed a few more minutes, asking Helmut if he'd seen the driver or noticed anything else about the car. He hadn't. She rose from the overstuffed sofa. "Thank you. I'm sorry to run. I want to follow up. And I promise. We'll catch up on the neighborhood gossip another time."

Helmut pushed the cat off his lap and stood. "Let me know if I can help." He walked Becks to the front door, oblivious to the clutter on the floor. "Good luck with your investigation."

"It's not my . . ." she started to say and stopped. Why go into it? She'd call the police and let them take it from there.

After letting herself into the house, Becks went to her office and picked up the phone to call Cole, then paused and held the receiver in midair. What would she tell him? Tommy hadn't seen the license plate. She had no proof the BMW in which Menny disappeared was the same one that lingered in her neighborhood. Cole would never act on such weak evidence. Just the same, it was all she had. She dialed and waited as the operator put her through.

"Detective Cole, it's Becks Ruchinsky," she said after his terse greeting.

"Yes, ma'am, how can I help you?"

"I just wanted to pass along something I learned today. When Menny was staying with us, I noticed a car, a black BMW, in our neighborhood. I hadn't seen it before. I just learned that Menny left the market in a black BMW the night he went missing. It might be the same one. My neighbor saw it in our neighborhood and said the license plate read shin." She spelled out the word.

"Why are you telling me this?" Cole's voice was icy.

"I just thought . . . that is . . . maybe Menny's death wasn't an accident. I told you he didn't ride a bike so finding one where he drowned was strange. Plus he was concerned about being kidnapped. I thought whoever owned the BMW might . . . know something."

"I appreciate your concern," the detective said, "but black BMWs are a dime a dozen in Boca Raton. And why would Menny go off in a stranger's car without telling you?"

"That's exactly my . . ."

"If something else comes up, let me know. I'm a bit backed up so you'll forgive me if I–"

"Wait a minute,' she yelled. "I'm not through."

"What is it?"

"Did anyone find the food Menny picked up at Shapiro's Market the night he went missing?"

"No. It was probably dragged off by raccoons."

"What about the bike. My son and Menny's mom said he couldn't ride."

"It may have been at the canal already. It was pretty rusted. Now if there's nothing more I have to run."

"Did you—"

The phone clicked off.

"Damn." Becks slammed the receiver into its cradle. She felt like a fool for bothering to call. It was her fault, she realized, for withholding information from the detective the year before when she was looking into her father's past.

Was he being vindictive? Who knew? Either way, she'd have to come up with something more substantial before he'd investigate. What made things worse was that his refusal to act on the BMW information meant more work for her. She'd already spent too much time looking into Menny's death, time she should have devoted to her work while the *police* investigated. Now she'd have to dig up more information on the BMW's license plate.

Perched on the edge of her chair, Becks googled the word "shin." The monitor lit up with hits. "The front of the leg between the knee and ankle." Nothing new there. "A Hebrew letter and symbol for the three-pronged weapons used by Poseidon and Shiva." Interesting. An hour later, she came across a website that mentioned Shin-Bet was an acronym for Israel's internal security agency and sensed she was on to something.

But what? If she knew who owned the car, she'd have a better idea. Years earlier, when she worked at the newspaper, she'd have called her contacts at The Department of Motor Vehicles. Unfortunately, most of them had probably moved on. She sank back in her chair and stared out the window. A sanitation truck pulled up to Helmut's house, its gears grinding as the driver scooped up and emptied her neighbor's bin with the mechanical arm. Minutes later, it moved on to the next house, the grinding repeated as another trash can entered the jaws of the large yellow truck.

Who could she call? There had to be someone. She rose and walked to the bulletin board where she pinned flyers and business cards she picked up along the way. One of the notices, written in black ink on formal cream card stock, caught her attention. A few years earlier, she'd received an announcement that her colleague Maya Dipaolo had left her job as a researcher at the newspaper to become a private detective. Despite her appearance—the woman favored tight skirts and revealing blouses—Maya had been brilliant on the internet, searching doggedly until she found whatever the reporter needed. Maya and Becks had gotten together for an occasional lunch while they were working together but hadn't touched base in years. She might be able to help.

Becks found Maya's business number on the notice and dialed. After three rings, the detective answered and, to Becks relief, seemed happy to hear from her. She listened as Becks described Menny's death, then explained she was busy but could meet for lunch in Fort Lauderdale the next day. They set up a date for noon.

Becks sat back in her chair and took a deep breath, letting it out slowly. Finally. Someone willing to help. She looked forward to seeing her old friend and felt sure Maya, of all people, would be able to identify the license plate owner. Becks would follow up with a few calls, see what she could learn about the owner and pass the information to Cole. He could take it from there. And she could get on with her life.

26

At noon the next day, Becks found herself trailing Maya through the waterfront bar at 15th Street Fisheries en route to the dining room. She knew she'd let herself go a little, rarely wearing makeup or styling the shoulder-length curly hair that flopped into her eyes. This morning, though, she'd applied foundation and lipstick and dressed professionally in a black pantsuit, one of the few outfits that complimented her six-foot frame. She thought she looked rather stylish until Maya, sashaying through the bar in a skin-tight black skirt and low-cut ruffled blouse, drew appreciative stares and a wolf whistle. Becks, who towered over the petite investigator, felt like a Neanderthal.

"Pretty good for fifty-five," Maya said as she slipped into a leather booth in an intimate corner of the restaurant. From her seat, Becks looked outside toward an open deck where young people at high-top tables sipped beer and ate from red plastic baskets. A scruffy man in cutoff jeans secured a red and yellow cigarette boat the length of the deck to the pier.

Daniel had taken Becks to the restaurant years earlier for an anniversary dinner but she hadn't paid attention to the prices. Today, she did a double-take. Maya was unperturbed, though, ordering a dry Martini, three olives, before turning to her friend. "Now tell me why you're so interested in this kid's death. Is he a relative?"

As they made their way through clams casino and lobster tails—no question, Maya treated herself well—Becks recounted Gabe's friendship with Menny and her sense of guilt at letting the boy leave her home alone. She also told Maya about the black BMW with the SHIN license plate. "All I have to go on is the plate, a dorm visit from a stranger, Menny's fear of being kidnapped and the fact that a bike—he couldn't ride one—was found near the canal. Call it a feeling if you like. Something isn't right."

Maya waved the waiter over and ordered a second Martini. "I remember your 'gut feelings' and they're usually on target. I'll help you out. First, though, promise me you won't be stupid. If you learn anything, tell the police. It's their job."

"Of course." Becks placed her napkin next to her plate and signaled the waiter for the check. "I'm just trying to light a fire under their lazy butts."

"Yeah, sure." Maya laughed. "I know you better than that."

After leaving Maya, Becks headed north to the *Broward Tribune* to bring her editor Hanley Stevenson homemade mango bread. He'd promised to ask the newspaper's publisher to release her from a contract that gave the *Tribune* all rights to her recipes. She thought she'd modified four from her column enough to skirt the paper's copyright policy and include them in her first cookbook but, so far, the publisher refused.

"Rankin still won't release the recipes," Hanley said after escorting her to the building's cafeteria and rustling up two cups of coffee. The room reeked of overcooked green beans and ammonia. Glancing around the room, she was disappointed at her inability to recognize a single person. Hanley had warned her the paper, like most others in the country, operated with a skeleton staff and most of her friends had moved on. The food editor she'd started with was long gone and Hanley, who'd been a general assignment reporter, had stepped in to handle the food section.

"It's bad enough every blogger can reprint my articles and recipes without being sued. Now I can't use them in my own book," Becks said as she took the paper cup from Hanley. She sipped the coffee and wrinkled her nose.

"You'll get the go-ahead eventually." He spoke with an authority Becks envied yet didn't quite trust. "We'll figure something out. Don't worry."

After catching up on each other's lives, Becks thanked him and returned to her car. She was worried. If approval didn't come through, she'd be forced to pull the recipes.

She resolved to wait two more days. If the publisher didn't change his mind, she'd come up with new recipes for the cookbook. That would be embarrassing: she'd already returned her final edits. Worse, though, it might ruin her chances of publishing another cookbook.

Meanwhile, she had enough to do getting her next article written and, if Maya delivered, tracking the owner of the black BMW.

27

As she pulled into her driveway an hour later, Becks' cell launched into an irritating brrrng. Jamming the gearshift into park, she scrounged around in her purse for the phone. "Yes," she yelled into the receiver, hoping to catch the caller before he gave up.

"Talk about an easy assignment," Maya said. "I've got news on your driver. Who do you want to hear about first? The old fart or the young stud?"

"Why don't you choose?" Becks said, digging into her bag for a pencil and paper. "You're the expert on men."

"All right then. Myron Northrop is eighty-five and lives in Fort Myers. I'm going out on a limb here but he probably wears Bermuda shorts and knee socks with white sneakers. Sidney Fox, your more likely choice, is forty-three and owns a night club in South Beach. Club Shukran, whatever that means. Probably wears all black. And you're going to love this."

Becks waited for the figurative drum roll.

"His club was busted a year ago. Patrons selling drugs. The guy must have connections because his name wasn't linked to the bust. Maybe he wasn't involved. More likely he greased the right palms."

"That was fast. You got anything else?"

"That wasn't enough?"

Becks laughed. "Thanks a million. I'll take it from here."

"Meaning what?"

Becks got out of the car and grabbed her purse from the passenger seat. "I don't know. See what else I can learn about Fox."

"How are you going to do that?"

"Go online. Call friends in Miami Beach. I suppose I'll call him." She grabbed the keys from her purse and climbed the steps to her porch.

"Good idea. Don't forget to ask if he killed the kid."

"I'll make a point of it."

"Let me know if you need anything," Maya's tone had turned somber. "And be careful. I remember how you used to run off half-cocked when you were on to something."

"Not to worry. I'm older and wiser now."

"Yeah, I believe that." Maya laughed and hung up.

Letting herself into the house, Becks considered the name: Sidney Fox. It sounded like a species of rodent or a cartoon character—a bushy-tailed creature in a golf cap? Fox tended to be a Jewish name so that was something. Still, where would Menny have met a night club owner?

She sat at the kitchen table and googled "Sid Fox" on her cell. There wasn't much. A *Miami Herald* article about the bust and an online Yellow Pages entry that listed Fox as an entrepreneur. Then she tried Club Shukran and found little more than photos of half-naked women. Next, she combined his name with a half dozen terms and got nowhere until, theorizing Fox might know Menny through religious connections, tried "Hasid." Bingo. His name came up; he'd been a Hebrew teacher at a school for religious youngsters, Yeshiva Sha'arei Avraham. How had Fox, if it *was* the same man, gone from Hebrew school teacher to night club owner? She smiled when she saw the yeshiva's address. Bingo again. The school was in Kleynshtot, the town mentioned in Menny's article on the education scam.

Finally, a connection between Menny and the BMW owner. That had to convince Detective Cole to investigate. She reached for the phone but withdrew her hand. He'd find it too easy to brush her off if she called. She printed out the school roster and drove to the police station.

The City of Boca Raton is recognized for its attractive landscaping and open spaces and visitors to its police station pass through a jungle of towering banyans to reach the building's entrance. Spotting Cole leaving the station as she pulled in, Becks jumped out of her car and called his name. He looked up and grimaced, then tried to hide his reaction behind a bland smile.

"What is it?" he said as she reached him. "I'm on my way to a meeting."

"I found a connection between Menny and a night club owner in Miami. A guy named Sidney Fox."

"Don't tell me you're still looking."

She ignored the comment. "Fox, the guy with the black BMW I told you about, lived in the same Hasidic village as Menny. It was just after community leaders were arrested on government fraud charges." She spoke quickly, afraid he'd cut her off.

"Were Menny or Fox involved?"

"I don't know."

"Did they know each other?"

"Not that I'm aware of."

"So what do you want me to do? Run to Miami and ask the guy if he knew Menny? Question him about driving around your neighborhood?" He nodded toward a passing officer. "I'll be a minute." Then to Becks, "I'm sorry, ma'am, but we've got thousands of New York transplants in

South Florida. If coming from the same town was all I needed to arrest a suspect for murder, I'd be on easy street."

"Couldn't you look into Fox's past? See if there's more?"

"I appreciate what you're trying to do." He sounded resigned. "No one wants to accept a tragedy like this. The case is closed. The medical examiner ruled Menny's death an accidental drowning. Our investigators found Menny's blood on the culvert where we suspected the boy hit his head before going in."

"So that's it? You won't consider murder?"

"The boy drowned." He enunciated each word.

Becks grit her teeth. She'd run out of arguments.

"All right." Cole sighed and looked in the direction his colleague had taken. "I'll do a criminal background check tomorrow. If nothing shows up, you'll let it drop?"

Becks nodded. More like leave him alone. "It's a deal."

She released her breath as she returned to her car. Becks hadn't realized how uncomfortable she felt in Cole's presence. The detective made no secret he found her nosy and intrusive. Too bad. She was going to get to the bottom of this. Never mind what Daniel or the great detective thought.

"Oy, Becks, you're such a pain in the *tuchus*," Tootsie said after dinner that evening. A splotch of icing dotted his chin. She touched a finger to her chin hoping he'd take the hint. When he didn't, she reached across the table and dabbed at his face with a napkin. He swatted her hand.

"What the hell are you doing?"

"You've got icing on your chin."

"You coulda told me. What do I look like? A senile old man?"

"I was trying to help."

It was Tootsie's birthday and he'd come over for his traditional birthday meal—ribeye steak and carrot cake. After dinner, Becks told her father and Daniel that Maya had identified the BMW's driver as a Miami night club owner named Sid Fox. Her voice rose as she announced he'd lived in the same Hasidic community as Menny.

Daniel listened in silence, then practically rolled his eyes as he cleared the plates and brought them to the kitchen. A minute later, Becks heard dishes clattering a bit more loudly than was strictly necessary. When she heard the water running, she turned to her father.

"How about it, Dad? Could you call your Hasidic friends in the restaurant business? One of them must know Sidney Fox from back in New York."

"You got to be kidding. It's not like they're one happy family and everyone knows everyone. You got almost as many Hasidic groups in New York as you got Jews. The Lubavitch. The Bobovs. The Satmars. And if you want to go way out, you got your Skverers."

"One or two calls. It's all I ask."

Tootsie shook his head and pulled the cake closer. He ran a finger around its base and popped the icing in his mouth. "Tell you what, Doll." He spoke with his mouth full. "I'll make a call or two. It doesn't mean I like your poking around. I'm only doing it because you're such a great cook."

After chatting with her father for a few minutes then seeing him to his car, Becks returned to the kitchen. Daniel was still washing dishes so she grabbed a dish towel and dried.

"Haven't you done enough already?" he said after a few moments of silence.

She looked up, startled by his tone. He hadn't seemed angry at dinner.

"The boy's dead. Let it go." He tossed a pot onto the

drain board. It bounced and landed on the floor. Becks picked it up and kept drying.

"I don't understand why you're so pumped up about finding the BMW's owner. The odds are slim it's the car in which Menny left Shapiro's if he even left in a car. The medical examiner said Menny drowned. Let it go."

"I don't——."

Daniel held up his hand. "This Fox guy may have something to hide. But it probably has nothing to do with Menny. The night club business attracts a criminal element. Start poking around and you don't know where it'll lead. Remember Custer Corporation?"

Becks winced. Of course he'd bring *that* up. During her last year at the newspaper, she'd discovered the owners of a Miami construction company had made illegal donations to city commissioners before winning a contract to build a municipal garage. When word of her investigation got out, she'd received anonymous letters and midnight calls warning her to drop the story. The newspaper ran her articles and two commissioners went to prison. Still, she had trouble sleeping for months.

It was one of many arguments Daniel used when he'd urged her to leave her job. It was bad enough, he said, that Gabe demanded constant supervision. What would happen if he lost his mother?

Becks folded the dish towel and draped it over a chair. "I'm sorry you feel that way, sweetheart. I'm not giving up until I find out what happened to Menny."

Daniel looked at her, scowled and looked away. "It's your call. Try to be careful at least. I'm sick of worrying you'll get hurt." He stomped out of the kitchen.

Becks sponged the counters more vigorously than usual. After hearing the shower run in the master bathroom, she headed upstairs.

28

It didn't take long the next morning to relocate Sid Fox's
website. The minute Becks googled Club Shukran, images
of girls with balloon-sized breasts and greased buttocks
flashed on the screen. Becks' stomach churned at a picture
of a teenage girl engaging in—or pretending to engage
in—oral sex with a sneering man. Did these women
realize how horribly the photos demeaned them, or that
their parents might see?

And what kind of scumbag posted such exploitative
photos on his website? Becks knew she had to contact Fox
about his relationship with Menny. But how could she
face the man without showing her revulsion? She had no
intention of spending time alone with the creep, who may
or may not have murdered Menny. She needed someone
neutral to accompany her. Recalling her father's promise
to contact Hasidic customers, Becks decided to ask if one
of them might come along to a meeting with Fox.

She dialed Tootsie's number.

"Why are you calling so early?" he asked, then
yawned so loudly Mulligan, curled up on her desk, pricked
his ears. "It's only nine."

"Sorry dad." She told him what she had in mind. "Do
you think you could reach someone today?"

"What's the rush?"

"I want to get this over with. Fox's website looks like a porno magazine and I'd prefer not to meet him alone."

"Tell you what. Hold off for an hour or two. I'll make a few calls. I've been out of the game for a while. I'd be surprised if any of my old customers know the guy."

Becks hung up and stood, hands on hips, leaning back to stretch her muscles. She considered calling Gabe to make sure he was recovering all right from his friend's death. They'd spoken two days earlier and he seemed fine. She'd read that one of the so-called "benefits" of Asperger's was that people with the syndrome tended to lack empathy and couldn't experience grief. Becks didn't buy it. In her heart of hearts, she sensed Gabe was too overwhelmed by the emotion to express it.

Glancing at the notes she'd scribbled while on the phone, Becks wondered if Gabe had been to Club Shukran. It seemed unlikely and not only because he was underage. The loud music would drive him crazy and the laser lighting she'd seen in photos of the dance floor would send him into a frenzy. She hated the idea of her sons spending time in such a disreputable venue. Still, it saddened her that clubbing was one more experience Gabe could never enjoy.

Her cell rang as she considered calling him.

"Sorry, Doll," Tootsie said, "no luck. I made a couple of calls and most of my customers are dead or out of business. I got one guy on the line who'd heard of the club and said the owner had put a king's fortune into the joint. He heard this Fox character likes playing big shot, hosting celebrities. But he wouldn't agree to meet with him. Does that help?"

"Maybe," Becks said, taking notes. "Anything else?"

"I've got one more call out. I'll let you know what I hear. You still want to meet the guy?"

"I'd like to."

"You sounded frightened before. Want me to join you?"

Becks hesitated. She didn't want to go alone. And how much safer would she feel with Tootsie along? He was old and wouldn't offer much in the way of muscle. On the other hand, Fox had to be a misogynist to post such disgusting photos on his website. He might act more respectfully in the presence of a man, especially an elderly one.

"I'd appreciate it. Let me get back to you when I have a time and place."

She hung up and dialed Detective Cole's number. If Fox had a criminal record, she wanted to know about it before her meeting. Another officer picked up and she left Cole a message. She knew she should wait until he returned her call but the prospect of coming face to face with Fox sent shivers of revulsion down her spine. If she didn't set up the meeting soon, she might never do so. Taking a deep breath, she grabbed the receiver and punched in the club's number.

"Club Shukran. What can I do?" A woman with a raspy Brooklyn accent answered.

"Is Mr. Fox available?"

"Just a minute, dear. I'll try to find him."

Becks resolved to approach the call dispassionately. She'd ask for a meeting to discuss a mutual friend. She hoped Fox wouldn't dismiss her request as too vague but wanted to hold off and observe the club owner's reaction to Menny's name.

As she waited for Fox to come on the line Becks reached across her desk for a silver-framed photo of her boys. It was taken years earlier in front of a horse barn. Josh, a curly-headed ten-year-old with a splatter of freckles, grinned into the camera, his arm draped over his brother's shoulders. Gabe stared stiffly ahead, arms pulled into his body, fingers splayed. Even then he found physical contact repugnant.

The nasal voice came back on the line. "He wants to know who's calling."

Becks hesitated. "Becks Ruchinsky. We have a friend in common."

A minute later, a gruff voice came on. "Sid Fox here. What can I do for yuh?"

"This is Becks Ruchinsky." Her face grew hot as she struggled to erase the pornographic images from her mind. "I'd like to set up a meeting to talk about a friend in common."

"Who is it?"

"I'd rather not say."

"Look, lady, I'm a busy man. How about you tell me what this is about? Then I'll decide if we meet."

Becks took a deep breath and slowly released it. She didn't want to blow her chance of catching Fox unawares. She also didn't want to give him time to search for her on the internet. He'd likely refuse to talk once he discovered she'd been a journalist.

"I won't take much of your time. Ten minutes. Whenever it's convenient. I can come today. I don't think you'll regret it." She hadn't meant her last words to sound like a threat but it was fine if Fox took them that way.

"Jesus Christ." It came out like the snarl of an irate German shepherd. "Okay, lady. You got me hooked. Come at three. There's a deli near my club, on the corner of Washington and Sixth. Bagels and More. We'll talk there."

"How will I know you?"

"Don't worry. You'll figure it out."

Finding a parking spot on Washington Avenue was a bigger challenge than Becks had anticipated and the pain that pierced her temples grew sharper as she circled the neighborhood. She'd picked up Tootsie at two-thirty, giving herself a half hour to cross the causeway to Miami Beach and find the deli. Gazing over the sparkling blue waters as she crossed Biscayne Bay, Becks tried to remember why she'd abandoned Miami. The bumper to bumper traffic on Washington Avenue reminded her. With five minutes to spare before meeting Fox, she pulled into a parking lot a block from the deli.

"Thief," Tootsie said after reluctantly handing the parking attendant a twenty. "We used to park free in front of the classy joints here."

Becks laughed. She didn't recall any "classy" restaurants in the area. Decades earlier, Tootsie had taken the family to a kosher restaurant on Washington Avenue every Sunday night after visiting Grandma Yentl. Back then, South Beach was a Mecca for Jewish immigrants who wanted to spend their golden years reminiscing about the old days while tanning to a leathery bronze. The kosher markets and tacky little tourist shops that had catered to elderly Jews now housed trendy cafes and chic boutiques.

Glancing over her shoulder to ask if Tootsie recalled those shops, Becks saw her father struggling to keep up. "Sorry Dad," she said, adjusting her pace. She remembered with a bitter sense of loss that he no longer was the vigorous giant she'd run to keep up with.

The crisp-sour odor of dill pickles and freshly-baked rye greeted Becks as she opened the glass door to Bagels and More and led her father past brightly-lit display cases of cheesecake and cookies. As she neared the hostess stand, Becks eyed the salad platters artfully arranged behind glass.

This late in the day, the lunch crowd was gone and a few young couples sat in booths nursing mugs of coffee.

Becks had no problem finding Fox. He *had* to be the towering, acne-scarred brute scowling at her from a corner booth. His hair, brushed back from a high forehead, was thin and shoe-polish black and a small black yarmulke struggled to maintain its position on the back of his head. Spotting Becks, he sneered and eyed her in a manner clearly meant to communicate his ability to envision her naked. She resisted the urge to slap him. Instead, she pretended not to notice and introduced herself before slipping into the booth with her father.

"So what's with this friend we have in common?" Fox said, pushing the metal bowl of pickles toward Tootsie. "Try one. They're delicious."

"Sorry to be so mysterious." Becks played along, feigning a friendly demeanor. "A young man who visited me for a few days drowned under my watch and I'm trying to learn more about him. Did you know Menachem Tannenbaum?"

She studied Fox's face. If he recognized the name, he was a better actor than Robert De Niro. The thug bobbed his head as though considering. "Nope. Sorry. Doesn't ring any bells."

Becks pulled the photo of Menny and his friend from her purse and slid it toward Fox. "Either of them look familiar?"

Fox looked and shook his head. "Nope." He handed it back."

An elderly waitress approached with billboard-sized menus, which Becks waved away. "Coffee for two." She turned to her father. "You want anything?"

"Cheesecake," he told the waitress. "Strawberry if you got it."

Becks nudged his knee. Tootsie ignored her. Damn, they'd be stuck there with Fox.

"So why are you asking me about the kid?" Fox asked, running a hand through his hair. "What's it got to do with me? You and pops looking for someone to lay it on?"

"Do you own a black BMW?" Becks asked.

"Yeah."

"With a plate that reads SHIN?"

His eyebrows drew together. "What's it to you?"

Becks sat back and folded her arms. "A black BMW with that plate drove around my neighborhood while Menachem was staying at my home. A few days later, someone saw him get in the same car." A white lie wouldn't hurt. "The next time anyone saw Menachem, he was floating face down in a canal. Does *that* ring any bells?"

Fox jerked forward, bringing his face within inches of Becks'. His breath stank of tuna fish and beer. Her legs grew weak but she refused to budge.

"Are you asking if *I* killed the kid?" Fox sat back and slammed his fist into the table. The waitress, arriving with coffee, stumbled back, sending the brown liquid and mugs clattering to the floor. She scurried away.

"I don't know what you're playing at. Wonder Woman and the Caped Geezer?" He laughed at his joke. "You'd better watch who you accuse. I never met your friend and, frankly, I don't give a shit if he's dead." He glared at Tootsie and Becks. "Now leave me the fuck alone."

He rose, revealing a large gut and a silver Star of David belt buckle, and stormed out.

A shiver ran down Becks' spine. Detective Cole had shown her an almost identical star when she'd gone with him to identify Menny's body.

A minute later, the waitress returned with the cheesecake.

"You still want this?"

"Sure. Why not?" Tootsie said. He turned to Becks as the waitress slapped a plate of cheesecake on the table and left. A chubby young girl with a mop replaced her. "Nice job, Doll. Real nice." He pierced a forkful of strawberry cheesecake and pointed it at her. "You just made yourself a nasty enemy."

After dropping Tootsie at his apartment and fighting the rush hour traffic out of Miami, Becks went up to her office. She was still shaken by her meeting with Fox and needed time to think things through. Grabbing a piece of paper from her printer, she wrote "Menny's death" in the center, circling the words. Then she surrounded it with the terms "kidnap," "dissident," "Rabbi Tannenbaum," "Sid Fox," "Club Shukran" and "Hasidim." After she circled them, she sat back and stared at the sheet.

What were the links? So far she had few ideas. Menny was afraid of being abducted. But who would benefit from the kidnapping? The dissidents who'd objected to his departure had left Crown Heights months earlier, according to Rabbi Tannenbaum. Were they still afraid Menny had created a sect? She drew lines linking "dissident" and "kidnap" to "Menny's death."

Sid Fox had to be hiding something. Why else would he be so upset by her questions? Still, how would Menny know a night club owner and why would Fox want the boy dead? Was Fox the man who'd visited Menny and Gabe's dorm? The next time she saw him, she'd show Gabe the man's picture from the Club Shukran website. The night club owner might be one of the dissidents afraid Menny would start a sect? Or a member of the group that had committed fraud in Kleynshtot. But he didn't look Hasidic. He looked like a thug.

Becks was still struggling to find links between people when Daniel stuck his head in her office. "I'm home."

She checked her watch. It was after six. "I had no idea it was so late."

He crossed to her desk and kissed her. "What's up?" He pushed aside her mess and sat on the old leather couch near her desk.

"I met Sid Fox today, the guy who owns the license plate with SHIN."

"You went to his office?"

"A deli nearby. Tootsie came along."

"Didn't we decide . . .?"

"Fox told us he didn't know Menny and was pretty convincing," she said, ignoring her husband's objection.

"You think Gabe knows anything about the man?"

"Maybe? If—"

She stopped speaking as a ball of fur flashed across the room and landed on Daniel's lap. Mulligan vanished most days only to reemerge upon her husband's arrival. Neither spoke as Daniel stroked the cat and the contented animal's purrs filled the room. The cat made no secret of adoring Daniel.

"Fox used to teach Hebrew at a yeshiva in Kleynshtot, a village where Menny lived for a few months." She didn't bother to mention the night club owner's rude behavior. "They may have met."

Daniel laughed. "That's perfect. An hour of Hebrew instruction followed by a field trip to the night club. Somehow I can't picture those black hats rocking out to hip hop?"

"I don't know." She spoke slowly. "Remember Josh telling us about the Purim party at Emory's Chabad House? The men got drunk and danced on the tables."

Daniel smiled. "That doesn't necessarily translate into clubbing." He rose. "Will you be down soon?"

"A couple more minutes."

Becks returned to her notes and drew a line and question mark between "Hasidim" and "Club Shukran." Did Hasidic youngsters frequent the club? There was no one she could ask. She considered her options and shuddered. Visiting the night club might mean running into Fox. She'd seen the website's photos of stylish young people lined up to get in and wondered if she'd be admitted. Didn't you have to know someone or be breathtakingly beautiful? She rose from her desk and walked to the stairwell but stopped before descending. Maya might know what to do. She had the moxie and connections to weasel her way into any situation. If that didn't work, she'd know whose palms to grease.

Becks returned to her office and emailed Maya. Relieved to have a plan, she went downstairs to make dinner.

29

The next evening, Becks couldn't decide if the writhing, half-naked bodies on Club Shukran's dance floor reminded her more of a Fellini film or a psychedelic acid trip. The sight was unlike anything she'd witnessed before. A network of flashing lasers swept across the two-tiered black marble dance floor, the heart of the circus tent-sized warehouse, changing colors in sync with the music. Becks found herself swaying to the Latin beat as the pounding bass reverberated like a conga against her chest.

They'd bypassed the block-long line of young people waiting behind a velvet rope to enter the club, giving their names to the bouncer and walking right in. After being temporarily blinded by the bright lights, Becks followed Maya up an expansive Lucite staircase toward the dance floor. The transparent stairway, illuminated from below, appeared to be suspended in air and she held her breath, fearful each step would send her tumbling to an ignominious death. She swore softly, cursing Maya for convincing her to dress like a South Beach prostitute. She was fifty, for God's sake. Who did Maya think they were kidding?

Once she reached the top of the stairs and felt steady enough to look around, Becks noticed a DJ suspended above the crowd in a gilt cage. His dark hair was electric with movement and his white sequined suit sparkled in the bright lights as he danced and spun records. Below him, the beautiful people—blacks, whites, Asians, Latinos and others too ethnically ambiguous to name—danced in synchrony, their arms and legs intertwined like a nest of eels.

That morning, Maya had surprised Becks when she phoned to announce success. One call to Club Shukran's publicist explaining she was covering South Beach for a Toronto newspaper got them through the door. Maya doctored both of their press credentials earlier in the day but no one asked to see them. Even so, Becks grasped Daniel's bulky Nikon to her chest, trying to remember if she'd removed the lens cap before taking shots of the crowd outside.

"Wow. Take a look at this," Maya called over her shoulder.

Stumbling in her stilettos, Becks joined her friend at the bar which, on close examination, turned out to be an enormous glass-topped fish tank extending the length of the room. Blue, green and purple fish swam through colorful coral, creating a mesmerizing seascape visible from the top and sides of the tank. Becks glanced around to see if anyone else was as awed as she was and did a double-take at her reflection in the mirrored ceiling. Was that her? The slinky red dress she'd pulled from the back of her closet and the heavy makeup Maya'd applied to her eyes rendered her almost unrecognizable. Damn. She *was* hot. Sid Fox would never recognize her.

"What'll you have ma'am?" A man's voice broke through her reverie, shattering her fantasy of youth and beauty. A smile played on the lips of the handsome tuxedoed waiter as he leaned across the fish tank. Maya was sipping a martini. She'd already attracted the attention of a swarthy young man with deep brown eyes.

"A Cosmo, please." She wanted a soda but something

pink and elegant seemed more appropriate to the new Becks.

The bartender retreated to the far end of the bar and returned with the drink.

Becks had taken a sip and placed her glass on the cocktail napkin when Maya tapped her shoulder. Becks' head shot up and she searched for Fox, her heart racing. She found no sign of the night club owner. Following Maya's gaze, though, she saw a young man in a yarmulke, black pants, and a white shirt below which strings dangled approach the dance floor. Once he reached it, he swirled rapidly, hands raised above his head as if beseeching the heavens. The other dancers stepped away and resumed their gyrations.

A minute later, Maya grabbed Becks' arm. "Over there," she whispered, pointing to the opposite side of the room. Another twentyish man entered the floor, this one in an immense fur hat and a calf-length coat. It swept away from his narrow frame as he spun. It was hard to tell from her vantage point, but his eyes appeared to be glazed. The dancers, again, made room for him.

Becks stared at one boy, then the other. What were these Hasidic kids doing in Fox's nightclub? They looked like dull gray horses lumbering around in a field of shiny black stallions

"Everyone seems used to them," she whispered to Maya.

"They must come here often." Maya waved at the bartender and pointed to her empty glass. "You think it's only Club Shukran?"

Becks shrugged. It was too noisy to talk. They'd discuss it on the drive home.

By the time Maya's martini arrived, Becks was exhausted. The flashing lasers and heavy bass beat were giving her a headache. The Cosmo, which she'd slugged back out of thirst, had worked its way south and she needed the lady's room.

"I'll be back in a sec," she yelled over the music, which seemed to grow louder as the night progressed.

"What?" Maya asked. She was elbowing her décolletage and fluttering her eyelashes at her new friend.

"The lady's room. You want to come?"

Maya shook her head.

Following the dimly lit signs for the restrooms, Becks descended another set of Lucite stairs to the first floor. It was quieter there and small groups of people were gathered around black lacquered tables covered with bottles of whiskey, glasses, mixers and snacks. The loud laughter that sprang from the clusters of young men and women suggested many had already imbibed in what the club's web site had described as "bottle service."

Becks skirted the drinkers to reach the lady's room. It was a relief to escape the loud noise and dizzying lights and she took her time washing and drying her hands. She was applying lipstick when a young woman stumbled out of the stall behind her and smiled at Becks' reflection. "I like your lipstick."

Becks returned the smile, self-conscious about how odd her appearance in the night club must seem. "Thanks," she said, then added, "Places like this weren't around in my day." She was embarrassed at her compulsion to explain but continued. "I feel like an anthropologist studying a primitive culture."

"That's cool." The girl's tone was a little too enthusiastic. "I tried to get my mom to come. She's not interested."

"You've been here before?"

"A few times. Mostly to celebrate birthdays." She

turned on the faucet too fast and giggled as water splashed her blouse. "I get so klutzy when I drink."

"It'll dry," Becks said and took a moment to check her lipstick in the mirror. She didn't want to seem nosy. Still, she *was* here to learn about the club. "I saw something odd out there. Two young men—ultra-religious Jews, I guess—were twirling around the dance floor. They seemed right at home. One looked stoned."

The girl shrugged. "Those weird-looking guys. They're here a lot." She tucked a strand of shoulder-length hair behind her ear.

"Isn't it against their religion?" She hoped the girl didn't realize she was being disingenuous. "A night club seems like such an . . . unlikely place for people like that."

"I don't know about that. But there are rumors." She looked around and lowered her voice. "I heard drug dealers hire Hasidic kids as mules. Who's going to suspect a bunch of super-religious kids of bringing in drugs, right?"

Becks nodded, struggling to hide her shock. "It makes sense, I guess. It seems awfully risky for the kids."

"The money's supposed to be huge." The girl switched her purse from one shoulder to the other. "And this seems to be the place to meet up with a dealer."

The girl started to open the door and then turned toward Becks. "Maybe I shouldn't have said anything. You're not, like, a cop, are you?"

Becks laughed. "God no. Just a curious old lady."

And that's what she felt like. A curious old lady who'd come face to face with a possibility she didn't want to consider. Had Menny been a mule? Her chest felt heavy as she recalled what Hannah had said about leaving his community in shame. The woman was insistent her son didn't deal drugs. Still, she couldn't be sure. Becks considered his situation: where did Menny get the money to move to Miami and attend an expensive private university? He claimed to have a scholarship. Maybe he lied. Or it wasn't enough to live on. She'd check with Gabe, see if Menny did any traveling or had visitors other than Fox.

It was past midnight. Pumpkin time. She hobbled upstairs, her feet in agony from the stilettos and found Maya where she'd left her. Her suitor was gone.

"Ready to take off?" Becks asked.

"Sure thing," Maya twisted her lips and nodded toward the far end of the bar, where the swarthy young man was flirting with a younger and bustier woman. "Can you believe that son-of-a-bitch ditched me?"

Becks patted her shoulder. "Sorry." And she meant it. So much so that she refrained from reminding Maya that her handsome suitor was young enough to be her son.

Maya fell asleep the minute her head hit the backrest of Becks' car and slept the entire ride before stumbling into the lobby of her condo. By the time Becks reached home, Daniel was blessedly asleep, his snores sonorous and steady as she crawled into bed.

30

The next morning, Becks grabbed a cup of coffee and ran up to her office to call Detective Cole. Once he heard about the Hasidic men and rumors of drug dealing at Club Shukran, he'd have to agree something was fishy. The phone rang once, twice, then another four times before a woman answered "Boca Raton Police Department." The detective wasn't in but she'd be glad to take a message. Becks left her name and number and a brief description of what she'd learned. She wasn't hopeful. Cole had dismissed her questions about Menny's death and hadn't bothered to respond to her request for information about Fox's criminal history. What were the odds he'd return her call?

She stared out the window, distracted by the roar of the lawnmower on Helmut's front yard. She waved at the man behind the machine, a cadaverous white-haired septuagenarian who'd been doing yards in her community for as long as she'd lived there. He returned her greeting. On the side of her neighbor's house, a slim, dark-skinned man in mud-splattered khakis walked the periphery of Helmut's flower beds, creating precise demarcations between the soil and sod with his edger.

The familiar sight helped relieve Becks' frustration at Cole's refusal to return her calls. With luck, she'd learn something else that might spur a police investigation. And

Maya's willingness to help relieved some of the pressure Becks had been feeling since Menny's death. Maya had access to much of the information the police had. Between the two of them, she'd find enough leads to get Cole interested. She smiled at her choice of word—leads. It *was* like the old newspaper days, Maya and her on the trail of a story.

The first order of business was contacting Gabe. He might know if Menny traveled. She picked up the phone but returned it to its cradle. It had been almost three weeks since she'd seen her son and this was as good an excuse as any for a personal visit. He had no classes on Tuesdays so she texted him she was coming. He didn't text back. Then again, he never did. She got dressed and, after a quick stop at the deli, headed south to Miami.

An hour later, she'd parked, made her way through the dorm's lobby and stood outside Gabe's room hugging a white paper bag to her chest. She knocked on his door. "Gabe?" No answer. She knocked again, louder. "It's Mom. I brought bagels."

The door opened and Gabe, his face puffy from sleep, stared blankly at Becks. "What are you doing here?" He grabbed his cell off the desk. "It's only noon." He turned and climbed back into bed, pulling a pillow over his head.

Becks laughed. Some things never changed. Gabe could get up early to make a class but if he had nothing scheduled he'd stay in bed all day. Seating herself at his desk she watched him, feeling such tenderness her heart ached. For a moment, she remembered him as a toddler, so trusting, his warm hand in hers as he sought protection from a playground bully. Would she ever get past this overwhelming need to protect him?

She glanced around for something to read and froze when she spotted the straps and boxes at the back of his desk. *Tefillin*? They looked newer than the grubby leather straps and boxes she'd seen on Menny's desk. What was Gabe doing with *tefillin*?

"Wake up." She nudged his shoulder.

He groaned.

She grabbed his pillow. He held on tight.

"Come on, sweetheart. You need to get up. I've got orange juice and bagels and lox."

He pulled the pillow from his head and eyed the juice bottle. "Oh, okay." He sat and swung his legs off the bed. "Why are you here?"

"I have a question about Menny. But first, what are you doing with these?" She held up the straps and boxes.

"They're *tefillin*." Gabe slugged down half the juice. "You use them for praying."

"I know that. What are they doing in *your* room?"

"I use them when I pray." He said it in such a matter of fact manner that Becks didn't know how to respond.

"You . . ." she gave them a shake . . . "you lay *tefillin*?" She repeated the term her grandfather had used.

Gabe nodded.

"Since when?"

"Since Menny taught me. We prayed together every morning."

Becks was speechless. How had she missed that? "I see." She spoke slowly, plagued with so many questions she didn't know where to begin. What had prompted him to adopt such an ancient ritual? Had he found new meaning in Judaism, or was this another passing fancy? Becks considered the practice old fashioned, something done by ultra-religious Jews and old people from Europe.

"Did you go to synagogue with him, too?"

Gabe shrugged, more concerned with devouring his bagel than discussing theology. As he chewed, he pulled his pillow onto his lap and rubbed its frayed hem between his thumb and index finger. It was a gesture he'd relied upon to comfort himself since childhood.

"So, tell me, are you finding religion?" She did her best imitation of a Yiddish accent. "Praying and going to shul?"

Gabe frowned and she realized she'd hit a nerve. His interest in religion had always been academic—a chance to study passages from the Torah and read scholarly commentary that addressed them. Now he was praying and going to synagogue and, if the tefillin was any sign, taking it very seriously.

"I told Dad I was going to shul with Menny, mostly to the campus Chabad."

"Mostly?" she asked. "Where else?" She remembered Daniel's mention of Gabe's foray into Chabad and hadn't given it much thought other than relief that he'd made a friend.

"A few weeks ago a junior took us to a Chabad in Miami Beach."

"How'd you like it?"

"It was okay." He shrugged and slid onto the bed, resting his back against the metal headboard. "Why are you here?"

She considered pressing Gabe on his interest in religion but let it go. The idea of his following his friend into Hasidism left her uncomfortable. She'd grown up in a secular Jewish family and ultra-orthodox Judaism seemed as foreign as Hare Krishna. How soon before Gabe grew a beard and peyos? Became kosher and refused to eat in her home?

Setting her concerns aside, Becks described her and his grandfather's meeting with Fox and discovery of the Hasidic men at Club Shukran.

"Do you think Menny visited the night club?"

Gabe narrowed his eyes. "Night club? No way he'd go somewhere like that."

"How do you know?"

"I just know."

"What about travel? Did he go on any trips?"

"He might have when he first moved in. I did not know him then."

"What about after?"

"I do not know."

Realizing she was getting nowhere, Becks tried another tack. Opening his laptop, she went to the Club Shukran web site and found a photo of Fox. She turned the computer and slid it toward her son. "Is that the man who was looking for Menny before you brought him to Boca?"

Gabe tilted his head to the left, then right. Between the weak lighting and the people crowded in the photograph, it was hard to make out Fox's features.

"I… I do not know," Gabe said. "The guy is big like that man. It is hard to tell. It could be."

Gabe reached for his pillow and rubbed the soft fabric between his fingers. "Is that the man who owns the night club?"

Concerned by her son's behavior but afraid to say anything, she answered, "Club Shukran."

"What did he want with Menny?"

"I don't know. He claims he never met your friend."

Gabe stared down at the frayed case. His rubbing had grown more rapid.

"One more question," Becks said. She could sense her son's growing tension. "I heard Mr. Fox sells drugs in his club. Do you think Menny was involved?"

Gabe's gaze swept erratically across the room, settling on his door, his desk, one of the Torah quotations posted above his bed. Everywhere except Becks' face.

"Menny hated drugs. If he saw someone smoking marijuana, he left the room." He flapped his hands against his chest for a minute then returned to the pillowcase.

Becks was taken aback by her son's response. He wasn't lying—-he didn't know how to lie. It went with Asperger's Syndrome. Even so, Gabe wouldn't react as he had without reason. Menny objected to drug use. Even so, that didn't mean he hadn't used or sold them in the past. Maybe he'd worked for Fox. That might explain Menny's fear when he learned of the stranger's visit. Why was Gabe so upset though? She bit her lower lip in frustration. If only she knew the right questions to ask.

"Come on honey," she said, rising from her chair. The muscles of his back were knotted beneath his tee shirt. Exercise would relieve his anxiety. "Let's go for a walk. I'll wait downstairs while you dress."

Fifteen minutes later, Gabe met her in the dorm lobby. The room had grown crowded and hip-hop music blared from speakers in the ceiling. Students were returning from class, she guessed, as jeans-clad youngsters raced past.

After leaving the dorm, Becks and Gabe worked their way around tall sleek buildings and crowded sidewalks to reach the arboretum that, Gabe informed her, botany professors had planted decades earlier. Tucked into a quiet, isolated corner of the large campus, the small woods felt like a world unto itself, a fairyland dropped into the cold, impersonal universe of a college campus. The grounds were thick with palms, some tall and graceful with broad luxurious fronds, others squat with trunks covered in spiny barbs and uneven foliage. Impressed by his enthusiasm for the forested landscape—Gabe could name every tree without reading its label—and afraid to upset her son further, Becks let their discussion of Menny lapse.

Driving home, Becks reflected that she hadn't gotten very far with Gabe. He'd been alarmed by the photo of Fox, which was suggestive. Still, he didn't admit recognizing him. She'd learned nothing about Menny's involvement in drugs or the names of friends he'd made at the university.

It wasn't much but she decided to call Detective Cole the next morning with what she had. If he refused to look into Menny's death, she'd figure out what her next step should be. Deep down, she knew the answer. Daniel would be angry. All the same, what choice did she have?

31

Daniel came home early that evening and surprised Becks by announcing he'd reserved a table at Bianchi's. It was her favorite restaurant and a family regular for birthdays and anniversaries. When he knew they were coming, the proprietor, a patient of Daniel's, held a private corner for them.

"What's the occasion?" she asked. They were in the kitchen and she discreetly returned the steak she'd defrosted to the refrigerator. "Our anniversary isn't for a month."

"No occasion. I want you to myself. No phones. No computers."

Becks slid her arms around Daniel's waist and kissed him, enjoying the warm pressure of his lips on hers. She'd been so preoccupied with Menny and, before that, getting her cookbook in shape for the publisher, that she'd ignored her husband. They needed time together. Tonight would be perfect.

She ran upstairs and changed into her red silk sheath and silver flats. Daniel smiled appreciatively when she came downstairs. He looked handsome in the gray wool pants and white shirt he wore for work. He ran several days a week and looked fit, his stomach flat and shoulders broad. Daniel's hair was gray now and fine lines surrounded his eyes but he still had the pronounced Slavic cheekbones and ready smile that made her fall in love with him as a young medical student.

Mr. Bianchi's welcome was effusive, as always, and he repeatedly thanked Daniel for his patronage as he escorted them to a private niche off the dining room. Becks loved this table, most of all because the crystal chandelier sent prisms dancing on the white tablecloth. Daniel ordered a bottle of Chianti then chatted about work and the cruise to Alaska they planned to take the next summer. Once their orders were placed and the wine poured, Daniel reached across the table and took Becks' hands. His were dry and rough and she felt utterly safe in their warmth.

"Sweetheart, I don't want to upset you."

"That's a great way to start a romantic evening."

He smiled gently. "Gabe called this afternoon. He sounded upset."

She pulled her hands from his. "You brought me here to tell me that?"

Daniel blushed and shook his head. "No. I made the reservation before he called. But we should discuss it."

Becks rested her chin in her hand and tilted her head. "All right. What did he tell you?"

"That he didn't want you to keep asking about Menny. He said his friend was dead and he was tired of your questions."

"Anything else?" Her jaw muscles tensed.

"He wasn't very articulate. He mentioned something about Fox and a night club. He said you visited him to find out if Menny was a drug dealer."

Becks leaned back in her chair and sighed deeply. Gabe had seemed calm enough when she left the university. What had happened between her visit and his call to Daniel? Now she'd have to tell her husband about the visit to Club Shukran.

He studied her, arms crossed and eyebrows raised.

"It's a long story."

He nodded.

"Maya and I went to Fox's club last night. I didn't learn anything during our meeting and I sensed he was hiding something. I thought I'd pick up information at the club."

"Are you crazy?" Daniel uncrossed his arms and leaned across the table. "You could've been arrested for trespassing."

Becks hid her grimace with a sip of wine. Of course, he considered the worst possible outcome. "Not likely. Imagine the headline. Middle-aged housewife arrested in South Beach night club. Not exactly great public relations. We were fine. Had a few drinks and left."

"And that's all?" His voice was edged with skepticism.

She kneaded her napkin under the table. The heavily-starched linen felt crisp and clean. "Pretty much. We saw two Hasidic men on the dance floor. One was stoned. Turns out Club Shukran has a reputation for hiring young men, including *frummers*—she used the Yiddish term for religious Jews—to transport drugs."

"That's terrific. Did you—"

Their appetizers arrived and Becks relaxed, grateful for the interruption. They ate in a silence punctuated by the dull clatter of forks and knives on china and the discreet murmurings of the restaurant's well-heeled patrons. Once they'd finished and the waiter disappeared with their plates, Daniel spoke. "I thought you were going to drop this. Let the police investigate."

"They're not interested."

"With good reason. Menny was *not murdered*." He dropped his voice. "I talked to the medical examiner this morning and he assured me Menny drowned after suffering blunt force trauma when his head hit the culvert. His parents have accepted his death as an accident. Why can't you?"

"Because I don't believe it."

The waiter stopped a few feet from their table, a tray balanced above his shoulder. Becks nodded and he set the tray on a stand and transferred the plates to the table. Bianchi's osso buco was unsurpassed and, despite Daniel's carping, she wanted to eat.

"You're upsetting Gabe. And me," Daniel said once the waiter left. "Please, Becks. Let it go. I'm afraid you'll get hurt. Tell the police what you learned and move on."

But Becks couldn't. She had too many questions. She'd promised to protect Menny and failed. An innate determination to keep digging, to peel away the layers of deceit and discover what lay beneath, had kept her going as a newspaper reporter. She sat straighter in her chair as she realized the same stubborn resolve was driving her now.

Becks took a forkful of osso buco and set the plate aside. She'd lost her appetite and the rich meat made her queasy. "I'm sorry, Daniel. I'll do my best to keep Gabe out of it. I can't let this go."

His eyes grew hooded and blotches of red stained his cheekbones. "I wish you'd consider my feelings for once. This Sid Fox sounds like a tough bastard. You could be dealing with a murderer. I don't want to lose you."

Had she sensed an unspoken "again?"

Daniel finished his meal and, fifteen minutes later, the waiter came over with the dessert menus. Daniel asked for the bill and quickly paid. As they neared the entrance, Mr. Bianchi strode across the room and thanked them for coming.

He placed a hand on Daniel's shoulder. "I hope you had a pleasant evening."

Daniel nodded. "Thank you."

"And you, Madam." He bowed ever so slightly.

Unlike Gabe, Becks could lie. "Thank you, Mr. Bianchi. Everything was lovely."

It had begun to rain during dinner and Becks jumped in the car the minute the valet pulled up. She slammed the door before the attendant could shut it. The only sound on the drive home was the swish of wet road and the metronomic beat of the windshield wiper.

32

Becks jolted awake the next morning, out of breath, her heart beating wildly against her chest. Menny had appeared in her dream, his skin translucent and his eyes sorrowful as he waved at her to follow. He started slowly and gained speed and she found herself chasing him through a lush green rain forest. He looked over his shoulder as though to tell her something but she somehow knew he had to reach his destination first. She stumbled over tree roots and brushed against damp vines while pursuing him. Only feet away from the boy, she woke with a start. She was panting and rolled over to check Daniel's side of the bed. His chest rose and fell beneath the white coverlet.

The dream left her jittery and depressed and she slid up against her pillows to assess what it meant. Cole hadn't returned her call the day before. No surprise there. She planned to talk to him that morning and wash her hands of the whole business. Was her subconscious telling her to find Menny's murderer? That no one else would?

On the ride home from Bianchi's the evening before, Becks had considered her options. Weeks earlier, when the police found Menny's body, she had no intention of pursuing a murderer. She wasn't sure Menny *was* murdered but wanted the police to consider the possibility.

That hadn't worked out and, at this point, she had no illusions about Cole pursuing the case.

Where did that leave her? Becks couldn't let go until she'd convinced herself Menny's death was an accident. She'd give herself a week or two and move on. If Daniel didn't like it, too bad. It was her life. During the year he was gone, she'd become accustomed to doing things her way and wasn't about to change.

Gabe was another story, though. She didn't want to further upset her son. He hadn't been much help so far and she had no reason to believe he knew anything more than what he'd told her. With Gabe, you didn't get answers without asking the right questions. And as far as she knew, she'd asked them.

Becks got out of bed and went downstairs to brew coffee. When it was done, she took a cup and joined Mulligan on the rattan sofa on the patio. It was one of a set she'd upholstered in bright tropical fabric to go by the pool. The colorful cushions were covered with cat fur and she brushed aside as much of the fine hair as she could before sitting.

It was a cool, crystalline morning and a spider web glistening with dew formed an arc between the two mango trees in her backyard. Despite the cheerful sunlight, Becks couldn't slough off the unease she'd felt since emerging from her dream. Images of a sad-eyed Menny looking over his shoulder at her in the jungle haunted her as she sipped her coffee and ran a hand over Mulligan's fur.

When Daniel came downstairs, Becks made him a western omelet—his favorite—to apologize for her anger the night before. She wouldn't change her mind about looking into Menny's death but she wanted him to know she loved him.

"I appreciate the breakfast," he said as he picked up his fork. "It's not going to make me feel better about this Menny business, though."

Becks pulled out a chair and sat across from him. "I'm sorry, sweetheart. I can't walk away after what I've learned. I'll give it a few more days, see what I can find out."

"Do what you think is best." He smiled grimly. "I know you won't change your mind."

Becks dialed Maya's cell the minute Daniel left the house. The women had been too tired to talk on the drive home from Club Shukran and Maya had been in meetings yesterday. Becks was anxious to get her friend's take on the evening.

"You are some hot mama," Becks said when Maya picked up. "Half the men in Club Shukran had their tongues out like cartoon wolves."

Maya laughed. "You looked great too. That's a terrific disguise."

Becks didn't know whether to take it as a compliment or insult. "I talked to Gabe yesterday. He doesn't know anything about the club or Menny's involvement with drugs but he tentatively identified Sid Fox as the man who was looking for Menny. When I asked if there was any chance Menny worked as a mule, he went a little crazy. Said Menny was rabidly anti-drug and hid in his room when anyone used them."

"Maybe Menny had a bad experience with drugs or knew someone who did," Maya said. "Or maybe he was afraid of getting caught with them. I think we need to look for a link between Menny and Fox. You have any ideas?"

"Maybe, though I don't know where to go with it. I told you Fox worked as a Hebrew teacher in a town called Kleynshtot. I learned Menny lived there for a few months too. That might be where they met. Can you look into that?" Becks knew she had a lot of nerve asking. But Maya had been supportive thus far.

"I'll need to run a few skip traces this morning then I'll look. How about I stop by tonight with whatever I find. I've got a date and I'd love you to meet him."

"Great. I'll do some work in the meantime."

Becks was at her computer reviewing recipes for kasha varnishkas when the phone rang. It was Hanley. The *Broward Tribune's* publisher had decided against letting her run the four recipes she'd adapted from ones she'd printed in the paper. Her heart sank. Now she'd have to spend hours developing new recipes. That was a pain and she could deal with it. The hitch was telling Betsy Weinstein, her editor. Her stomach churned at the prospect of calling the woman this late in the game. Betsy had no choice but to accept the revised recipes. Still, she'd be livid.

Betsy answered on the first ring. "Speak to me."

"It's Becks Ruchinsky."

"What is it?"

Becks' palms felt clammy. "I just got word I have to change four recipes. Do we have time?" She explained what had happened.

After what felt like hours but was probably a minute, her editor cleared her throat. "Do I have a choice?"

Becks wiped her palms on her skirt.

"Have them to me by tomorrow afternoon. And make sure the word count doesn't change."

Resigned to spending the day cooking, Becks pulled half a dozen cookbooks off her shelf and devoted the next three hours to perusing them and creating recipes to replace those she was removing. By the time Daniel got home at six, she'd visited two supermarkets and a kosher grocery and had the zucchini kugel, Moroccan fish and legume salad on the table. A Sephardic-inspired barbequed brisket would be ready in a half-hour. The aromas of spicy garlic sauce, earthy potatoes and fragrant paprika filled the kitchen.

"Smells great," Daniel said as he tossed his mail on the kitchen table. Then, turning to Becks, he laughed. "What happened to you?"

She caught her reflection in the window over the sink and cringed. In the rush of cooking, she'd run her hands through her hair and clumps rose from her head like spikes on the collar of a large vicious dog. Her tee shirt was splattered with tomato and cranberry sauce.

Once the brisket was done, Becks filled both their plates with her "experiments." Daniel's praise for the meal came as an almost physical relief; he was a reliable critic and didn't shy away from telling her when a recipe didn't work or a little more salt or lemon was needed. Exhausted, she decided to wait until the next morning to email the recipes to Betsy.

At nine o'clock, as Daniel and Becks were drying the last of the dishes, the doorbell rang. The two exchanged mystified glances as Becks left for the door. "Damn," she said after looking through the peephole. She'd forgotten about Maya's visit. Her friend stood on the patio, dressed in red leather pants and a matching jacket. A large, loose-limbed man with a gray ponytail held her hand.

"Come in. I'm glad you could make it." Becks struggled to hide her exhaustion behind a veneer of cheerful expectation. The smell of cooking permeated the hall. "I've got your dinner waiting."

After a minute of weak protests, Maya and the man she introduced as Guillermo came into the kitchen, where Becks quickly assembled plates of leftovers. As usual, she'd cooked more than needed and there was plenty to go around. The two ate with gusto, complimenting Becks on the meal. As they ate, Becks and Maya gave the men a brief history of stories they'd worked on years earlier.

After dinner, when Guillermo offered to help Daniel with the dishes, Maya signaled Becks to join her in the family room. Once the two women were seated on the couch, Maya drew a legal sized envelope from her red leather handbag.

"I'll call tomorrow to discuss this. I want you to take a look first. This Sid Fox is quite a hustler. Miami Beach police busted his club twice for drugs and he got off scot-free."

"Anything about how he knew Menny?"

"I don't think so but you read it and decide."

The men emerged from the kitchen arguing over the final inning of a Marlins' game that had taken place two years earlier and Becks slid the envelope behind a cushion. Guillermo smiled at Maya. "Ready to hit the road?"

She took his arm in answer. After saying their goodbyes, Maya and Guillermo announced their departure with a throaty roar of the Harley they'd parked out front. Daniel announced he was heading to bed.

Becks waited until his steps sounded on the upstairs landing before returning to the family room. Dropping onto the couch, she retrieved the envelope from behind the cushion and emptied it on her lap. Maya had left her copies of two *Miami-Herald* articles. She'd underlined the date, September 18, 2009, on the first and scrawled "local section?" across the top. The first read:

Miami Beach police arrested eight club patrons and employees of a popular South Beach venue early Sunday for the alleged sale and possession of controlled substances. Among the drugs confiscated at Club Shukran

*were ecstasy, cocaine and heroin, according to Miami
Beach police detective Alonzo Perez.*

*The undercover drug bust came after a two-month
investigation that involved more than 50 drug sales.*

*"I was shocked because I've been visiting the club
since it opened and haven't noticed drug use," a man who
asked not to be identified said. "That was unusual for
South Beach clubs."*

*At a news conference Sunday afternoon, Deputy
Police Chief John Suggs talked about the epidemic of drug
abuse in South Beach.*

*Charges in the case include drug possession and
drug sales. Police say other drugs seized in the club
include marijuana.*

The second article was dated six months earlier. It
reported that five Club Shukran patrons, three of them
Hasidic Jews, were charged with possession and sale of
heroin. Fox's name wasn't mentioned in either story.
Becks went back and reread both. That was odd. Most
reporters would've gotten at least a nominal quote from
the club owner. More often than not, he or she would
disavow knowledge of drug use. How had Fox kept his
name out of the paper? In Miami, drug busts at popular
clubs made the front page. Why had the paper buried Club
Shukran's busts in the local section?

Becks was dying to know how Maya got her hands
on the third item in the envelope, a spreadsheet with Club
Shukran's employee schedule for September 2009, when
the second raid took place. The photocopied page included
the names and work schedules of the club's bartenders,
waitresses, janitors and security detail. Maya had
underlined the security guards' names along with the
hours they worked. Becks shifted forward on the couch
when she saw one of the names, Alonzo Perez, the

detective who'd commented on the club's second drug raid. Perez had worked twice as many hours as the other security guards that month and wasn't scheduled for the night of the bust. Maya had circled "Perez," "Hodges" and "Deluca" and scribbled "MB cop!" next to each name. They hadn't worked the night of the bust either.

Her message was clear. Fox had become cozy with the Miami Beach police. How cozy wasn't obvious. In any case, he'd made enough friends to keep his name out of the paper and his club open despite charges against his patrons and employees.

Becks hugged a pillow to her chest and sank back on the couch. Fox may not have sold drugs at Club Shukran but he had to be getting a cut of his employees' and patrons' take—including whatever the Hasids brought into the country.

Maya's findings shed light on the club owner's character and contacts. Still, they did not establish a link between Fox and Menny. A cascade of ideas raced through her mind like a dealer shuffling a deck of cards. She felt so close and yet so far from the proof she needed to get the police interested. She was fairly certain Fox was the stranger who'd visited the boys' dorm. But Gabe never looked into people's faces—Asperger's again—so his identification of the man could be challenged. The clerk at Shapiro's Market said Menny left in a car like the one Sid Fox owned. Moreover, the butcher was certain the boy had left with a short, bearded man in a black hat. Fox was beefy and tall.

Did Fox have a confederate who looked Hasidic? Was the club owner waiting in the car when Menny left the market?

Becks sighed and returned the materials to the envelope. It was almost midnight. She'd call Maya and decide what to do tomorrow. Remembering her promise to email Betsy the revised recipes early the next morning, she scowled. What if the editor didn't approve them? It might mean the end of her career as a cookbook author. She also needed to finish the knish article she'd promised Hanley. Her life was becoming too complicated. Convincing the police to investigate Menny's death was becoming an obsession. It was high time she found some answers and moved on with her life.

33

The Boca Raton Public Library is a leviathan of a building. Set off the road among queen palms, giant oaks and fiery red Royal Poinciana trees, its orange, barrel-tiled tower looms over Spanish River Boulevard like a castle in a tropical forest. Approached through a columned porte-cochere, the Spanish Colonial-inspired building is one of the most graceful structures in a town known for architectural excess. Inside, its proportions feel more intimate, with meeting rooms, cozy chairs and small tables where patrons can contemplate the turquoise lake through floor-to-ceiling windows.

Arriving at the library the next morning, Becks set her computer on a table near a window then sniffed and looked around. A homeless woman who stopped by two or three times a week sat a few feet away. It was seventy-five degrees outside but the elderly lady wore a black watchman's cap and a heavy wool coat that was long overdue for a cleaning. She snored faintly, her head pillowed by a pile of large books. Becks scanned the room. A man she'd nicknamed the Maori because of his elaborately tattooed face wasn't at his usual table. She sat there.

Every winter, Boca Raton's libraries become havens for homeless people who prefer its air-conditioned comfort to the sunny beaches South Florida's more conventional snowbirds enjoy. Becks came to the library once or twice a week to avoid the distractions at home and was familiar with its dispossessed clientele. Most days, she smiled or waved when she passed.

Today, though, she got right to work searching the library's database of Jewish publications for information about Fox. Pairing his name with the word "Hasid" worked before so she tried it again. Yes! The author of a blog about South Florida's Hasidic community wrote that Fox had donated a sterling silver breastplate to the Washington Avenue Chabad. He'd made the gift to decorate a Torah donated by the owner of an erotic art museum. Photos of bearded, black-hatted men carrying Torah scrolls ran above the story.

Becks was surprised. It was strange enough that an erotic art museum proprietor supported a Chabad. But a night club owner who dealt drugs? After reading a few more posts and finding no further mention of Fox, she searched the erotic museum's website. Things were getting weirder and weirder. The erotic art collection was owned by a Jewish grandmother and Holocaust survivor named Fanny Berkowitz.

A night club owner. An erotic art museum proprietor. A Chabad house. And a murdered Hasidic boy. She recalled Gabe's favorite "Sesame Street" song, "One of These Things (Is Not Like The Other)." What was the relationship between them? And what, for that matter, was an erotic art museum? She'd visit Mrs. Berkowitz to see if she could shed light on Sid Fox's connection to the Hasidic community. And if time permitted, she'd check out the museum?

Becks packed up her computer and left the room, ignoring the nattily-dressed octogenarian who, one of the librarians had told her, was expelled a month earlier for downloading pornography. Driving home, she called the museum and explained she was a freelance writer interested in publishing a story about the art collection. Who knew? It *could* turn into a story. The operator put her through to Mrs. Berkowitz, who agreed to meet the next day. Becks was surprised by the woman's heavy Yiddish accent. She sounded more like a *bubbe*, an Old-World Jewish grandmother, than an erotic art aficionado.

Ten minutes later, as she pulled up to her house, Becks' cell rang. It was Maya. "So what do you make of the material I left?"

"Fox has some good connections with the police. Do you think the cops lied about finding drugs on patrons and not Fox?"

"Don't be naive." Maya laughed. "A cop can make a fortune if he works enough off duty detail. And that's if he's honest. You notice the name Alonzo Perez, the detective who handled the first bust at Shukran?"

"I saw it." Becks got out of the car and pulled her purse strap over her shoulder. Her gardener was mowing the lawn and she pulled the phone closer to hear over the engine.

"He wrote a character reference for Fox after the bust. Talk about conflict of interest. I can't say who told me but you owe me a hundred bucks."

"You've got it." Becks scrabbled around in her bag for the key, let herself into the house and made a beeline for the kitchen. After dropping her purse and computer case on the peninsula, she threw together a turkey sandwich and told Maya about Fox's donation to the Chabad and her plan to visit the erotic art museum the next day.

"A sex museum?" Maya asked.

"Erotic art."

"With penises and pornography?"

"I'd assume so."

"You're going to need my help there," Maya said. "Pick me up at ten."

Becks laughed and hung up. Maya was always ready to lend a hand.

34

Becks took a moment to check in both directions before following Maya into the erotic art museum the next morning. Crammed between a Burger King and a Cuban bodega, the drab white office building on South Beach's Washington Avenue looked unassuming enough. It could've held law or accounting practices for all the exterior revealed. Once inside the black- and gold-tiled lobby, though, Becks' eyebrows arched. Maya snorted. What at first glance appeared to be a classical nude statue in the center of the room turned out to be a life-sized sculpture of a leering satyr chasing a naked woman.

This was *not* going to be her grandmother's museum.

Climbing a flight of narrow stairs to the exhibit space, Becks felt a trace of trepidation at the prospect of viewing pornography. She'd seen dozens of paintings and sculptures that bordered on porno at conventional museums. How different could this be?

When she stepped into the museum's brightly-lit vestibule and gazed into a display case, she found out.

"Holy cow!" She motioned Maya over. Dozens of exquisitely rendered porcelain and metal figurines depicted men and women engaged in sex, many with members of other species. Every position in the Kama Sutra, Becks guessed, was represented along with some she suspected the artist had dreamed up.

After purchasing tickets from a bespectacled twenty-something, Becks and Maya made their way down a narrow hallway, stopping to stare at the pen and ink drawings of Snow White and the seven dwarves in the midst of an orgy. Moving on to the next display, Becks laughed as she realized each item in the museum's collection of brass, wood and pottery apples had a vagina.

The erotic art went on for room after room and by the time the women reached the exhibits of Egyptian phalluses their titillated giggles had given way to yawns. Maya walked ahead while Becks took a moment to examine a violin with breasts. A few minutes later, she found her friend sitting cross-legged on a carved wooden bed, leaning back against one of its penis-shaped posts as she tapped at her cell phone.

"Had enough?" Maya said, looking up. "Let's find the owner and get out of here."

Becks was about to argue—after all, *she'd* paid the admission fee—when a soft voice sounded behind her. "Becks Ruchinsky?"

"Yes." She turned to find a petite woman in the doorway.

"I'm Fanny Berkowitz."

Becks stepped back. She'd pictured the museum's patron as a flamboyant, albeit older, blonde woman in bright red lipstick and flashy jewelry. In Becks' imagination, Mrs. Berkowitz wore a tight flowered dress that showed generous cleavage.

Instead, she saw an elegant matron in an expensively cut, pink designer suit. A simple gold cuff encircled her wrist and tiny diamonds studded her ears.

Mrs. Berkowitz laughed as Becks blushed. "It's all right. This is the last thing *I* expected to be doing at my age," she said as though reading Becks' mind. "The collection started when my son asked me to find erotic art for his apartment. I got carried away."

Becks smiled.

"Come along. We can talk in my office."

Becks and Maya followed Mrs. Berkowitz through a collection of scrolls to a large office, where the older woman settled herself behind an expansive marble desk and motioned her guests to sit in the stainless-steel chairs opposite. The room was spare and the desk uncluttered, a significant departure from the hodgepodge appearance of the museum she curated.

"What can I do for you?" Mrs. Berkowitz asked, folding her hands on the desk.

"I'd like to be honest with you. I *am* a freelance writer but that's not why I'm here," Becks said. "Recently, a young man—a Hasidic friend of my son—died under my watch. I want to make sure it was an accident."

Mrs. Berkowitz placed the tips of her fingers on the desk. "What does that have to do with the museum?"

"I think you know someone who might be involved. Sidney Fox. I read that he donated a silver breastplate to decorate the Torah you gave to the Washington Avenue Chabad."

Sunlight streamed into the room through plate glass windows, its unforgiving light revealing the fine lines that draped the older woman's eyes and mouth. Still, the museum owner appeared healthy and vigorous and the glint in her eyes suggested she was no one's fool. She tipped her head to the side and frowned. "Tell me more."

Becks told her about Menny's death and let Maya explain how she'd identified the owner of the BMW with the "shin" plate as Sid Fox. Once Maya finished, Becks described their visit to Club Shukran and discovery of the Hasidic men.

Mrs. Berkowitz sat upright, hands folded on the desk, throughout their recital. Once Becks finished, she leaned back in her chair. "Well, I must admit I *am* surprised at the presence of Hasidic youngsters at the night club. Still, young people will experiment at that age. I can't tell you much about Sid Fox. He's active, as I am, in the Washington Avenue Chabad." She removed a photo from the top drawer of her desk and slid it toward Becks. It showed Mrs. Berkowitz holding a Torah. Fox stood to one side and a bearded man to the other. "The man to my right is the rabbi, Shimon Haziz. He's been at the Chabad for two years. My husband and I supported numerous Jewish causes and, when he passed away, I gave the Chabad a Torah to honor his memory. Sid was gracious enough to donate the breastplate."

"Do you have any idea why he did that?" Maya spoke, returning the photo.

Mrs. Berkowitz slid the photo into her drawer and smiled gently. "Mr. Fox seems a bit rough around the edges so I understand your curiosity. He attends services almost every Saturday and participates in our outreach programs. I assume he was raised in a religious home and, as with many of our young members, decided to return to the fold. He was simply showing his gratitude."

"Does he have friends there?" Becks asked.

The older woman shook her head and waved away her question with a flick of her wrist. "My goodness, you girls are suspicious. He and the rabbi seem friendly. They may have met before Mr. Fox moved here. I understand the rabbi provided him a character reference before he opened the night club. Mr. Fox chats with some of the men after services. I don't know what they discuss." She shrugged. "Sadly, I don't speak Hebrew."

"Does he leave the Chabad with anyone?" Becks said.

"I don't know." She sounded fatigued or, Becks theorized, tired of their questions. "I never stay for more than a few minutes after services." She rose in an evident sign of dismissal. "Why don't you come to Chabad and see for yourselves? Women tend to arrive on Saturdays at ten and stay for lunch. You might enjoy it."

Becks wasn't thrilled at the prospect of sitting through an orthodox service but couldn't pass up the chance to learn more about Fox. It might be her best opportunity to catch the man unawares and when his defenses were down.

"Thank you. I'll try to make it this weekend."

"It's called the Washington Avenue Chabad," Mrs. Berkowitz repeated, rising and offering her hand to both women. "You can find the address on the website."

On their way to the exit, Becks and Maya passed two more exhibits, one of African fertility symbols, the other with a seven-foot metal phallus Maya insisted on standing next to as Becks photographed her.

When they emerged from the staircase into the downstairs lobby, Maya turned to Becks, hands on her hips, head tilted. "I don't get it. What is that nice old lady doing with all that fucking junk?" She snorted with laughter as she opened the door to Washington Avenue.

Becks shook her head and followed Maya outside.

As they returned to the car, Becks reflected that her search was becoming stranger by the moment. The erotic art museum owner seemed genuinely fond of Fox. Maybe Becks' visit to the Chabad House would yield more insight into the man.

That or a morning of excruciatingly dull prayer.

35

Becks deliberately took her time stuffing lipstick, her cell phone and a notepad into a small black leather clutch while Daniel, his arms folded, glared from the foot of their bed. Getting dressed for temple, he'd made no secret that he'd rather spend Saturday morning on the tennis court than in a synagogue. But Gabe had made a surprise visit the night before and offered to join his mother at the Chabad. Daniel, not wanting to give up time with their son, agreed to join them.

At a quarter to nine, Gabe knocked on the bedroom door then stuck in his head. "We need to leave now. It'll take fifty-seven minutes to get there and ten minutes to park." He glanced at his watch. "I'll wait in the car."

While she hadn't forced the issue, Becks was relieved Daniel was going. She was nervous about running into Fox and knew she'd feel out of place in the ultra-religious synagogue. Though he rarely attended synagogue, Daniel had grown up in an observant family and was familiar with the orthodox service.

Over coffee that morning, he'd questioned her motives for visiting the synagogue. "Fox will suspect you're there because of him. You think he'll talk to you?"

"Maybe not," Becks said. "Just the same, I'll be more comfortable approaching him. If he's such a big shot at the

Chabad, he won't stomp off like he did at the deli. I'd like to meet the rabbi, too. The Hasidic world seems pretty small. He might have heard something about Menny's disappearance."

Five minutes later, as Daniel was backing out of the driveway, Becks' cell rang. Tootsie was calling to announce he'd be heading up to Boca Raton in a half hour. A few weeks earlier, she told her father he was showing up too early on Saturday mornings and he agreed to call before leaving Miami. He'd been surprisingly agreeable about giving Becks advance warning. When Becks informed him the family was heading in his direction for services, he laughed. "When did you turn into a super Jew? What's the holiday? Purim? Sukkot? Sandy Koufax's birthday?"

"We're checking out the Washington Avenue Chabad. You want to come?"

"Sure. Why not? We can have lunch when it's over. Let me know why we're going when you pick me up."

An hour later, after picking up Tootsie and circling the block twice, Daniel pulled in front of a modest, fifties-era house with jalousied windows and a cracked cement driveway. The only landscaping was a row of dead bushes—most now twigs and brown leaves—in front of the building.

"Are you sure this is it?" Becks asked. She'd read that the Chabad met in a South Beach home but hadn't expected such a small, drab structure.

Daniel checked his GPS. "It's the correct address."

The house sat on a narrow, tree-lined street of pale pink and yellow homes and low-rise apartment buildings four blocks from the erotic art museum and a short walk from Club Shukran. Scrutinizing the renovated Art Deco homes that signaled the neighborhood's gentrification, Becks wondered if the house—the website said it belonged to a Chabad member—would go on the market once real estate prices rose.

When she entered, Becks was surprised to find that the house's interior walls had been removed to create room for a sanctuary. The entry led directly into a large sterile space filled with folding chairs and bisected by louvered wooden screens. A few dozen men stood to the right of the screens, rocking back and forth, mumbling prayers, while three women sat quietly to the left of the divider.

The stocky, bearded rabbi Becks had seen in Mrs. Berkowitz's photo swayed in front of the congregation at a chest-high table covered with a velvet purple cloth. A white tasseled prayer shawl covered his head and most of his face and he chanted in a monotone as he rocked back and forth. Behind him, a tall armoire-like piece of furniture with wooden doors stood open, revealing a Torah encased in a white silk cover. A small silver breastplate etched with the tree of life hung like a necklace from the two wooden dowels that held the scrolls. Fox's gift? It looked expensive.

"See you after the service," Daniel whispered as he and Gabe left to join the men on the right side of the divider. Becks walked to the women's section, where she stood a moment before finding her way to the front row to get a better view of the rabbi. Even there, she had to crane her neck to see the rabbi on the far side of the screen.

Five minutes later, Tootsie, who'd gone in search of a bathroom, sat in the chair to her left. Leaning toward her as if to share a confidence, he whispered, "Okay if I join you?"

She took him up on his challenge. "Be my guest." He knew where to sit. After a minute, he slapped his head in feigned confusion and left to join Daniel and Gabe in the men's section. As he left the women's area, he winked. Becks bit off a laugh. He knew exactly how she felt.

Becks had picked up conversational Hebrew during a summer studying in Israel but was lost as the rabbi droned on in the language. She was about to nod off when a clatter of dishes rose from the back of the room. Turning, she spotted a tiny kitchen. Grateful for an excuse to abandon the service, Becks rose and joined the handful of women preparing lunch. A slow cooker bubbled on a narrow counter.

"Is that cholent?" Becks whispered. The aroma of meat and vegetables was unmistakable. Her grandmother had made a big pot of the savory beef and barley stew every Friday to comply with religious laws prohibiting cooking on Sabbath.

"It's Yael's recipe," a fortyish woman in a calf-length navy dress said. It took Becks a minute to realize the woman's lush, brown shoulder-length hair was a wig. Another girl, this one wearing a ponytail and a short denim dress, gave a brief wave. "I'm Alina. Are you a new member?"

"I'm just visiting. I've been to the Chabad near my house and am curious about others." She wasn't lying. She *had* gone to a Boca Raton Chabad to pick up Ava when her car wouldn't start after services.

As they chatted, the door of the Chabad opened and Becks froze. It was Fox. He didn't appear to notice her as he found his seat and draped a prayer shawl over his Hawaiian shirt. Many of the congregants smiled and nodded, clearly pleased he'd arrived. When the rabbi removed the Torah from the ark and handed it to Fox, she realized why. Fox was a *Kohanim*, a descendant of the priestly Israeli tribe whose members are the first called to read from the Torah.

A priest by day. A drug dealer by night. Wasn't South Beach great?

Figuring she'd have to confront him eventually, Becks returned to her seat. She sat in the front row of the women's area and leaned forward so she could be seen, then fought off a smug grin when the night club owner stared at her. A few minutes later, he looked her way and mumbled to the rabbi.

The service continued for another half hour but the room grew noisy as mothers with strollers and toddlers filed into the women's section. They were soon joined by young women, only a few of whom wore the wigs or scarves required after marriage. When she caught young men glancing over their prayer books at the girls in the front row, Becks realized the Chabad was turning into a singles scene—albeit under the watchful eye of young matrons.

Becks debated her next step as the rabbi led the congregation in closing prayers. Her stomach churned at the prospect of coming face to face with Fox but she was determined to talk to him. If things got rough, Daniel would step in. Her mouth grew dry.

Becks had left her seat and was in the back of the sanctuary looking for a water fountain when an anguished cry rose above the hum of prayers. Her heart leaped as she turned and saw Gabe on his feet, staring at Fox. His facial muscles had stiffened into a terrified mask and his skin had grown pallid. He flapped his hands before uttering an earsplitting wail and sinking to the floor, groaning.

Ignoring the customary restrictions on women entering the men's section, Becks raced to where Daniel knelt by their son, his fingers on Gabe's wrist. Nothing mattered now—not the rabbi, not Fox, not the stupid orthodox rules. Her child was in pain. Touching Gabe would make matters worse so Becks spoke softly, assuring him he'd be fine. After a few minutes, his groans subsided. Ten minutes after his meltdown, Gabe rose from the floor. Eyes wide and mouth ajar, he scanned the room. Becks followed his gaze. Fox was gone.

Guiding her son to a chair, Becks tried to fathom what had provoked his meltdown. He'd spent the morning staring into space, lost in his private world as usual. Had he noticed Fox at the end of the service and reacted to the man? It seemed likely. Any doubts she had about Gabe's identification of the night club owner disappeared. Fox *had* to be the man who'd sought Menny at the university. Had he killed the boy as well? And what had Fox done to provoke such a dramatic response from Gabe? She shivered. Menny's death was awful enough. Was Gabe in danger?

Heart pounding against her ribs, Becks realized she'd had enough. The police weren't looking for Menny's murderer and no amount of evidence would convince them to do so. Now Gabe might be in jeopardy. *She* had to find Menny's killer.

36

"Is the boy okay?" Rabbi Haziz asked, approaching Becks and her family. They were kneeling next to Gabe, waiting for the boy's breathing to return to normal. "Can I get him a glass of water?"

He's fine." Becks snapped, sounding more annoyed than she'd intended. She was irritated that he hadn't come over earlier, choosing to chat with members of his congregation instead. Still, she understood his reaction. Most people were frightened or embarrassed by Gabe's outbursts and tried to ignore them. She considered explaining her son's behavior but Gabe hated it when she discussed his problems with strangers.

"If you're up to it, we'd like to have you join us for lunch." The rabbi motioned toward a pair of tables at the side of the room where a dozen young men and women laughed and joked between forkfuls of food. A foil pan of roast chicken and a paper plate with challah sat at one end of each table near pitchers of grape juice. Suddenly hungry, Becks' stomach growled as the aroma of cholent floated over.

"I don't know—." Daniel began.

"We'd love to," Tootsie interrupted. "It smells great." He headed toward the table.

Becks, unsure of how Gabe might react yet anxious

to speak with the rabbi, turned to her son. "Do you mind if we stay? They have roast chicken." It was one of the few foods Gabe would eat.

He surprised her by nodding and trailing his grandfather to the end of the table away from the other diners.

"Thank you. I guess we will." She rose from the floor and followed Daniel to the table.

After having a word with the younger guests, Rabbi Haziz slid into the seat next to Becks. "Did Gabriel tell you we've met before?" he said, leaning around her to smile at the boy. Becks looked toward Gabe when he didn't answer and cringed at the sight of her son eating with his hands.

"Gabe," Becks called loud enough to get his attention. "You didn't tell me you knew Rabbi Haziz."

He looked up from his plate. "You didn't ask."

Turning toward the rabbi so Gabe couldn't overhear, she said "I'm sorry your congregation had to witness Gabe's meltdown. He has Asperger's. You've heard of it?"

"Yes. I'm afraid I've never seen behavior like that."

She decided to skip an explanation. "Where did you meet Gabe?"

"I filled in at the university's Chabad a few weeks ago. Their rabbi was out of town. We had quite a turnout. The fact that one of our congregants was serving spaghetti didn't hurt." He laughed. "There's nothing like a free meal to attract college students."

As the rabbi spoke, Becks realized the picture in Mrs. Berkowitz's office didn't do the man justice. She'd assumed he was her age but, up close, he appeared to be in his late thirties or early forties. His thick beard failed to conceal a square jaw and strong cheekbones and his hazel eyes sparkled as he spoke. Becks felt herself responding to the warmth and magnetism that she imagined drew young people to his congregation.

Watching the rabbi chatting with her father, she debated asking him about Sid Fox. As horrendous as Gabe's meltdown had been, it did provide her with an opening to inquire about the night club owner.

"I'm trying to figure out what happened with Gabe today," she said after he'd finished with Tootsie. "Something about the man in the Hawaiian shirt set him off. I think he may be the same person who came to my son's dorm looking for his friend, a Hasidic student named Menachem Tannenbaum."

"You mean Sid Fox?"

Becks nodded. "This boy stayed with us after the man's visit. He was afraid the visitor planned to kidnap him. A few days later, Menachem disappeared. His body was found in a canal near our home."

"*Baruch dayan haemetz*," the rabbi said, bringing a hand to his chest. Becks didn't know what the words meant but sensed the compassion behind them. "His family must be devastated."

"Of course." Why mention her lack of success in contacting them? "Do you have any idea why Mr. Fox would've been on campus?"

"He owns a night club a few blocks from here and it might have something to do with that. What don't you ask . . ." He scanned the room. "He didn't stay for lunch?"

"Maybe he was upset by Gabe's meltdown." *More likely, avoiding questions.*

"Possibly."

Becks picked up a piece of challah and tore it into small pieces as she formulated her next question. "Do you have any idea how Fox and Menny could've met? Maybe in Crown Heights where Menny lived?"

The rabbi shook his head. "I wish I could help. Unfortunately, I didn't meet Sid until I moved to Miami. He hasn't told me much about his past."

A roar of laughter rose from the far end of the table and Rabbi Haziz smiled. She liked the man. He seemed sincere about wanting to help her. Yet she sensed he was holding something back—perhaps out of loyalty to Fox.

The rabbi rose. "Forgive me. It's time for the closing prayers. Please join us again. I know it's a long drive from Boca Raton but you're always welcome." He took two steps and turned. "I am sorry about the boy's death. And I'm certain Sid had nothing to do with it. He has a temper and you don't want to be around when he's angry. Even so, he has a good heart."

Once they'd left the Chabad—Tootsie scurried out the moment prayers began—Becks turned to Daniel. "Did you say anything to the rabbi about driving down from Boca?"

"I didn't have a chance to talk to him. Gabe must have mentioned it when they met before."

Becks shrugged. "Maybe." Looking over her shoulder to see if her father was keeping pace, she caught Tootsie handing Gabe a fifty-dollar bill.

"You don't need to do that, Dad. You'll spoil him."

Tootsie laughed and reached for Gabe's shoulder but his grandson jerked away. "Don't be a spoilsport." Her father winked at Gabe. "I told him to spend it on a girl." Then, bringing his lips to Gabe's ear, he staged whispered, "You like girls, right?"

They'd dropped Tootsie off at his apartment and were driving north on I-95 when Becks glanced into the back seat. Gabe stared down at his laptop, fingers flying across his keyboard like a piano virtuoso. Becks caught Daniel's eye and nodded toward their son. Gabe was okay.

Becks twisted around to watch him. He seemed lost in his game and she knew he'd entered a realm where he felt safe, where no one yelled at him or mocked his odd behavior. His obsession with video games concerned her but she didn't have the heart to deny him the one domain where he felt secure and had at least virtual friends.

"Gabe," she said.

He didn't answer.

Then louder. "Sweetheart. I want to talk to you."

"Later."

"You can go back to your game when we're finished." She reached over the seat for his computer and he pulled it away.

"Shit. You made me lose my place." He tossed the computer on the seat. "What do you want?"

"I want to know if you remember the rabbi."

"What rabbi?"

"The man we met today. Rabbi Haziz. He said he led services at school when your regular rabbi was out of town."

"Oh, yeah. I went with Menny." His gaze traveled from Becks to the floor. "We were seven minutes early. Menny had to leave because his stomach hurt. I told him he should not leave. I got up early to go to services and he should have stayed with me. A lady served spaghetti after the service. She gave me three chicken meatballs. They were better than the ones you make. Will you make chicken meatballs?"

"Gabe." Daniel's tone was brusque.

"We should have chicken meatballs. The lady said mom should call her for the recipe. She knows you. She said she lives in our neighborhood and knows me too. We could call her."

"Hold on, Gabe," Daniel broke in. "You want to back up a little. What lady are you talking about?"

"She's fat and the hair close to her head is a different color from the rest. Most of it is red. She said she belongs to a Chabad in Boca Raton and you should bring me there."

"Why was she serving spaghetti at your school if she lives in Boca Raton?"

"I do not know. The sauce looked like your sauce. I think it had tomatoes in it and –"

"Wait a sec. Let me ask a question," Becks said. "I know the man who frightened you today was the same man who asked about Menny. Did he come to your school's Chabad that day?"

"When?"

"The day the lady served spaghetti."

"No."

"Did you see him after Menny moved in with us?"

Gabe clenched his jaw and flapped his hands against his chest.

"Sweetheart. It's okay. Tell us what upset you. Dad and I will keep you safe. If something bad happened, we need to know. Do you understand?"

Becks took a deep breath, waiting for the inevitable meltdown as Gabe rocked back and forth. That went on for a few minutes.

"It was that guy." He spoke quickly as though summoning the courage to tell them. "The man in the flowered shirt. He said . . . he would hurt me . . . if I told Menny . . . he was looking for him. And then . . . I told Menny."

"Oh, honey. Of course, you were upset."

"Don't worry about Mr. Fox," Daniel said. "Mom and I will take care of him. Let us know if he comes around again. I can set up a meeting and . . ." He looked into the rearview mirror, then over his shoulder. Becks followed his gaze.

Gabe was back on the computer, lost in whatever

cyber world he'd decided to enter this time. The computer was his refuge, as crucial to his security as the one-eyed teddy bear his brother Josh had clung to through nursery school.

Becks decided to drop the subject. She couldn't tell if Gabe had registered her or Daniel's words. It didn't matter. The game was doing its job, calming Gabe.

What concerned her now was how she and Daniel would keep their son safe.

It was a question that ran through their lives like the chorus of a familiar song. How do we protect Gabe—from the bullies at school, from the danger of roaming their neighborhood at night, from the isolation and loneliness he might experience in college?

He'd been doing so well before Fox's visit. He hadn't made friends other than Menny but he was attending classes and doing his homework. Could they safely send him back to the university? Becks sighed. She and Daniel had some tough decisions ahead.

37

It was past midnight and the light from the kitchen chandelier threw a dim glow onto the porch where Mulligan, a lizard dangling from his jaws, waited to be let in. Inside, Becks and Daniel glared at one another across the kitchen table. It hadn't taken long for their discussion of Gabe's return to campus to escalate into an argument about whether Becks was wasting her time by looking into Menny's death.

"You know as well as I do that there's always room for error," she said when Daniel cited the medical examiner's report. "The autopsy may have missed something." Becks rose from her chair and threw on an apron. "Fox's reaction to my questions about Menny was too violent. Then leaving the Chabad during Gabe's breakdown? Does that sound like an innocent man?" She opened the dishwasher.

"You practically accused the guy of murder the last time you saw him. I doubt he wanted a repeat performance."

Becks looked over her shoulder and stuck out her tongue. That always cooled off a fight.

Daniel laughed. "He might have hired Hasidic kids—including Menny—to transport drugs. But murder? What was his motive? Where's the evidence?"

"You want evidence?" She ticked the items off on her fingers. "First, Menny was so frightened when Fox showed up that he ran away from the campus. Then the man threatened to hurt Gabe if he told anyone about Fox's search for Menny. And, third, why were those stoned Hasidic kids hanging out at the club? Something's fishy."

"You don't know that. And I don't see how any of this adds up to murder." Daniel shouted to be heard above the clatter of the plates. "Come on, Becks. You can do better than that."

Becks put a plate on the bottom rack, then straightened, hands on her hips. "How's this? Fox decided to return Menny to Crown Heights but something went wrong and he killed the boy."

Daniel frowned. "Okay, you've made your point. Does the fact that Menny and Fox lived in Kleynshtot fit into any of your theories?"

"Not yet."

"You're going to let it dangle?"

Becks raised the door of the dishwasher and punched the start button. "Certainly not. There's still a lot I don't know. I'll figure it out eventually."

If Becks had learned anything as an investigative reporter, it was that you followed each lead until it led somewhere, even if it was a dead end. At some point, she'd uncover a lie, an odd coincidence, an unexpected relationship and move forward with that. She was just starting to piece out the relationships between Menny and Fox, Fox and Mrs. Berkowitz and Fox and the rabbi. In due course, she'd figure out what they all meant.

Not tonight, though. She was exhausted.

"So tomorrow we tell Gabe he's staying in Boca," she said, confirming the decision they'd made earlier. She'd drive Gabe to Miami Monday morning to collect his textbooks and arrange to get notes and assignments for the classes he'd miss. Luckily for him, it was mid-semester and none of his professors gave midterms.

Daniel nodded. "I'll contact Fox tomorrow. Figure out what he thought he was doing threatening Gabe."

"I'd like to be there when you talk to him."

"That's not a great idea. One angry parent is enough and you've already alienated the guy."

Becks smiled weakly. "Now there's an understatement. Let's get some sleep."

Daniel followed her upstairs and they prepared for bed without speaking. When he rolled onto his side and reached for her, she moved closer to her side of the bed. She was tired and worried and craved the safety of his arms but was afraid that snuggling might lead to more.

It had been six months since he'd moved back home and she wasn't ready to make love. She didn't know if she ever would be. The trust and security she'd shared with him for thirty years would take a long time to return—if it ever did. And she still harbored more resentment than she cared to admit. The man with whom she once thought she'd spend the rest of her life had erased almost all possibility of sharing unconditional love.

And his unwillingness to support her theories about Menny's death was eating away at what remained.

38

Becks was in the laundry room folding towels the next afternoon when the doorbell rang. She wasn't expecting company and was surprised to find Tootsie on the front porch, a bucket of fried chicken in one hand, a bottle of black cherry soda in the other.

"You'll never in a million years guess who I talked to today," he said as she opened the door.

Tootsie hadn't mentioned anything about bringing dinner that night but she let it slide. He had an annoying habit of making plans with her, at least in his own mind, and forgetting to tell her about them. He'd show up at a random hour of the day or night and grow cross when she wasn't ready. When she argued he hadn't told her about their date, he accused her of lying. Tonight wasn't a problem, though. She'd planned to send out for pizza.

Becks followed her father into the kitchen, her mouth watering like a Saint Bernard's. She loved fried chicken and its spicy aroma evoked memories of childhood picnics on the beach.

"Go ahead. Guess who called," Tootsie said, settling into a chair at the kitchen table and plopping the chicken and soda in front of him.

"I don't know."

"Just guess."

"The Dalai Lama?"

"Don't be an idiot."

"Esther?"

"I wish." He rarely talked to her sister. "Give up?"

Becks nodded. Was she really playing this stupid game?

"Herb Moscowitz." He waved his hand as if Moscowitz was the most obvious answer in the world.

"Who's Herb Moscowitz?" Becks pulled out a chair and joined him at the table.

"Jesus Christ, Becks. Talking to you is like talking to a salami. Don't you listen?"

Becks laughed. A salami? Sounded like Gabe.

"Herb's an old customer, one of the curlies I told you about. He moved here from New York twenty years ago and opened a deli in Miami Beach. What was its name? Everyone went there."

"Does he know Fox?"

"You bet. I called him a while ago when you asked and he was at his grandson's bar mitzvah in Brooklyn. Herb says Fox is a wheeler-dealer. Co-owned a couple of clubs in New York that were raided. Herb thought they'd closed."

"Is your friend still in touch with Fox?"

"Nah. Herb can't stand the guy. Says Fox likes to brag, hint that he's ex-Mossad. Israel's intelligence agency," he added at her raised eyebrow. "No one buys it. Herb says it's part of his tough Jew *shtick* as if being religious and ex-Mossad makes him a big shot."

"What did he say when you mentioned Fox's visit to Menny?"

"He didn't have much to contribute. Said Fox could have been a family friend, that most Lubavitch visited Crown Heights at some point. When I told him you suspected Fox was involved in Menny's death, he was surprised. He said Fox might be a thug but he didn't strike Herb as a killer."

"So that gets me . . ."

"Nowhere I guess."

Tootsie rose and retrieved a paper plate from an overhead cabinet before rummaging through the pantry for a plastic fork and knife. The drone of a lawnmower sounded in the distance, probably a neighbor rushing to finish the lawn before it got dark. Tootsie had just served himself a thigh and mashed potatoes when Daniel walked in.

"You'll never guess who I talked to today?"

Father and daughter exchanged glances.

"Sid Fox?" Becks said.

"Good guess. I finished up with patients early and called him. We decided to meet halfway between our offices at the Denny's on Sheridan."

"And?"

"It went okay, I guess. I was steaming mad when I got there. Fox looked stunned when I accused him of threatening Gabe. He claims he asked Gabe to keep his search secret so Menny wouldn't leave campus before Fox reached his father."

"How does he know Menny's father?"

"He doesn't. Fox said someone—he assumed it was Menny's dad—posted a note on a Lubavitch website looking for the boy, who was seen in South Florida. Fox checked the university because it seemed like a good place for Menny to hide."

"Why is it any of his business?"

Daniel shrugged. "I guess he wanted to be helpful."

"Did he find Menny?"

"He claims he didn't."

Becks twisted her lips. "What about threatening *our* son?"

"Like I said, he was shocked when I said he'd frightened Gabe. You know, it *is* possible Gabe over-reacted. He does that."

"You believe Fox?"

"I have no reason to doubt him."

Becks was stunned by Daniel's naiveté. Sure, Fox was being a Good Samaritan and helping Rabbi Tannenbaum find Menny. And Gabe had overreacted to the man's so-called "request" he keep quiet.

"What about those Hasidic boys? Were they visiting Club Shukran because they felt at home drinking and dancing to techno music?"

I mentioned that and Fox seemed surprised. He said Hasidic youngsters are welcome but he's never seen any at his club.

She opened her mouth to object then stopped and stared at Daniel. She didn't have the words to explain how betrayed she felt by her husband's decision to believe Fox's account over hers.

"So you *want* to send Gabe back to the university?" she asked. If he heard the scorn in her voice, he pretended not to notice.

"I'm sure he'll be fine."

"All right. Fine with me." It wasn't. Still, she felt better now that Fox knew he was being watched. Gabe could not afford to miss classes. She'd warn campus security and Gabe's residence advisor to keep an eye out for the club owner.

Becks rose and set the table, then went to the stairwell and called Gabe to dinner. He'd spent the day sleeping and playing video games.

"I talked to that man who upset you," Daniel said as Gabe slipped into his seat.

"The one who was asking about Menny?" Gabe seemed remarkably calm, given yesterday's histrionics.

"Mr. Fox. Yes. He didn't mean to threaten you. He was trying to help Menny's father find him and had no intention of hurting your friend. He didn't want you to mention his visit because he was afraid Menny would leave campus before he could tell Menny's father where he was."

Gabe shot a questioning look at his father. Daniel was too deeply engaged in eating a chicken thigh to notice.

"Are you okay going back to school?" Becks asked.

"If you think it's safe." Gabe grabbed a leg from the bucket.

Becks stared at Gabe. He seemed so calm about returning to school. Had she misjudged his reaction to Fox the day before? Or was he mature enough now to recover from emotional turmoil?

"Your dad thinks so and he'd never place you in danger. Why don't you drive back in the morning? If you're uncomfortable for any reason, call me. Come home whenever you want. "

"All right." Gabe returned to his chicken.

Becks reached into the bucket and pulled out two wings. Two *scrawny* meatless wings. Daniel and Tootsie had scarfed down the best pieces. Tomorrow, after Gabe left, she'd pick up her own bucket. It wasn't the healthiest choice. After what she'd been through with Menny and Gabe, though, she deserved it.

39

Becks was stepping out of the shower the next morning when the phone rang. Grabbing a towel, she raced through the bathroom to her end table and snatched up the receiver.

It was Gabe.

"Everything okay?" She tried to disguise her panic. He'd left for school an hour earlier.

"Not ex . . . exactly. Someone touched my things."

"What do you mean touched your things?"

"They moved my books and took papers out of my desk."

The obsessive-compulsive disorder that had compelled Gabe to alphabetize the family's CD collection and bookshelves in high school had flourished since he left for college. He'd arranged everything in his dorm room so precisely that he practically twitched when he saw an item out of place.

"Was anything stolen? Did you call campus police?" Her heart pounded as she pictured Fox racing from his meeting with Daniel to Gabe's dorm. Had Daniel mentioned their son's absence from school?

"Nothing's missing. I told Meredith and she called campus police. They think it's a prank and I shouldn't worry."

Becks searched her memory. Meredith? Right. The heavyset girl with a thick gold braid who'd introduced herself as Gabe's residence advisor. They met the first week of school and Becks briefed her on what the girl had termed Gabe's "idiosyncrasies."

"Do you want me to come down and check things out?" Becks said.

"No. Meredith wants to talk to you."

Becks heard voices in the background before Meredith came on the phone. "Hello, Mrs. Ruchinsky. This is Gabe's RA." She spoke with forced cheerfulness. "Gabe seemed a bit upset before but he's fine now. The campus police sent a woman out to look around. She asked a few students if they'd seen anyone enter Gabe's room. No one did." She paused. "You know what a neatnik Gabe can be?"

Becks frowned at the euphemism. "Yes."

"Well, it appears his door was unlocked and someone, probably another student in the hall, noticed and did a little rearranging. The room isn't messy or anything and Gabe's already put his stuff back where it belongs."

Becks cradled the phone between her shoulder and chin and secured her towel. "Does it look like the person who entered his room was searching for something?"

"I can't say for sure. Gabe says some papers he kept inside a drawer were on his desk. Other than that, there is no reason to think it was anything except a prank."

Becks considered what Meredith had said about the papers on Gabe's desk. Whoever entered his room had plenty of time to look around if they'd left it in good order. She didn't want to alarm Gabe or Meredith but she doubted the break-in was a prank.

"Was anyone else's room touched?"

"No," Meredith said. Then she quickly added, "Wait a sec. One of the girls in the hall told me she saw an older man knocking on Menny's door. That was Saturday morning. She assumed he was Menny's father. To be honest, I didn't give it much thought."

"Did you check Menny's room?"

"Yeah. It was a mess but, then again, that's how Menny kept it. I couldn't tell if anyone was in there."

Becks drew her towel closer and sat on the bed. The girl had described the visitor as an old man. Could it be the same one who'd driven Menny away from the kosher market?

"Mrs. Ruchinsky?"

"Sorry. I was thinking." Becks ran a hand through her hair. It had dried while she was on the phone. "Thank you for handling all this. I meant to call later today. Do you have a minute?"

"Sure."

"I wanted to fill you in on what's been going on. Gabe seemed upset a few weeks ago when a man came to the dorm asking about Menny. That was a day or so before Menny came to stay with us."

"Another girl on our floor said a man asked her about Menny," Meredith said. "It was around the same time."

"My husband and I figured out who the man is—a Miami Beach night club owner named Sid Fox. He told my husband he heard Menny's father was looking for him and came to the university on a hunch Menny might be there. He probably doesn't pose a threat to anyone, but I'd appreciate your letting me know if you see him." She didn't want to worry Meredith. "Gabe felt threatened by him and I'm concerned about what'll happen if he sees Fox again. He's overweight and tall, looks like a gangster from an old movie."

"This man got inside the dorm?"

"According to Gabe."

"That's not supposed to happen. I'll get in touch with campus police and tell the students who work at the front desk to be alert for him. Is there anything else I should know?"

Becks hesitated. She hated playing helicopter parent but Gabe was a special case.

"Could you keep an eye out for Gabe? Make sure he doesn't wander at night and that he returns to his room after classes. I know we talked about this before. Menny's death has upset us all."

"Not a problem."

Becks thanked the girl and hung up.

She remained on the bed, staring into space. Someone had broken into Gabe's room and tried to enter Menny's. It had to be Sid Fox or the older man working with him. She glanced toward the bureau where she'd left Menny's articles on the Kleynshtot scam. Could those be what the visitor sought? She hadn't learned anything from the articles that implicated Fox or anyone else. Which didn't mean Fox was innocent. Was Menny killed because of something he knew about the diversion of government funds?

The possibility had been playing in the back of her mind for days. Menny held on to those articles for a reason. She didn't know what it was. Still, she was fairly certain of the night club owner's involvement. Had Menny threatened to go to the police with information about Fox?

Becks had to find out. And the only way to do that was to visit Kleynshtot and look into Menny and Fox's relationship. As an investigative reporter, she'd learned the only way to uncover the truth was to speak directly with the people involved.

Daniel would be livid. After talking to Fox, he seemed even more convinced that Menny's death was accidental. She was sick of trying to convince him and Detective Cole otherwise. They'd written her off as a crank and wouldn't lift a finger to find out if the boy was murdered. Becks chewed her lower lip in frustration. As much as she hated to admit it, it was up to her. *She* had to discover why Menny died. And who killed him.

40

Becks shivered and pulled her collar closer around her neck as she paused in front of Menny's parents' house the next afternoon. She'd flown into New York that morning and dropped her suitcase at Milt's before jumping on the subway to Crown Heights. The Tannenbaum home looked bleak, the paint on the front door peeling and the porch dusted with damp, grimy cobwebs. The glum faces she'd seen on the subway had left her in a lousy mood, made worse by the leaden cast of low-lying clouds.

She climbed the icy steps to the house and took a deep breath before knocking. Becks had left Hannah a message the day before to say she'd be in New York. After her game of "gotcha" with Rabbi Tannenbaum, she didn't know what kind of a welcome she'd receive.

"You must be freezing. Come in," Hannah said, stepping back from the door to let Becks enter. Becks relaxed as the younger woman embraced her then hung her coat in a cramped closet. Asher and Schmulie barely looked up from their puzzle as the two women entered the kitchen.

"What happened?" Becks said. "The boys found me so fascinating the last time I visited."

"They'd never seen a lady in pants." Hannah smiled as she gazed at Becks' legs, now swathed in black tights beneath a calf-length skirt. "It looks like you're becoming one of us. Sit and I'll make tea."

Settling herself at the wooden table, Becks took in the burned metal scent of furnace-heated air as Hannah bustled about the kitchen. Watching the boys play—Asher officiously telling his younger brother how a puzzle *should* be done—she remembered how Josh and Gabe fought at that age. She couldn't leave them alone for a minute. Hannah was doing something right.

Gazing past the children into the back yard, she caught sight of a rusted swing set, the area below each swing barren and muddy from the constant scrape of little feet. Beyond it, a row of denuded oaks stretched skeletal branches toward the sky. Becks pictured the red ginger that bloomed in her yard. She'd forgotten how bleak winter could be.

Once she'd lit a fire under the tea kettle, Hannah turned to the boys. "How about a movie?" The toddlers were on their feet in seconds and, five minutes later, the opening strains of "Toy Story" sounded.

Hannah returned to the kitchen and served tea. "So tell me. Have you learned anything new about Menachem?" She put a hand to her mouth.

"Not as much as I'd hoped. I thought you might be able to help me put some bits and pieces together."

"I'll try." Hannah took a sip of tea and set her mug on the table. "What would you like to know?"

"Well, first—how did Menachem pay his tuition at the university? That's a pricey school." She smiled, trying to make light of the question. "I should know. I'm paying for Gabe."

"He told me he got a scholarship. A teacher at City College, where he started university, helped him apply. Why do you ask?"

Becks wrapped her hands around her mug and took a sip before setting it on the table. "I . . . This is hard."

"It's all right." Hannah reached for Becks' hand. The woman's palm felt warm and damp. "Ask."

"I told you about the man who frightened Menachem and Gabe at the dorm?"

"I remember."

"His name is Sid Fox and he runs a night club in Miami Beach."

Hannah frowned.

"He also belongs to a Chabad in Miami Beach and claims someone—he thinks it was your husband—posted a request on a Lubavitch website asking anyone who'd seen Menachem to contact him. I went through several sites and couldn't find the post. Do you know anything about it?"

Hannah shook her head. "I'll ask my husband and tell you unless you'd like to—"

"Later. There's another thing that bothers me. I paid a visit to the club one night and saw two religious men who seemed to be stoned." Did Hannah know the term? "High on drugs. Later, I heard rumors Mr. Fox hired Hasidic youngsters to bring drugs into the country. The girl who told me said police don't usually stop people who look . . ."

Becks stopped speaking as Hannah gasped and swept her hands to her face. Her eyes widened. "Levi!" She whispered the name.

"What? You know Sid Fox?"

Hannah shook her head and sank back in her seat, breathing heavily. She looked toward the room where the children watched their movie.

"Levi was Menachem's best friend. A few summers ago, he got a job and wouldn't tell his mother what he did. Only that he would make enough money to get married. Menachem later told me Levi flew to Amsterdam a few times to bring in drugs." Her voice dropped to a whisper. "He got caught at the airport and went to prison after refusing to tell the police the name of the person who sent him to Amsterdam. Menachem thought Levi was afraid the man would kill him or his family if he revealed the name."

"You don't think . . ."

"Was Menny . . . ?"

The women spoke in unison.

Hannah rose and went to the stovetop. She added water to the teapot and turned up the flame. Then she turned around and smiled sadly. "When Menachem left, I worried he was selling drugs and ran away to avoid embarrassing our family. But he was too angry and upset over what happened to Levi to make the same mistake. Menachem wouldn't sell drugs."

Becks decided there was no point in pursuing it further. Hannah was probably right. Still, she'd have to check for herself. Instead, she pulled out her cell and showed Hannah the photo of Fox she'd downloaded from Club Shukran's website.

"That's the night club owner. Does he look familiar?"

"No."

"How about the people with him?" She clicked on a photo of Fox with Fanny Berkowitz and Rabbi Haziz.

"Sorry. Who are they?"

Becks explained, omitting details about the museum's collection.

"Do you know if Menny had friends in Kleynshtot?" Becks asked, moving on. "I'd like to get in touch with anyone who knew him."

"He wasn't there long. I don't know if he made friends. Why?"

Becks hesitated. She felt uncomfortable admitting she'd searched Menny's room. "Gabe told us Menachem was researching a case of fraud in Kleynshtot. It was an old case and he might have been writing a paper for class. Did he say anything to you about it?"

Hannah shook her head. She returned to the stove and turned the flame down before looking over her shoulder. "Are you saying it has something to do with Menachem's death?"

"I don't know. I'm looking into it."

"You should talk to Faigy," she said, wiping her hands on her apron. "She has a friend in Kleynshtot who might be able to help."

Becks' spirits lifted. She'd been dreading the trip to Kleynshtot since reading that residents rarely spoke to outsiders. Faigy might be her "in."

"I will." She rose. "I should probably get going. First, though, I'd like to ask Rabbi Tannenbaum a few questions."

"Certainly." Hannah stood. "I don't know if it's worth mentioning but one of Menachem's professors called a few days ago. Trevor . . . I think it was . . . Northbrook. He told me he'd heard about Menachem's death and offered his condolences. He said Menachem was a gifted mathematician and that he'd been a great help with the man's research at City College."

"It's probably the professor who helped him get a scholarship to Miami," Becks said. "I'd like to talk to him."

"I'm sorry. I didn't get his number."

They chatted for a few more minutes before Hannah led Becks to the back of the house and knocked on the door to the rabbi's study. She opened it as he called "come in." The rabbi started to rise from behind his desk but Becks stopped him. "Please don't get up. I have a few quick questions."

He sat, sighing as though he could feel every muscle in his body settle into its usual spot on the chair.

"Someone I talked to in Miami claims he saw a post on a Lubavitch website asking for help finding Menachem. Did you send that?"

The rabbi raised his eyebrows. "No."

Becks considered herself a good judge of people but couldn't tell if he was lying.

"Do you have any idea who might have?"

"None."

"It could be important. Perhaps one of the dissidents you mentioned. It would be helpful if I had a list of those people."

The rabbi twisted his lips and glared at Becks. "We've discussed this. That kind of talk ended years ago. I see no reason to revisit it." He glanced at his watch. "So if there's nothing else . . ."

Becks clenched her jaw. The man was so arrogant, so sure of himself that he refused to share information that might help her find his son's killer! She looked at Hannah, who'd grown ashen. The rabbi opened the book on his desk.

Regretting her action even as she took it, Becks crossed the room and smacked her fist on the man's desk. His head jolted up.

"Rabbi Tannenbaum." Her voice quivered with rage. "Do you, or do you not, want to know what happened to your son?"

He glared at her. "Of course I do."

"Then you need to give me those names."

The rabbi met Becks' gaze and scowled. Becks refused to lower her eyes. Finally, the rabbi pulled a legal pad from the middle drawer of his desk and jotted down a few names. Ignoring Becks' outstretched hand, he tore off the top sheet and gave it to Hannah. "Make a copy for Becks," he ordered, "and return it immediately."

Becks bit her lip to hide a smug grin.

The rabbi returned to his book. They were dismissed.

Becks waited outside the closet-sized room adjacent

to the rabbi's study as Hannah copied and handed her the list. She folded the page into quarters and slipped it into her purse.

"I'm sorry he was rude," Hannah said as the women approached the front door.

"Not your fault." Becks put on her coat. "I'll let you know what I learn."

"Please." Hannah closed the door halfway then swung it back open. "Call me if I can help. I mean it." She shut the door behind Becks.

Becks was beginning to feel like a hamster on a wheel, running back and forth between Boca Raton and Crown Heights and getting nowhere. Now she had five more men to contact. She hoped the people on the list would be more forthcoming than Fox or Rabbi Haziz. If she was lucky, one of the men would provide a piece of data, a scrap of information that pointed her in the right direction.

Until then, she'd keep riding the wheel and searching for answers.

41

Trudging up Kingston Avenue toward Faigy's store, Becks pulled the rabbi's list from her purse. Two of the "dissidents" lived in Kleynshtot and three in Crown Heights. She'd already arranged to rent a car to drive upstate the next day so would start by contacting dissidents who lived in the outlying village. She dreaded the visit, fearing members of the community would refuse to talk to her. She clenched her fists. She'd go from shop to shop and house to house if she had to. She hoped Faigy would help.

Becks was in front of the Judaica shop reaching for the knob when the door flew open. "Darling, I've been expecting you." Faigy took Becks' elbow and guided her inside. A jangle of bells sounded as the door closed. "Hannah told me you were coming. I've put on the kettle."

Becks kissed Faigy's wrinkled cheek and followed the shopkeeper to the back of the store, passing through a curtained doorway to a small office and storage room. Metal shelves crammed with cardboard boxes lined one wall and a large wooden desk filled the other. A red Victorian settee with carved legs rested against the back wall, next to a TV table with an electric kettle. Steam rose from its spout.

"No tea for me," Becks said. She lowered herself on to the settee, releasing a musty odor. "Did Hannah mention —"

"I'd love to join you in Kleynshtot," Faigy said, her eyes sparkling. "I haven't left Brooklyn in months."

"But your store? Who'll watch it?"

"No one. My customers can come back when I'm here. It's not like anyone died for lack of a candlestick." She laughed merrily. "So *nu*, what's our plan?"

Becks shifted her weight on the sofa, trying without success to find a comfortable spot between the springs that poked through the fabric. "I thought I'd start at the town's government office then go to the library and synagogue. I don't know where Menachem worked or lived."

Faigy fluttered her fingers in dismissal. "Oh dear, you do need my help. You won't learn anything at the town hall or library. Rebbe Sadowsky runs Kleynshtot. If you want to know anything, you need to contact one of his . . ." she struggled for the word . . . "advisors."

Becks tilted her chin. "Advisors?"

"Oh, yes, he surrounds himself with people who advise him about everything, from who attends shul to how much the village spends on electricity. You can't move to Kleynshtot or change jobs or buy a house without the rebbe's permission. You're going to an old-fashioned village."

Old-fashioned? It sounded Orwellian, with Rabbi Sadowsky as Big Brother. Faigy appeared to take the rabbi's power for granted.

"How do *you* think we should handle this?" Becks asked. "I want to find out what type of work Menachem did there, who he knew, who his friends were, that sort of thing."

Faigy folded her hands on her desk and remained silent, staring down. Becks took the opportunity to leave the settee and take a look at Faigy's s inventory. Expecting to find a trove of Jewish treasures, she was disappointed to find most of the boxes on the shelves empty. Was Faigy running low on inventory? Becks studied the diminutive woman, whose gaze was glued to her age-spotted hands, then smiled. Faigy wasn't peddling Judaica for money. She may have sold a few items here and there. But she came in each day for another reason. From her little perch along Kingston Avenue, she could chat with neighbors, see who passed and catch up on gossip.

"I've got it." Faigy broke into Becks' musings. "We'll visit my friend Pauline. She'll give us lunch first so no one will suspect us of spying." She smiled mischievously. "She can call around to find out where Menachem lived and worked. It's a small town and everyone knows everyone else's business."

Kleynshtot sounded a lot like Crown Heights. "Will you let her know we're coming?"

"I'll tell her to expect us at eleven."

Relieved to have a plan, Becks arranged to pick up Faigy the next morning and, after pulling on her coat and scarf, left for the subway station. She planned to stop in Zabar's on the way home for the knishes and sour pickles her father-in-law loved. She felt a tinge of guilt. It wasn't the healthiest choice for a man with cardiac problems. Still, an occasional treat wouldn't hurt and she loved to make Milt smile.

The subway pulled up as she reached the platform and Becks slid into a bench between two stocky teenagers in black baseball caps.

"Spying," Faigy had said, describing their forthcoming trip to the religious community. Becks chuckled, drawing the quizzical stares of her neighbors. Tomorrow, she'd learn about Menny's time in Kleynshtot—and whether it had any bearing on his death.

With any luck, her "spying" would finally pay off.

42

The route to Kleynshtot took Becks and Faigy along the Hudson River before crossing the George Washington Bridge and turning north on the broad expanse of the Palisades Parkway. In minutes, views of massive apartment buildings bisected by city streets gave way to open forests where a few stubborn leaves clung to denuded branches. The gentle whoosh of the road and steady hum of the heating system left Becks relaxed and a little groggy.

"So then my parents left Warsaw and took a train to Paris, where Papa worked as a janitor to earn passage to New York," Faigy said, continuing the narrative she'd started the minute she stepped inside the car. She told Becks her family had come to Crown Heights to join a famous Lubavitch rabbi who was trying to recreate the life he and his followers had left in Europe. The woman seemed bright and articulate and Becks shot her a look of disbelief when she admitted she didn't learn English until she was forty.

"There was no need," Faigy said. "Everyone I knew spoke Yiddish. Girls weren't allowed to leave Crown Heights without their fathers or husbands, so there was no point."

"You didn't mind?"

"What was to mind? I had my family, my friends and my shul in Crown Heights. I married the man my parents chose and stayed here. It was a great sorrow not to be blessed with children but my husband understood and stood by me."

"Why shouldn't he?"

Faigy didn't answer and Becks dropped the subject. She'd read enough about Hasidism to know that centuries of tradition separated her and this woman, whose every act was proscribed by her religious beliefs. Becks found the idea of living under such rules abhorrent. Yet Faigy and Hannah seemed content. Menny had spoken longingly of his life in Crown Heights. He'd said that Lubavitch customs gave him a sense of purpose and security just as his religious beliefs made life feel sacred and meaningful.

An hour after leaving Manhattan, the interstate gave way to a two-lane highway of tawdry strip malls, low-rise office buildings and auto repair shops. Here and there, the landscape opened to brief stretches of forest where discreet signs on clapboard houses advertised drapery and furniture showrooms. When they passed a small grocery with two gas pumps, Faigy told Becks to take a right. They'd reached the outskirts of Kleynshtot.

Becks didn't know what to expect. The night before, she'd googled the town and learned that half its population was on welfare. Even so, she was taken aback by the condition of houses along the road. Most looked well cared for. However, overgrown lawns, blistered siding and sagging roofs suggested many were abandoned. The rundown structures reminded her of dilapidated houses her family had passed on a road trip that had inadvertently taken them through West Virginia's coal country.

"Take a right here," Faigy said as they reached an intersection crammed with small shops and restaurants advertising falafel and kosher food. "Park at the end of the street."

Becks pulled into a space near a drab low-rise apartment building. Its dun-colored walls and blocky lines resembled Soviet-era structures she'd seen in documentaries. After following Faigy up a narrow stairwell, she stepped into an uncarpeted hall that reeked of roach spray. An elderly woman waiting by the stairwell pulled Faigy into a hug and launched into a verbal barrage of Yiddish. Becks stepped aside and smiled at their thick-throated chatter.

After a few minutes, the woman—Faigy introduced her as Pauline—smiled shyly at Becks. "Please to come in." She opened the door to her apartment. "Ve havink lunch."

The apartment was clean though small and sparsely furnished. Crocheted doilies sprinkled the arms and backs of the threadbare floral chairs like faded snowflakes. While the older women set out lunch, Becks glanced at the framed family photos that filled every table and wall. Most were grainy and, as with the sepia-toned photos in her Grandma Yentl's home, showed unsmiling people in formal nineteenth-century dress.

Faigy and Pauline continued to chat in Yiddish as they ate and Becks was surprised to find she didn't understand a single word. The words and expressions she'd learned from her grandmother were useless for carrying on a conversation.

Once the women finished their sandwiches, Faigy set her glass of tea on the table and turned to Becks. "Pauline has good and bad news," she said, tapping a gnarled finger against a small pad of paper covered with indecipherable scribbling. Becks hadn't noticed the pad among the condiments and dishes that littered the table. "She called around last night and learned Menachem worked for a bookkeeper. We can walk to his office from here. The owner's son, Yossi, speaks English and is willing to talk to you."

"Thank you." Becks nodded at Pauline. Then, looking at Faigy, "and the bad news?"

"Menachem tutored at a yeshiva but you're going to have a hard time getting anyone to talk. An administrator told Pauline his staff was tied up and wouldn't be free for a few days."

"Damn." Becks brought a hand to her mouth.

Faigy ignored her slip. "Not to worry. We'll figure out something."

Five minutes after thanking Pauline and promising to report back, the women were walking along Kleynshtot's main street, a narrow road lined with bookstores, kosher butchers and Judaica shops. Groups of bearded men walked briskly along the sidewalk in striped frock coats and large fur-trimmed hats beneath which sideburns emerged. Becks had read that men in certain Hasidic sects dressed like members of the eighteenth-century Polish nobility. Still, she was not prepared for the strange effect this created of traveling back in time. The young women pushing strollers and ferrying young children along the road resembled peasants in their drab coats and oversized headscarves.

"Over there," Faigy said, taking Becks' elbow and pointing to a two-story house set away from the street by a small plot of grass. With its freshly painted front porch and polished brass doorknob, it was in much better shape than most of the buildings along the road. Becks followed Faigy up the brick walkway and knocked.

A tall, lanky man with a short dark beard and scanty mustache answered, then ducked under an interior doorframe as he led the women from the hall to his office. The strings of his prayer vest fell haphazardly below his shirt and his eyes looked bleary, as though he'd been working through the night. Removing stacks of paper from the chairs across from his desk, he invited the women to sit.

"My father told me what happened to Menachem," he said after introducing himself as Yossi Stern. "I can't believe he's dead."

"Yes, it's terrible," Becks said. "Were you a friend?"

"Not really. We worked and went to shul together, but he never spoke of his past. He kept to himself and I could see he was unhappy."

Becks frowned. "Any idea why?"

"Are you a reporter?"

That was an odd question. Becks chose her words carefully. "Menachem stayed in my home shortly before his death. He and my son were friends and I'm trying to find out what happened to him."

Yossi tugged at his peyos as he studied Becks, looking at her in a sidewise manner to which she was becoming accustomed as she visited Hasidic communities. He seemed curious about her relationship with Menny and Becks suspected he was discomfited that a woman would leave her family to look into a stranger's death.

"It's hard for outsiders to understand how things work in our community." He continued to tug at his sideburns. "Everyone here has relatives who've lived in Kleynshtot for at least two generations. Word got out that Menachem left Crown Heights and his family to live here and people were curious. Residents rarely leave our village. I think he felt we were judging him." Yossi shrugged, his loose-limbed elbows and shoulders flopping like those of a marionette.

They spoke for a few more minutes, discussing Menny's role at the firm and his unhappiness living in Kleynshtot.

"Did you hear from him after he left?" Becks asked.

"No. He might have stayed in touch with someone at the yeshiva. He tutored there a few times a week."

Becks rose and extended her hand but—catching Faigy's frown—withdrew it.

After getting directions to the yeshiva, they thanked Yossi and returned to the car.

The temperature had dropped during their visit and Becks sat in the driver's seat, teeth chattering, as she waited for the heat to kick in. She marveled at how well Faigy, who was so much older, coped with the cold, then remembered the multiple layers of clothing she'd donned before leaving Pauline's.

"What do you think? Should we go to the yeshiva?" Becks asked. She was anxious to visit the school but loath to embarrass Faigy, who had friends in Kleynshtot and might hesitate to violate male territory.

"Of course we should, darling. That's what we came here for. The worst they can do is throw us out."

Becks laughed nervously. Fox and Rabbi Tannenbaum hadn't greeted her with open arms. She had no reason to believe the yeshiva's staff would be any more welcoming.

43

It took Becks less than ten minutes to find the yeshiva where, Yossi informed them, Menny had worked with youngsters beginning their Torah studies. It stood on a rise twenty feet above the road amid dense trees. The structure looked more like a penitentiary than a school, its three windowless cinder block buildings linked by enclosed breezeways. A sign in Hebrew and English identified the central building as Sha'arei Avraham Yeshiva. She parked next to a late model Buick and suggested Faigy wait in the car while she looked for the entrance.

A few minutes later, she returned. "It's around the corner a few yards." She helped Faigy out of the car and led her to an unpaved path off the parking lot.

The architect couldn't have done a better job if he'd intentionally designed the yeshiva to discourage visitors. Even its setting far from the road and among gnarled trees and large gray boulders seemed meant to intimidate. The growl and whine of trucks shifting gears on a distant highway was the only sound to penetrate the thick forest. Becks felt a chill as she stepped from the unpaved path to the cement walkway that led to the school's entrance. Something felt wrong. The yeshiva's isolation? Its concealed entrance? She fought an urge to turn and flee.

"You sure you want to do this?" Becks looked over

her shoulder at the elderly woman. "I can drop you off at Pauline's and come back."

Faigy smiled grimly. "I want to know what happened to Menachem."

The walkway ended at a terrace where double glass doors reflected the drab gray walls of the opposing building. Becks' spirits sank at the prospect of entering the forbidding structure. Faigy, undeterred, marched through the doors, Becks in tow.

The interior of the yeshiva felt as barren as the exterior, its concrete walls broken only by a collection of black and white group photos. Black tile flooring extended into three corridors, at the intersection of which a gnome-like man sat at a small wooden desk, reading a leather book. Becks cleared her throat.

He looked up and frowned. "*Vos ton ir viln?*" Becks knew enough Yiddish to translate. What do you want?

Faigy responded. "*Mir zenen kukn far a iung mentsh.*" We are looking for a young man.

The conversation went on for a few minutes. Becks didn't understand a word but knew things weren't going well when Faigy's voice grew loud and insistent. The gnome responded in an unpleasant nasal tone and brandished his fist in the air. The heated exchange came to an abrupt halt when an obese man in a black suit and skullcap stormed into the reception area yelling in Yiddish. He glared at Becks and Faigy then released what sounded like a stream of guttural invective at the elderly man.

After a few minutes, his face red, he turned to the women. "Leave. Vomen are not permitted." His voice was low and threatening.

"I have a few questions first. Do you know Menachem Tannenbaum? He taught here."

"I know of no such person. Now go."

"Is there anyone else I can ask? He worked here for several months."

The man—Becks assumed he was a teacher—pointed toward the door, back arched with the effort of extending his arm. "Leave."

Becks was about to refuse when Faigy broke in.

"I'm sorry, Rebbe. We're not going anywhere until you answer our questions."

Becks spun around to find the shopkeeper approaching the man. Her torso was angled forward with determination and her fists were pressed to her sides, a tiny missile in a pink sweater honing in on a human target. Becks' mouth dropped open as the man turned purple with rage and raised his hand to strike the elderly woman. Speechless, Becks raced to intercept the blow. Despite raising an arm to block him, the man struck her shoulder.

"Jesus Christ," she yelled, leaping back. "What do you think you're doing?"

The teacher hesitated and then walked toward her, his eyes black with rage.

She stepped back.

"Get out," he roared, clearly out of control.

The elderly man who'd greeted them cowered behind his desk.

"Fine." Becks spit out the words. "This isn't over."

She turned and retreated toward the entrance, taking her time. The son-of-a-bitch could damn well wait. Faigy stayed at her side as Becks stopped in front of a row of group photographs. She heard her attacker breathing nearby and resisted the urge to glance back.

One of the men in the first photo she examined resembled Rabbi Haziz. She squinted and brought her eyes closer. It *was* him, only much younger and with the scraggly beginnings of a beard. She noted the date on the photo, 2008, before checking the 2009 group shot, in which Haziz also appeared. Studying the 2009 photo through narrowed eyes, Becks caught her breath. Sid Fox was in it as well, looking younger and leaner and wearing a skullcap over close-cropped hair. Neither man appeared in the 2010 group shot.

That was odd. The rabbi claimed he met Fox in Miami.

Becks tapped the glass over Haziz's face and whispered. "That's the rabbi I met in a Miami Chabad."

"I don't care who he is." Faigy looked over her shoulder and flinched. "We need to get out of here."

Becks followed her gaze. Their attacker stood where they'd left him, his arms rigid at his sides. His nostrils flared like those of an angry bull. Becks grabbed Faigy's elbow and fled the yeshiva.

44

Becks winced as she extended the seat belt across her chest. Her shoulder stung where the sanctimonious bastard had struck her but she felt a certain satisfaction in what it signified. She was on to something.

Why had the obese man reacted so violently to her visit? Was it outrage that the women had violated the yeshiva's sacred space? Or anger over her questions about Menny? She pulled to a stop sign in front of the yeshiva and considered what she knew about the institution. She'd learned of it a week or two earlier when looking into Sid Fox's past. He'd been on the faculty at one time. The school's name also came up in the articles she found in Menny's dorm; several of the government fraud's conspirators worked at Sha'arei Avraham Yeshiva. Problem was, they'd been convicted and sentenced years before Menny came on the scene. Then she remembered: two of the conspirators fled the country and were convicted *in absentia*. If they returned, they faced prison.

Could Fox be one of the fugitives? The fleshy Israeli seemed devious enough to *plan* the conspiracy. How about Rabbi Haziz? The fact that he lied about not meeting Fox until after he'd moved to Miami raised questions. Even if the two hadn't worked together, the Hasidic communities in Kleynshtot and Crown Heights seemed too entwined for the men not to have met.

The most important question, though, and the one she wasn't any closer to answering remained: what was Menny's role in this? Had he recognized Haziz and Fox as the fugitive conspirators and threatened to report them? If so, both had a strong motive for killing the boy.

She'd go to the library tomorrow and find out.

"Becks. Are you all right?"

She startled at Faigy's voice.

"You were staring into space."

"Sorry. I was thinking."

"Good. Have you solved the case? We've been sitting here five minutes."

Becks smiled and pressed the accelerator. "I have some ideas. But I need more information. Maybe Pauline can help."

Becks drove slowly, filling Faigy in on the newspaper articles in Menny's dorm and her suspicions about Fox and Rabbi Haziz.

"I heard about the conspiracy," Faigy said. "People talked about it for months. Such a shanda." She used the Yiddish term for disgrace. "How can Pauline help?"

"She knows everyone in town?"

"Almost."

"She might recognize the men I saw in those group photos?"

"You have pictures of them?"

Becks parked in front of Pauline's building. "I'll show you when we get inside."

Twilight had descended on Kleynshtot and the buildings surrounding the apartment house looked even seedier beneath the feeble yellow glow of the streetlamps. Behind the building, pale pink clouds hovered near the horizon and faded into the gunmetal gray of the darkening sky. Becks checked her watch. Only three o'clock? She'd forgotten how short the winter days became. The evening air was chilly and damp and she yearned to return home where the cheerful greens and reds of tropical foliage would sweep away her winter blues.

"Why don't you call Pauline and ask if we can come up?" Becks said, shaking off the sadness that had enveloped her.

She handed her cell phone to Faigy. The elderly woman returned it. "I don't know from these phones. You dial and I'll talk." She gave Becks the number. After chatting in Yiddish, Faigy left the car and Becks followed.

Pauline's welcome was less effusive but she smiled warmly as she welcomed Becks and Faigy into her apartment, which now reeked with the sulfurous odor of boiled cabbage. Becks pulled a chair up to the sofa on which the older women had settled, wondering if cabbage was all Pauline could afford and struggling not to let her distaste show. Neither of the women had seen a Google search before and laughed and chattered as Becks scanned Club Shukran's site, directing them away from pornographic images as she sought a photo of Fox.

After a quick glance at the club owner, Pauline shook her head and spoke to her friend. "*Afshr yo, afshr nit. Ikh bin aoykh alt tsu geyn aoys.*"

"She apologizes and says she's an old lady who doesn't go out much," Faigy translated. "He might be here. She hasn't seen him."

There was no mistaking her recognition of Rabbi Haziz, though. Pauline screwed up her face in horror and brought a hand to her chest before spitting twice on the floor. "Badt man, very badt man." She pushed the phone away. "You don't go near."

"What did he do?"

Eyes wide, Pauline shook her head.

Becks pulled her chair closer to the sofa and tried to remain patient as Faigy took Pauline's hand and spoke calmly in Yiddish. Her voice, inquisitive at first, grew pleading and angry. Pauline turned red, then shook her head and put a hand over her mouth. After a few minutes, Faigy threw her hands up in surrender.

"What did she say?" Becks asked.

"She knows who he is and says he's evil. He lived here for a short time before the rebbe made him leave. She refuses to tell me why"

"Can you convince her?

"She won't budge."

"Is there anyone else we can ask?"

Faigy smiled sadly. "I doubt it. The rebbe made it clear that no one in Kleynshtot is to mention the man's name. Rebbe Sadowsky is very powerful and no one disobeys him."

"That's crazy."

"No, it's *mesira*. Jewish law says you can't turn in a fellow Jew."

Becks leaned forward, hands grasped between her knees. She hadn't expected this. What had Rabbi Haziz done to get himself banned from the village? Instigated the conspiracy to embezzle educational funding? This might be the clue she was looking for. She'd have to find out what this *mesira* business was and if she could find some way around it. It sounded like omerta, the mafia's practice of taking the law into their own hands.

As the older women chatted, Becks pulled Rabbi Tannenbaum's list of dissidents from her purse. Two lived in Kleynshtot. They'd been dissatisfied with the Hasidic community and might be willing to tell her what Pauline wouldn't.

Rising from her chair, Becks turned to Faigy. "Could you excuse me for a few minutes?" She retired to a corner of the kitchen with her cell and punched in the first name on the list. When no one answered, she moved on to the second.

"Mr. Brezlau?" she asked when a man answered.

"Yes?"

"My name's Becks Ruchinsky. Menachem Tannenbaum stayed with me shortly before he died. I wondered if I might ask a few questions. His father gave me your number."

"*Who* is this?"

"I . . ." She hadn't prepared her spiel. She explained that Menny was a friend of her son's and added, "Menachem seemed frightened when he stayed with me and wouldn't say why. I'm trying to find out."

She told him what Rabbi Tannenbaum had said about the community's concern over Menny's departure. "Menachem told us there'd been talk of kidnapping and bringing him back to Crown Heights. Did you hear about that?"

She expected Mr. Brezlau to become angry or hang up. Instead, he laughed. "*Oy vey*, not that again. We were upset when the boy left and concerned he'd get some younger members of the community to leave, too. No one talked seriously of kidnapping, at least not when I was around." Brezlau's voice was faint and raspy and she guessed he was well in his eighties.

"It was just a couple of hotheads mouthing off. After a while, they dropped the subject," he said. "I was upset to learn about Menachem, of blessed memory. His death was God's will. If you'll pardon my saying so, a young lady like you shouldn't be running around asking such questions. It isn't nice."

Nice?

"There's one more thing if you don't mind," she said.

"Depends."

"Do you know Rabbi Haziz? Rabbi Sadowsky made him leave Kleynshtot?"

"No. I moved here a year ago."

Becks thanked the man and hung up.

What Brezlau said supported Rabbi Tannenbaum's claim that no one in their community would abduct Menny. Becks wasn't ready to rule kidnapping out but it sounded less and less likely. The fraud conspiracy was another story. If Fox and Haziz were the fugitive conspirators, had they murdered Menny to avoid prison? She'd go to the library tomorrow to find out.

Turning back toward the sofa, Becks smiled. Her companions were fast asleep, Faigy listing to the right, hands in her lap, head drooping forward. Pauline slept with her arms akimbo, snoring gustily.

Becks nudged Faigy. "We need to leave," she whispered. "It's getting late."

Faigy rose and the women tiptoed from the apartment, closing the door silently behind them. On the drive home, Faigy slept while Becks stayed alert for the demons and ogres who prowled the New York State highway system.

She felt it in her gut now: she was getting close to finding Menny's killer.

45

Despite the cold wind gusting down Fifth Avenue the next morning, Becks reduced her pace to study the majestic lions that flanked the entrance to New York City's main library. Over the years, the regal statues staring imperiously ahead had come to symbolize the New York City she loved, its energy flowing through a network of streets and alleys like blood coursing through the veins of an enormous beast. After passing through a columned archway into the library's hall, she climbed the marble staircase to the reading room. Light flooding in from tall windows and grand chandeliers gave warmth to the room while gleaming brass lamps threw a cozy golden glow across oak worktables.

Although she'd never lived in New York, Becks loved the New York landmark and had renewed her card every three years since applying for it decades earlier. She found an unused computer monitor and, after locating articles on the Kleynshtot conspiracy, jotted the names of the eight men convicted. The rest of the morning was spent matching names to faces—most of them middle-aged men with unkempt facial hair—on Google and in the *New York Times* website. By noon, she'd satisfied herself that Sid Fox and Rabbi Haziz were *not* the missing conspirators.

Frustrated by her lack of success, Becks considered her options. Her theory that Fox killed Menny to hide his role in the conspiracy no longer seemed likely. So why did she remain uneasy about him and Rabbi Haziz? Rabbi Sadowitz must have had a strong reason for forbidding the people of Kleynshtot from mentioning Haziz's name. But what was it? The man she'd met hardly seemed the type to commit a horrible crime. Then again, plenty of women found Ted Bundy charming. She'd talk to the rabbi when she got home.

Becks had logged out and was loading pencils into her purse when her cell phone vibrated. Betsy, her editor's name, appeared on caller ID. Becks picked up the call too late. She'd emailed Betsy that she'd be in town and would like to discuss her next book. Racing downstairs two steps at a time, Becks hit the callback button.

After apologizing for missing Betsy's call, she got down to business. "Did you get my proposal for the Southern dessert cookbook?" she asked, heart pounding. After the last-minute changes to her upcoming book, she was afraid to hear Betsy's response.

"Haven't had time to look at it. Can you stop by today?"

Becks checked her watch. It was noon and she needed to eat before meeting the editor.

"One okay?"

"Fine."

Becks was too nervous to finish the sandwich she picked up at a small deli across from the library and handed the untouched half to a homeless woman on her way up Fifth Avenue. She'd found a phone number for Menny's math professor while in the library and decided to give him a call.

He answered on the first ring. After introducing herself and explaining her relationship with Menny, she asked if the boy had any problems at City College.

"What do you mean?" The street was noisy but she sensed leeriness in his tone.

"Did he argue with professors or students?"

"I don't know. Menachem was my student and he didn't discuss his personal life."

Becks thanked the man and hung up. Why had he sounded so defensive? Had Menny and the professor argued? She'd worry about that later.

Arriving at the publisher's office early, Becks paced in front of the glass and metal skyscraper for a few minutes before taking the elevator to the eighth floor. Becks knew Betsy worked for a respected publisher but still was impressed by the rich burgundy carpeting that led to the firm's heavy glass double doors. She entered and found Betsy in the reception area with a young woman. The girl left the office in tears.

Damn, Becks thought, her throat swelling. Was Betsy culling her authors? Had she come all the way to New York to lose her contract?

At Betsy's signal, Becks followed the woman, stylishly dressed in Manhattan's regulation black dress and stiletto heels, into a narrow office with floor-to-ceiling bookshelves. She recognized the names of well-known authors Betsy represented and felt a surge of pride at the prospect of her book joining theirs.

"Your cookbook's at the printer now," Betsy said, "and everything's fine. You nearly gave me a heart attack with that last set of changes." Her voice, if not warm, at least wasn't distant.

"I know and I'm sorry. I had no idea the newspaper would raise objections."

Betsy waved away Becks' words. "This can't happen again. If it does, I won't handle your work."

Becks' spirits rose. Handle her work? That sounded good. "It won't, I promise."

"Okay then. Let's discuss your next project."

The women spent a half hour kicking around ideas

for a Southern dessert cookbook and, after setting up a few deadlines, parted. The book would include dump cakes, chess pies and several of the coconut-heavy recipes she'd collected from her Savannah-born mother.

As she took the elevator downstairs, Becks considered catching a cab to Milt's and curling up with a book and hot chocolate. She was tired and it would help her stop fretting about Betsy's warning. But she was flying home at noon the next day and had promised to see a movie with Milt that evening. This would be her last chance to meet with one of Rabbi Tannenbaum's "dissidents."

Becks walked to a quiet corner of the lobby and turned her back to the crowd swarming in and out of the building. She pulled the rabbi's list from her purse and dialed the first person.

Schlomo Hirschberg was less than receptive.

"What's the point?" Hirschberg said after Becks explained why she wanted to meet. "The boy's dead."

"I heard there was talk of kidnapping Menachem and the idea was rejected. All the same, he seemed frightened when he stayed with me. I'd like to find out what happened after he left Crown Heights." She was starting to sound like a tape recorder.

"I don't know . . ."

"Please. Menachem's father gave me his blessing to call." She looked up, stunned to see a small man in a purple suit and lavender hat pass the window on stilts. When Becks smiled and waved, he stuck out his tongue. Only in New York. "I'm leaving town tomorrow and would prefer we speak in person."

"Can you come now?"

She jotted down his directions and, five minutes later, was on a subway heading south.

Hirschberg's home was a fifteen-minute walk from the subway station, and Becks had no trouble following the man's directions to the three-story yellow brick set back from the road amid mature oaks and maples. The house was well-kept and the landscaping more elaborate than the scrappy yards she'd passed in Crown Heights. A dark-haired woman in her early thirties balancing a toddler on her hip greeted Becks warily at the door. The aroma of freshly baked challah and roast chicken filled the hall, reminding her it was Friday and Mrs. Hirschberg would be preparing for the Sabbath. Afraid her host wouldn't have much time to talk, Becks hurried down the hall, dodging a double stroller and yellow dump truck to reach Mr. Hirschberg's office.

Becks had expected a young person but was surprised by the elegant urbanite who rose from behind his desk and apologized for the disarray of his office. She tried not to stare at his long lashes and solid jaw as he retrieved a folding chair from the closet and brought it around for Becks. Although a small yarmulke rested atop his head, he bore little resemblance to the shaggy-bearded, ultra-religious men she'd met so far. His pants, though black, were denim and fit as though tailored for his slim frame.

"So what would you like to know?" Hirschberg asked as Becks settled into her seat.

"Did anyone take the idea of kidnapping Menachem seriously?" she asked, getting right to the point, "or talk about how it might be arranged?"

Hirschberg shook his head. "For a few months, some of the younger men talked about bringing him home. There was so much fear and suspicion then. He was the most promising young man to leave our community."

Becks nodded encouragingly.

"You've probably heard that Menachem comes from

an old Hasidic dynasty. His grandfather was the third member of his family to lead our community in Poland. Menachem had a hereditary right and obligation to do the same. He was also brilliant and kind and the students at his yeshiva looked up to him. He would've made a fine rabbi."

Becks crossed her legs as she tried to reconcile the Menny she knew with the charismatic leader Mr. Hirschberg described. She realized with a pang that years of hiding and struggling to survive in an unfamiliar environment had taken their toll. The Menny she knew, though bright and kind, seemed world-weary.

"Back then, members of our sect feared we'd be left without a leader and our community might fade away. Worse, Menachem might attract our brightest boys to any group he started. Young men are always eager for something different and he had the charisma to draw people in."

"Did anyone pursue him?"

"Not to kidnap. Just talk. A lawyer who does some work for the rebbe, a man we thought Menachem respected, spoke to him. He didn't have any luck convincing him to return."

"So that's all that came of it?"

Hirschberg rubbed his chin and picked up a brass letter opener embossed with what appeared to be a college seal. He shifted it from hand to hand, keeping his gaze down as though searching for words among the papers and books spread before him. The spear-shaped object caught what little light there was in the room and its constant movement made Becks edgy. Finally, he set it down and looked up.

"A member of our group talked to a man he'd heard about through a friend. The man—he wasn't religious—offered to track Menachem down and bring him home. His fee was exorbitant."

"What happened?"

"Nothing. By that time, most of us agreed Menachem wasn't a threat and would return. It's tough out there and many of the young people who leave wind up living on the street or working menial jobs."

"Did you meet the man who offered to kidnap Menachem?"

Yes, he came to a meeting. Most of us were put off by him. He was a big guy, an Israeli who claimed he'd served in Mossad."

Becks took a deep breath and leaned forward. "Did you get his name?"

Hirschberg squinted and ran a hand through his hair. "I think so. I'd seen him in Crown Heights once or twice. It was an animal. Wolf?"

"Does Fox sound right?"

"That's it. You know him?"

Becks sat ramrod straight. "We've met. He owns a night club on Miami Beach and attends Chabad there."

Her heart beat wildly. That had to be why Fox was on campus. He hadn't seen a post from Menny's father. He'd learned about the boy through Hirschberg's group. Did he hope to collect a reward for recovering Menny?

"Do you remember *when* you saw him in Crown Heights? Was it around the time Menachem left?" Becks asked.

"Not then." He picked up the brass letter opener and tapped it against his palm. "Earlier. Around the time that kid went to prison. A friend of Menachem. Lieb . . . no Levi."

Becks rose, sending her chair scraping across the floor. "Are you certain?"

"I wouldn't swear to it—it's been almost two years."

Becks stared at Hirschberg, trying to wrap her mind around what he'd told her. Fox's presence in Crown Heights must have had something to do with Levi's trial.

A warning? Was Fox the dealer Levi refused to name? Did she have it all wrong? Was Fox searching for Menny to prevent him from revealing the night club owner's role in Levi's drug bust?

Becks felt dazed but managed to thank Hirschberg and call goodbye to his wife as he escorted her to the door. Walking toward the subway, she shivered. She dreaded the noisy, crowded rush-hour ride to Manhattan and looked around for a taxi. None were in sight. The longing she'd felt a day earlier for warm weather and sunny skies had blossomed into full-fledged homesickness. She yearned to wake up in her own bed with Daniel beside her.

Riding the train to Manhattan, Becks considered Mr. Hirschberg's revelations. Fox, whom she'd begun to rule out, was back in the picture. Pauline had thrown a curve ball with her announcement of Rabbi Haziz's expulsion. But she couldn't see a link to Menny's murder.

Becks had a lot to mull over. And not just about Menny's death. She was returning home with a new perspective on the Hasidic community. Hannah and Faigy seemed perfectly content living in a cosseted world defined by family, community and tradition. It left little room for independent thought or action. Yet the daily cycle of religious practice and custom offered the women meaning and structure. She could appreciate Menny's yearning to return to a community where everyone's role was defined and the rules were unambiguous.

At least for people who obeyed them.

So who had violated the most basic rule and killed Menny?

46

Pineapple dump cake. Hello dolly bars. Doctor Bird cobbler. Buttermilk chess pie.

Leafing through her box of recipe cards, most smudged from years of use, Becks sighed. She'd been collecting recipes since she was a teenager and it was going to be tough to pick the fifty or so that best represented the American South as Betsy suggested. Pecan pie was a must, of course. And coconut cake. She had a dozen variations of that alone.

It was Sunday morning and Becks' plane had landed in Fort Lauderdale the night before. On the drive home with Daniel, she'd tiptoed around the subject of her visit, instead telling her husband about the movie she'd seen with his father. Now Daniel was playing tennis, a treat on his rare Sundays off, and she'd risen at eight to work on her new cookbook. By ten thirty, she was so lost in reviewing recipes and remembering the friends who'd shared them that she was startled by the phone's jangle. Wiping her hands on her apron, she grabbed the phone off the counter.

It was Maya. "About time you got back. Learn anything useful?"

"Yes. And hello to you too." She recapped her visit, telling Maya about Fox's offer to kidnap Menny and Rabbi Haziz's expulsion from Kleynshtot. "I'm planning to visit the rabbi and Fox sometime this week. Want to come?"

"Let me know when you're going and I'll let you know. Promise you won't go alone."

"We'll see." Becks rang off before Maya could respond. Realizing the recipes had piqued her appetite, she opened the refrigerator to make a salad. Darn. The crisper held only a few limp vegetables. Why hadn't Daniel gone to the grocery store while she was in New York? Her irritation at his leaving a nearly empty refrigerator turned into panic as she considered another possibility. This was the longest she'd been away from home since their reunion. Had he taken advantage of her absence to have dinner with . . . she caught herself. This was crazy. Daniel would've sent out for a pizza before he'd have gone to the supermarket. That's why the refrigerator was empty. She had to let go of her misgivings and trust her husband.

The memory of Daniel's affair left Becks depressed and jittery and she realized she needed to get out of the house. Before leaving New York, she'd promised herself she'd spend a few days working on the new cookbook before acting on what she'd learned about Menny. But why wait? Word might reach Fox and Haziz that she'd been asking about them. She'd delay meeting Fox—any excuse to avoid the thug—and start with Rabbi Haziz. She picked up the phone.

"Washington Avenue Chabad." Becks was startled to hear the rabbi's voice. In most synagogues, a secretary answered.

"This is Becks Ruchinsky, Gabe's mother. I'm sorry to bother you again but I have some questions about Menachem's background and would appreciate it if we could get together."

"I'd be delighted. Let me look at my schedule." She waited. "I've got a funeral tomorrow. Can you meet me at the Chabad House today at three?"

"Yes, thank you." Becks clicked off and quickly punched in her father's number. She didn't want to go alone.

The phone rang six times before he picked up. "What time is it?" His voice was groggy.

"About noon. It's Becks. Did I wake you?' Tootsie often napped after breakfast.

"No. I always sound like shit this time of day."

"Sorry. Are you awake enough to talk?"

"I am now." He paused and she imagined him putting on his glasses. "So what's so important you had to wake an old man? I was having a great dream. A woman in a long white dress was walking toward me on the beach and—."

"I need your help, Dad," she interrupted. She had to get moving to make the appointment.

"What is it, Doll?"

"I'm going to see that rabbi from the Chabad. He's being shunned by a community in upstate New York and I want to find out why?"

"How's that any of your business?"

"Menny lived in the same town, Kleynshtot, when the rabbi was thrown out. No one will tell me what the rabbi did and I'd feel safer if you went along."

Silence.

"Dad! Did you hear me?"

"Give me a sec. I can't believe you're still messing with this. Don't you have anything better to do?"

"Are you coming or not?" She checked her watch. It was twelve-thirty.

What time?"

"I'll get you at two."

"Fine. I've got to be back for poker at six. I'm beating those schmucks and want to play while my luck's running."

"See you soon. And, Dad . . ."

She heard the click as he hung up.

She'd thank him later.

When they pulled up to the Chabad House that afternoon, the neighborhood was silent except for the faint squeak of the double stroller a young mother was pushing along the sidewalk. Becks saw Rabbi Haziz approach the house as she left her car. Spotting them, he waved Becks and Tootsie over. He seemed to be wearing the same coat and fedora he had on during services a week earlier and smiled warmly as he held the door.

A musty odor filled the empty room, which looked shabbier in the absence of congregants. Spotting the rusty metal folding chairs and scarred flooring, Becks realized the Chabad survived on a shoestring. Even so, the room looked as though someone had made an effort to keep it tidy. Books were neatly arranged on shelves along the walls and prayer shawls were folded and draped across a metal rack near the entrance.

"So what can I tell you about Menachem?" Rabbi Haziz said after adjusting the thermostat and flipping the switches that controlled the overhead lights. He'd joined them at the table where they'd sat for lunch. "I understand he was a Lubavitch but I don't know him or his family."

"I visited . . . that is . . . I'd like to know. . ." Becks blushed as she fumbled for words. She caught Tootsie's eye.

"Spit it out, Doll. The rabbi won't bite."

She scowled. "To be honest, I didn't come here to discuss Menachem. Last night, I returned from a trip to New York, where I visited Kleynshtot and saw your picture in one of the yeshiva's faculty photographs."

The rabbi nodded. "Yes, I taught at Sha'arei Avraham for a number of years."

"I saw a group shot that included you and Sid Fox. I was surprised."

"Why?"

"You told me you hadn't met Mr. Fox before moving to Miami. Wouldn't you have run into each other at the yeshiva?"

The rabbi frowned and stared at Becks. Then he laughed. "Oh, I see what you're getting at. Sid and I were— what's the expression—ships passing in the night. He joined the staff a few weeks before I left. In fact, he took over one of my Hebrew classes. I don't think he stayed long. Too much of a temper for the younger children."

"So you knew he was there?"

"I didn't know who he was at the time. We made the connection after we met here."

"There's something else I'd like to know." She hesitated and watched Rabbi Haziz. His brow furrowed and his chin rose. "A woman told me you were banned from Kleynshtot. She wouldn't say why, only that Rebbe Sadowsky forbids any mention of your name. I was shocked by her reaction." Becks ran damp palms over her thighs. "Can you tell me what happened?"

The rabbi's jaw tensed and released. "I hoped it wouldn't come out." He stared out the window a moment, then leaned forward and lowered his voice. "Since you've heard some of it, you might as well hear it all. Only I'd appreciate your keeping it to yourselves."

Tootsie nodded. "You bet."

Becks was silent.

"About three years ago, I was caught up in a case of fraud. You may have heard about it."

He didn't wait for a reply.

"Kleynshtot and the men involved were in the news for weeks. I learned about it before the news broke. In fact, I played a part, though I didn't know at the time. Several members of our community had obtained federal education grants to, among other things, offer Jewish history courses at a community college. My job was to recruit young people from Kleynshtot and neighboring areas to teach. Then one day, when I asked my supervisor for the teachers' contracts, he refused to provide them. One thing led to another and I realized the program was a scam. No course was planned and I'd been wasting my time."

Becks nodded.

"I was shocked. And angry," the rabbi said, pulling at his beard. "I made an appointment with Rebbe Sadowsky but he didn't want to hear it. He said I must be mistaken and accused me of lying. He refused to acknowledge the fraud and threw me out of his office. In hindsight, I realize he knew what was going on all along. When I said I was going to the police, he struck me. After a few minutes, though, he apologized."

"He let you report it to the authorities?" Tootsie asked.

"Of course not. He said he'd throw me out of Kleynshtot and let other communities know I was a troublemaker if I called the police. Who were people going to believe—me or the rebbe?" Haziz placed both hand on the table and sighed. "He threatened to prevent my parents and siblings from attending shul and make sure they were shunned. Members of our community follow the rebbe's orders. I couldn't let that happen to my family."

Becks recalled Pauline mentioning the rabbi's influence over his community. "So you left?"

"I had no choice."

Haziz dropped his head and stared at his hands. Becks felt sorry for him. She'd heard Hasidic leaders maintained rigid control, solving problems themselves rather than contacting the authorities. Rebbe Sadowsky sounded like a mafia don.

The rabbi's predicament didn't seem all that different from Menny's. Both had unwillingly left their communities, though Menny's reasons were still unclear. If the boy had lived, the rabbi might've helped him come to terms with his sense of isolation.

Tootsie cleared his throat.

"Do you have any questions, Dad?"

"Nope. I heard enough."

Becks was reaching to pick her purse up from the floor when she heard the door fly open and crash against a wall. She looked up to find Fox, his face red, stomping across the room.

"You son of a bitch," he snarled at the rabbi. Spotting Becks and Tootsie, he stopped speaking.

"Sorry," he said, glaring at the rabbi before glancing warily at Becks and her father. He took a deep breath. "Didn't see you. How's Daniel? Nice guy, your husband."

Becks decided to play along. "Thanks. How are you?" Then, before he could respond, "I'd love to stop by this week if you have some time. Would Tuesday work?"

Fox scowled and eyed his cell. "Can you come to the club late in the day? I'm meeting workmen earlier. Six thirty?"

Becks agreed and said her goodbyes. She wasn't sure how she'd approach Fox but didn't want to blow the opportunity to nail down a meeting time.

Five minutes later as she pulled out of her parking spot Tootsie snorted. "What a pile of crap."

Becks stared at him. "What do you mean?"

The rabbi's story. Like hell he didn't know about the conspiracy. Probably has millions squirreled away in the Holy Land."

"You believe that?"

"Don't you? He knew the police were closing in. The

old rabbi played right into his hands, banning him from Kleynshtot."

Becks considered her father's accusations as they drove across Biscayne Bay. Staring ahead, she took little notice of the workers teeming over the ocean liners, preparing the ships for their next cruise.

She didn't know what to make of her father's theory. Tootsie's instincts were good—that's how he'd survived in a tough business. The rabbi had seemed straightforward about admitting his role in the scam. He could have lied. Rabbi Haziz might have his secrets but she doubted they had anything to do with Menny's death.

After dropping her father off, Becks headed home. Her cell rang as she pulled onto the exit ramp in Boca Raton.

"Becks?" A woman spoke in a low, breathless voice. "It's Hannah."

"Is everything all right?"

"I'm not sure. I wanted to talk while the children were eating. I attended a wedding yesterday and ran into Leah Horowitz. Levi's mother. The boy who went to jail?"

"I remember. What did she say?"

"She visited Levi a week ago. When she told him about Menachem's death, he became so distraught he threw up. The guards had to take him away to wash up."

"That's understandable. They were old friends."

"There's more. Leah said Levi's hands were shaking when he returned. He begged her to be careful and to watch out for his brothers and sisters. He thinks they're in danger."

"Why?" Becks' heart fluttered as she recalled the break-in at Gabe's dorm.

"He refused to say. Leah thinks it has something to do with Menachem. Levi knows something about his murder and won't talk about it."

Becks paused to consider. "You may be right. The

man who hired Levi to transport drugs may have been involved in Menachem's death."

"You know who it is?" Hannah asked, her voice rising.

"I'm not sure yet. I think it's the night club owner I told you about but I need more proof."

"Let me know if I can help."

"Of course." Becks hung up and drove home. It was after seven and Daniel, who usually called when he ran late, wasn't home. She dialed his cell.

"Where are you?"

"At the hospital. Where else would I be?"

"Should I start dinner?"

"Sure. Why not?"

"It's after seven. I thought maybe you'd gone out with a friend."

"What friend? Who would I go out with?"

She didn't answer.

"Come on, Becks. I had to round on a lot of patients and lost track of time."

She didn't say anything.

"Becks, I'm telling the truth."

"All right. I'll have a sandwich. You can fix something when you get home."

She hung up before he could respond.

Becks hated the fact that, even now, more than six months after he'd moved home, she worried when Daniel was late. She'd imagine him with his nurse, an attractive drug rep, another doctor . . . the list went on and on. Daniel had reassured her of his love and faithfulness a thousand times. Even so, she couldn't let go. And the worst of it was, each time she questioned his fidelity, she relived the desolation she'd experienced at discovering his affair.

Too edgy to eat, she went upstairs to shower and read. By the time Daniel walked in, she was fast asleep.

47

"Becks. Wake up."

A warm hand shook her shoulder.

"I'm tired," she groaned, pulling a pillow over her head and squeezing it against her ear.

Daniel was having none of it. He removed the pillow. "Come on, sweetheart. We need to talk."

"What do you want?" Becks mumbled as she reached for her glasses then hiked herself up against the headboard. The foot of the bed sank under Daniel's weight.

"You sounded angry over the phone last night. I didn't want to wake you when I got in. What's going on?"

Becks shrugged. "What do you mean?"

"First you hang up on me. Then you go to sleep before I get home. You're avoiding me."

Becks adjusted her flowered nightgown and swung her legs off the bed. Daniel had opened the shutters and the early morning sun threw a ladder of shadows across the comforter. She felt a little silly about the way she'd treated her husband. Now and then these fits of resentment flared up and she realized how bitter she still felt. They both knew what troubled her but she was loath to admit it. It was easier to redirect the conversation.

"You could have called last night. It's common

courtesy to let me know what time you'll be home. I mean, how do I know when to start dinner?"

"I got busy and forgot. You know how crazy things get in the hospital. I will try harder."

"I'd appreciate it." She tried not to sound grudging.

"Sweetheart, I don't know what to say to you anymore. I made a mistake. It's in the past."

She refused to meet his gaze.

"You have to realize it by now. I've never loved anyone except you and never will."

"Right," she said, then relented, "I know."

"Want me to write it in blood?" He smiled crookedly, then pulled a pen from his pocket and pretended to pierce his thumb.

Becks laughed. "Sure. Go ahead"

He rose from the bed. "I'm in a rush this morning. Why don't we go out to dinner tonight and talk? We haven't had time together in awhile."

"Well, I'm . . ." She recalled her plan to meet Fox but decided against telling Daniel. She'd explain during dinner. "Let's make it eight thirty. I've got a lot to catch up on."

"It's a date." He kissed her, his lips lingering, and left. Watching him leave, she felt oddly satisfied and curious. Would tonight be the night? She rose from the bed and washed her face. Her stomach fluttered. Damned if she wasn't nervous as a schoolgirl.

"Stupid Miami traffic," Becks grumbled, swooping around the semi-trailer that had been trundling in front of her at fifty miles an hour. The drivers on I-95 were a nightmare, cutting too close or driving so slowly that traffic backed up for miles. She was grateful she only had to head south on rare occasions. She'd go nuts on a regular diet of Miami drivers.

She'd finally reached Gabe on the phone that

morning. Becks was stunned when he informed her he'd just finished S*hacharit,* his morning prayers. He said he was praying before and after meals and had bought a special cup so he could perform his ritual hand washing. Gabe tended to go overboard on whatever he did but what was this about? Was he trying to *become* Menny, to fill his friend's shoes as a way of dealing with the boy's death? It was disturbing yet within the realm of possibility. She decided to pay him a visit before her meeting with Fox.

When Gabe opened the door to his dorm that afternoon, Becks' jaw dropped. His hair had grown to below his ears and was greasy and unkempt. His once-smooth face sprouted an unsightly beard that merged into wispy sideburns.

She stepped inside and closed the door. "What's going on here?" She fought to sound calm. "What happened to you?"

Gabe's brow furrowed as he studied his mother's face. "You look angry. Something is upsetting you?'

"Have you seen yourself in a mirror lately? The sideburns and the beard. You look so . . ." she hesitated ". . . different."

Gabe rubbed his chin. "You do not like them? The Torah teaches 'Ye shall not round the corners of your heads, neither shalt thou mar the corners of thy beard.' It's in Leviticus."

Becks had no answer to that, at least nothing she could say without upsetting her son. "When did you decide to become Hasidic? That *is* what you're doing, isn't it?"

Her son smiled and her stomach roiled as she recognized the smug, self-righteous expression she'd resented on Menny's father. Did they teach *that* at Chabad?

Too upset to get into a discussion about his "conversion," Becks asked Gabe how his classes were going. He assured her they were under control.

"And what about that man you saw at the Chabad in Miami Beach? Has he been around?"

Gabe tilted his head and stared at the ceiling. "Oh yeah. I meant to tell you. On Sunday. I looked out my window and saw him walk up to the dorm, go inside and leave. I do not know what he wanted."

A trickle of fear filled Becks' chest. Fox had returned! How could Gabe not have mentioned that? "Did you tell anyone?"

"Tell them what?"

"That you saw the man who threatened you."

"But he did not do anything."

"I know and . . ." Becks paused and tried to remember what she'd told Gabe. She'd asked the campus police and Gabe's residence advisor, Meredith, to be on the lookout for Sid Fox. She had not instructed Gabe to call her if the man showed up. And being literal-minded, he hadn't.

"All right, Gabe. Listen to me. If you see him, stay away. Walk in the opposite direction or go inside a building where he won't be admitted. Then call me. Do you understand?"

"I understand."

She prayed he wasn't parroting her words.

After leaving Gabe, Becks stopped by the residence advisor's room to tell her about Fox's visit. Meredith promised to be on the alert and to inform campus police. In the meantime, she'd tell Gabe to contact her if he saw Fox or anyone else who looked suspicious.

Becks didn't bother to mention Gabe didn't know what suspicious looked like. He'd barely flinch if Genghis Khan rode up to the dorm with a Mongol horde. She couldn't prepare her son for all of life's possibilities. Much to her regret. But she was determined to keep him away from Fox.

48

Becks arrived at Club Shukran a few minutes early for her appointment and knocked on the metal door she'd entered with Maya. The rapping echoed in the empty street and, after a few minutes, she looked around for another entrance. Finding none, she was dialing Fox's number when the door clanged open.

"You made it," Fox swept an arm across his body in an exaggerated gesture of welcome.

Becks hesitated.

"Come in for Christ's sake. I'm not a monster."

She blushed and followed Fox up the Lucite stairs she'd taken with Maya, past the dance floor and bar to a flight of steps she hadn't noticed before. The warehouse-sized building felt cold and abandoned without the loud music and flashing lights that had transformed it into a neon circus. Walls that had blazed with colorful neon lasers were a disappointing dingy gray and exposed ductwork nearly hid a corrugated metal ceiling. They passed the aquarium bar, now concealed by stacked chairs, and went upstairs where Fox unlocked a door and ushered Becks into a spacious office. In addition to the large black marble desk at the back of the room, low-slung couches and chairs of soft black leather formed seating groups. An entire wall was comprised of floor-to-ceiling windows that afforded a bird's eye view of the dance floor, the cage on which the gilded DJ spun records and the bar where she and Maya had spent the evening.

Becks stared at Fox, who nodded and raised an eyebrow. "Not a big drinker, are you?"

Her neck grew warm.

"Your hot little friend sure put them away."

"I'll let her know you found her attractive." Becks lowered herself into one of the chairs near the window. She crossed her legs and motioned toward the chair across from her, sneaking a glance at the door. It hadn't clicked when Fox closed it and she comforted herself with the knowledge she could leave quickly. "Aren't you going to sit, Mr. Fox?"

The large man smirked and ran a hand over his hair. "Sid is fine." He took the seat.

"I imagine Rabbi Haziz told you I was in New York?"

Fox nodded and crossed his arms, forcing his biceps to strain at the fabric of his tee shirt.

"Then you know what happened at the yeshiva and how I learned of your time there."

"The photo, sure. I spent a year at the yeshiva, trying to teach those blockheads Hebrew." He laughed. It was a contemptuous grunt and his smile was that of a coiled cobra. "I heard one of the rebbes gave you a hard time."

Becks' arm—and pride—stung at the memory but she refused to give Fox the satisfaction of acknowledging it. "A yeshiva seems an odd place for a night club owner."

"Yeah, well, a guy's got to make a living. My night club in Manhattan went under and I needed a job. I speak Hebrew so why not teach?"

"In Kleynshtot?"

"I got news for you lady, that's where my mother grew up."

She blushed. "Sorry. I didn't know. It's just that you . . ."

"Seem so Israeli," he finished for her.

"How about Crown Heights?" she asked. "Did you spend much time there?"

Fox's eyes narrowed. "Enough about me. Why are you here?"

Becks uncrossed her legs, trying to find a comfortable position on the ludicrously low chair. "I appreciate your talking to my husband but I still have a few questions. For example, why were you back on campus last weekend? My son saw you near his dorm."

Fox didn't flinch. "He must be mistaken. I haven't been on campus in months. Not since I went looking for Menachem."

There was no point in challenging him on the visit or his claim to have looked for Menny in response to Rabbi Tannenbaum's post. At least he knew she was aware of his lies. Maybe she'd have better luck with the government scam.

"Did Rabbi Haziz mention he told me about the fraud conspiracy in Kleynshtot and the reason he was forced to leave?"

Fox's eyebrows shot up. "He admitted it?"

"He said he told Rebbe Sadowsky about the scam and was accused of lying."

"Isn't that commendable?" Fox curled his upper lip in amusement.

"What do you mean?"

"Nothing. If Rabbi Haziz said that, it must be true."

Becks stood, her dignity compromised by the challenge of raising herself from the low-slung chair. "If there's something you want to tell me, why don't you just say it?"

"What would I know? I'm a simple night club owner." Fox tapped his chest in a less-than-convincing show of humility.

She walked to the door and turned around. "Is the downstairs exit locked?"

"It opens from inside."

"Well, thanks so much for your help. I'll let myself out."

Becks took a deep breath, relieved to have left the dark and mustiness of Club Shukran for the twilight of Washington Avenue. Young people in suits and ties raced by, forcing her to step up her pace. The exotic aromas of falafel, saffron and curry drifted from small cafes along the street. Walking to the lot where she'd left her car, Becks tried to figure out what she'd learned. Fox had played a cat and mouse game with every question she asked, so it wasn't much. She was curious about Fox's cynicism regarding Rabbi Haziz's expulsion from Kleynshtot, though. The rabbi had been so forthcoming about his involvement in the scam that she assumed he was telling the truth. Tootsie might be right, though. The rabbi may have stolen thousands of dollars in federal funding. The problem was that Fox seemed like a thug, while the rabbi came across as sincere. She didn't know who to believe.

It was almost seven thirty by the time Becks pulled onto Washington Avenue. The street felt like a parking lot, cars barely moving as the light changed from green to red and back again. She realized she'd never make her eight thirty dinner with Daniel and texted him that she'd call when she was closer to home.

It took fifteen minutes to travel the two blocks to Fifth Avenue but the traffic on the main artery moved swiftly and she mounted the ramp to McArthur Causeway. Her frustration at Fox's evasiveness and irritation at being stuck in traffic had soured her mood. It lifted a little at the sight of passengers waving from the upper decks of a cruise ship as it left port for the open ocean.

A half-hour later, Becks was on I-95 passing under a multi-highway interchange when a flash of light nearly blinded her. She glanced into the rearview mirror to find a large SUV drawing uncomfortably close. Figuring the driver was anxious to pass, she moved from the left to the middle lane. The SUV followed, its high beams blazing. That seemed strange. Did the driver intend to pass from the middle lane? She shifted into the outside lane. It made no difference. The driver remained on her tail, honking his horn and flashing his brights.

She ducked her head and checked the mirror. No sign of a roof light, so it wasn't a patrolman. Just what she needed. A nutcase in a fit of road rage. She'd call the police.

Angry and scared, Becks reached for her cell and felt a jolt. Looking in the rearview window, she swallowed. The SUV was on her tail. Her heart leaped into her throat as the driver dropped back, then accelerated and plowed into her bumper. She gasped as her seat belt dug into her chest. Though desperate to call 911, she was afraid to release her grip on the steering wheel. She looked out her side window: no one seemed to have noticed. A minute later, a third crash sent the Mercedes sliding onto the shoulder. Adrenalin rushed through her veins as she wrestled the car back on the road.

Her breath coming in loud gasps, Becks gunned the Mercedes' engine, hitting seventy, then eighty. When the car started shimmying at ninety she dropped back. The SUV was still on her tail. Her spirits rose at the sight of the sign, "Stirling Road. Three Miles." She'd exit there and find a police station.

A quarter-mile' from the exit, the Mercedes jerked,

slamming Becks' head into the backrest. Her hands flew off the wheel. She jammed on the brakes but it was too late. A squeal of tires and a high-pitched scream filled the car as her Mercedes skid off the road and flipped. The dizzying roll and crunch of glass sucked the air from her chest.

When Becks came to, her left arm throbbed and her limbs felt sore and weak. The pain in her head kept growing. Taking stock of her surroundings, she realized she lay on her side wedged between the driver's door and steering wheel. Fluid filled her eyes, blocking her vision.

A sound of tapping reached her as though through a dense fog.

"Are you all right?" A man's voice. She shook her head. "I'll call for help."

Then darkness.

When Becks regained consciousness, she was on her back staring up at a bright expanse of ceiling, the high-pitched blare of a siren surrounding her. Every bone in her body ached. She tried to sit but the stiff collar that encased her neck prevented any movement.

"How are you feeling?" The words came from an olive-skinned woman who was adjusting an IV in her arm.

Becks winced.

"You were lucky to survive that accident. We're on our way to the emergency room."

"My husband, does he . . ."

"We found the emergency number in your cell. He'll meet us there."

"Thank you." Her head spun.

Ten minutes later, the doors of the ambulance swung open and a man in hospital greens helped the olive-skinned woman whisk Becks' gurney through the sterile halls of a hospital, past a nurses' station and into a curtained bay. Becks groaned as the two transferred her to a hospital bed, where a nurse helped her change into a flimsy hospital gown. She lost track of time as men and women rolled her from room to room for a dizzying array of scans and examinations.

Hours, or perhaps minutes, later Becks was back in her original bay floating in and out of consciousness when a familiar voice broke through her haze. "Becks." Then louder. "Sweetheart."

She opened her eyes and smiled at Daniel, who stared down at her, his brow wrinkled with concern. Why did he look so upset? And she was cold. He needed to turn up the thermostat in the hall. Then she blinked and, realizing where she was, registered shock, then a flush of relief. Daniel was here. He'd take care of things.

He took her hand and kissed it. "Becks, I was so worried. What happened?"

"An SUV ran me off the road," she said. She closed her eyes to block the blinding overhead light that pierced her skull. "It started harassing me at the Golden Glades Interchange."

"Did you see the driver? Or notice the car's make?"

"It was big. An Escalade? I couldn't see who drove."

Daniel squeezed her shoulder and she realized she'd dozed off. "You need to stay awake, honey. You might have a concussion."

She glanced around, more alert now, and realized she was in a small room with three walls and a green curtain behind which phones rang. A narrow counter to her right held gauze pads, a box of gloves and a pink plastic water jug. Pain pierced her left wrist as she pressed it into the mattress to sit. "Jeeze!" She grimaced. "How bad is it?"

Daniel pulled a chair to the side of the bed. "You're bruised and battered and you'll be sore for weeks. Your forehead suffered a gash when it hit the window. I've promised to keep an eye out for signs of concussion. Other than the sprain in your wrist, though, it's not too bad. The doctor is almost ready to send you home. They've given you something for pain and I'll fill a prescription tomorrow."

"We can leave soon?"

"After the police talk to you." He nodded toward the curtain. "Are you up to it?"

She felt awful—nauseated and sore—and furious at whoever had done this to her. She doubted she'd feel better any time soon.

"No, but send them in."

Daniel left the room and returned a minute later with a smartly dressed, middle-aged woman with a slight limp. She wore a red pants suit and chunky gold earrings that nearly disappeared in a shock of curly, black chin-length hair.

"This is Detective Rodriguez," Daniel said, motioning the woman to the chair he'd abandoned.

Becks answered the detective's questions, describing the SUV as best she could along with the events leading to the accident. She told the officer she hadn't cut anyone off in traffic but couldn't swear the episode hadn't been provoked.

"Lots of crazies out there," Det. Rodriguez said, "It could have gone a lot worse."

When the woman finished questioning her, Becks told Rodriguez about her investigation into Menny's death and suggested the accident might be related. Daniel's face flushed when Becks said she'd met with the night club owner before the accident.

"My God, Becks," he broke in, "I thought you were going to be careful."

She shrugged.

When Becks finished talking, the detective rose and

stood behind her chair, hands resting on its back. "You realize, Mrs. Ruchinsky, this *is* a matter for the police. Why didn't you go to them with your concerns about the boy's death?"

"I did. The Boca Raton police weren't interested."

Rodriguez eyed her curiously. "You might want to try again. Give me the detective's name and I'll send an accident report with a note about our conversation. I'll check to see if Fox owns an SUV. "

When the detective was through, Daniel went off to sign Becks' discharge papers and pull up the car. A nurse helped her dress and rolled her to the hospital entrance in a wheelchair.

"Thank God you're okay," Daniel said once they were on the expressway. "I don't think I've ever been that frightened. And don't worry about the car. It's not important."

Becks felt terrible. The car was probably totaled. Daniel had fallen in love with the vintage Mercedes five years earlier and bought it for her as a birthday present.

She dozed on and off during the drive home and made it as far as the family room before collapsing on a couch. Too exhausted and sore to climb the stairs to bed, she fell asleep in her clothes. Two hours later, she awoke, trembling at the memory of bright headlights driving her off the road. Frightened, she started to call for Daniel but fell back to sleep at the sound of faint snoring in the chair beside her.

49

The next morning, Becks was at her desk gazing through the window at her neatly clipped lawn when two women, one with a Labrador puppy, stopped to chat on the sidewalk. She fought the temptation to go outside and play with the dog. Her head ached and every muscle felt sore from the accident. Plus she'd promised Daniel and Detective Fernandez she'd contact the Boca Raton police department first thing in the morning. She'd slept late before making her slow way downstairs for breakfast, then procrastinated for half an hour at her desk. It was time to call.

She dialed and, shoulders tense, waited for the officer to answer.

"Detective Division. Cole."

His voice made her stomach roil. Becks gave her name. "I don't know if you remember me from a few weeks ago. I called to find out if you'd investigated the death of the young Hasidic man who drowned."

"I remember." His voice held poorly-disguised resignation.

"Last night, an SUV drove me off the road. I think it was an attempt—"

"Where'd it happen?"

"On I-95, south of Stirling Road."

"That's not in our jurisdiction."

"That's *not* why I'm calling."

He didn't respond.

"I talked to Menny's friends and family in Miami and New York. I'm certain he was murdered. Then, last night, someone ran me off the road after I'd met with Sid Fox, the night club owner I told you about. Menny was in Fox's car the last time anyone saw him."

"You're sure it was Fox's car?"

"I can't be positive but it was the same make. I told you before that I'd seen it in my neighborhood."

She paused, debating whether she should mention that Maya had tracked down the car's owner. Better not. She didn't want to get her friend in trouble.

"I learned that Fox and Menny lived in the same New York village. And I've heard Fox hires Hasidic men to transport drugs."

"Was Fox driving the SUV?"

"It was night. I couldn't see."

"Did you recognize the make?"

"I told you it was dark."

She looked outside. Helmut had joined the neighborhood gathering.

"I still think the boy's death was an unfortunate accident but I'll check around, see if a surveillance system picked anything up. I'll also have someone from narcotics contact you."

"What about last night?"

"Do you or your husband keep a gun?"

Was he serious? "No."

"Well, it could be a coincidence, being run off the road after your visit to Fox. All the same, I'd be careful."

"Meaning what?"

"Stay away from Fox. And call me if something happens." He rang off.

Becks stared at the phone before returning it to the cradle. She was surprised. Cole had at least pretended to take her seriously. That was good *and* bad. It meant he'd look into Menny's death. If Fox found out the police were investigating, though, she and Gabe might be in more danger.

Becks rose from her chair, thighs aching. Her arm felt clumsy and unnatural in the splint she'd worn home from the hospital. The pow wow in front of her house had broken up but it was a beautiful day for a walk. She'd have to take it easy.

She went downstairs and left through the garage. At this time of the morning, the joggers and dog walkers were gone and Becks looked forward to a walk unimpeded by any obligation to stop and chat. She moved slowly, relieved to find the pain in her legs dissipating. She'd gone a half mile and stopped to admire a staghorn fern when a voice called out.

"Becks. Becks Ruchinsky?"

She turned. A vaguely familiar woman waved from the porch across the street. A yellow and blue scarf restrained the bright red curls that threatened to escape from beneath the fabric. Becks narrowed her eyes to make out the woman. It was Kiki, a neighbor she'd run into at their synagogue a few times. She'd considered the woman shallow and superficial and had been surprised to learn Kiki had become *frum*— devoutly religious—after her husband's death a year earlier. Becks stared at her neighbor. It was hard to reconcile this frazzled hausfrau with the elegant woman who had shown up at temple events with Chanel purses and St. John's suits.

Becks' legs ached and she took her time crossing the street.

"What happened there?" Kiki said, gesturing toward Becks' splinted arm.

"An accident." Why go into detail?

"I'm glad I saw you. I've been meaning to stop by," Kiki said as Becks drew close. "Did Gabe tell you I ran into him?"

"No, but he never tells me anything."

"It was a few months ago. Rabbi Haziz from my Chabad in Miami Beach led services at the university when the school's rabbi had to leave town. He asked us to prepare a Shabbat meal for the kids. Your son loved my chicken meatballs and asked me to give you the recipe. I completely forgot."

Becks laughed. "He didn't know your name but he remembered the meatballs. He raved about them."

"I'm glad he enjoyed them. Come inside and I'll copy the recipe."

Unable to come up with an excuse, Becks followed Kiki through the foyer and into the kitchen. As with most of Becks' neighbors, Kiki had updated her kitchen with sleek cabinets and granite counters. Gazing at the ultramodern stainless-steel appliances, she noticed two dishwashers and realized Kiki was serious about keeping kosher, using one for meat and the other for dairy dishes.

"Here it is." Becks turned to find Kiki flourishing a dog-eared index card. "Give me a second to copy it." She reached into a drawer for a pencil and a fresh index card. After a moment, she looked up. "Goodness, I forgot. I heard that young fellow who stayed with you drowned. I meant to come by and offer my condolences."

"How did you hear?" Becks asked, taking the index card from Kiki's outstretched hand. Menny's death hadn't been in the news.

"No secrets in this neighborhood. I ran into Helmut a few weeks ago. He said Gabe came home with a young man in a skullcap and fringes under his shirt." She shook her head. "A few days later he told me what happened."

Becks stared at Kiki. Something seemed to be falling into place and she waited for the cogs in her brain to slip into the right notches.

"Do you belong to Rabbi Haziz's Chabad?"

"Why yes. Isn't the rabbi a love? I told him a religious young man was visiting our neighborhood."

So that *was* it. Helmut had mentioned Menny's visit to Kiki and Kiki had told Haziz about the boy.

Becks considered. Had Rabbi Haziz told Fox about Menny's visit to her home? It seemed likely. How else would the night club owner know where to find Menny? But that still didn't explain Menny's abduction. The butcher and Tommy were certain Menny left the market with an older man. Fox didn't look a day over forty. It had to be someone who was working with Fox.

"Becks, dear, are you all right?"

She turned to Kiki and smiled. "Sorry. I'm tired. Thanks for the recipe." She waved the card as she walked to the door. "Gabe will be thrilled."

On the walk home, Becks' legs felt stiff and her back ached. Still, she buzzed with excitement at the realization she'd discovered how Fox located Menny. Tomorrow she'd call Hannah and find out if Rabbi Tannenbaum was in New York when Menny vanished. She hated questioning the woman about her husband. But the key to finding Menny's killer was discovering who'd left the kosher market with the boy. And, assuming Fox had contacted Menny's father after the young man moved into Becks' home, Rabbi Tannenbaum seemed the most likely prospect.

Becks clenched her right fist to her hip. She was closing in on the answer. A few more calls and she'd know who killed Menny.

50

From her seat at the kitchen table the next morning, Becks had an unobstructed view of her neighbor's orange trash bins. They sat next to a stack of gray roof tiles and a mound of terracotta pots Teresa claimed she was saving to start a vegetable garden. A half dozen Tiki torches from a long-forgotten luau rested against the side of the house, their bamboo posts brown with rot. Becks sighed. She'd given up begging Teresa to move the junk. When the next hurricane struck, they'd become projectiles and go sailing through Becks' kitchen window.

Another problem over which she had no control.

Becks took a sip of coffee and wrinkled her nose. She'd slept late and the coffee, made hours earlier, was bitter. Daniel had come home the night before with Chinese takeout and sent her to bed after dinner.

Recalling her plan to call Hannah that morning, Becks gazed at the phone. The woman would, naturally, be less than forthcoming if her husband was out of town when Menny disappeared. Becks hoped she was wrong about Menny leaving the market with his father. But with whom else would he go? Rabbi Tannenbaum admitted members of his Chabad considered kidnapping Menny. Maybe they hadn't abandoned the idea. Rabbi Tannenbaum wouldn't hurt his son. Still, accidents happened. Tempers flared. Hands slipped.

She grabbed the phone and dialed Hannah.

"Becks? Have you heard anything?"

"No." She paused. "I'm still trying to find out who drove Menachem away from the kosher market."

"Why call me?"

Becks chewed on a cuticle, considering. "I can't think of anyone he'd go with except his father. The butcher at the market was very clear about Menachem leaving with an older, bearded man. The person he described fit Rabbi Tannenbaum's description."

It also fit the description of thousands of religious Jews.

"You think my husband kidnapped our son?"

Becks cringed at her tone. "Of course not. But he might have heard rumors." Her voice sounded foreign as she forced out the words: "Did Rabbi Tannenbaum leave town in the middle of October? Around Sunday, September seventeenth?"

Silence.

"Are you there?" Becks asked.

"Yes." Hannah spit out the word. "I'm checking his calendar."

Was she checking the dates—or coming up with a story to prove her husband hadn't left town?

"He had a funeral in Queens October seventeenth. A member of our Chabad, Chaya Lieberman."

"Thank you." Becks was torn between relief and confusion. If Rabbi Tannenbaum hadn't taken Menny, who had?

"You're quite welcome." Hannah's tone was cold. "Anything else?"

"Can you tell me when Menachem lived in Kleynshtot? Two of the men I met in Miami taught at a yeshiva there."

"Who are they?"

"One's a rabbi at a Chabad on Miami Beach, Rabbi Haziz. The other is Sid Fox, the club owner I told you about."

"Menachem never mentioned those names."

A childish voice sounded in the background, followed by Hannah's muffled response. Becks smiled. How did she get anything done with seven children?

Hannah returned to the line. "Menachem moved to Kleynshtot after I had Asher, in September 2009. He didn't like it there and left after a few months." She resumed her icy tone. "Does *that* help?"

"I think so and thanks. I'm sorry to have . . ." She heard a click.

Becks returned the receiver to its cradle. She didn't blame Hannah for being upset. Becks had essentially accused her husband of kidnapping his son.

Becks rose and poured a cup of coffee but started as a flash of red caught her eye. A cardinal had landed on her neighbor's trash can. It fluffed its feathers and flew off.

She had no reason to doubt that Rabbi Tannenbaum officiated at a funeral the day Menny went missing. Still she'd check the New York obituaries around that date. Which brought her back to her earlier theory that Fox had a confederate, an older man willing to help with his dirty work.

The question was who?

The Hasidic world was small and she'd assumed it was a member of South Florida's ultra-religious community. But it could've been anyone in a false beard and hat. A man or a woman. At this point, she was open to all possibilities.

Becks rose and poured a glass of iced tea, spilling a few drops on the floor. She groaned as she squatted to wipe it up. This investigation was turning into a pain in the rear, literally. Her wrist ached despite the splint and she was fed up with hitting blank walls and with having people hang up on her. She still suspected Fox. But why had he acted so cynical when she told him what Rabbi Haziz said about his expulsion from Kleynshtot? Was he playing games, trying to distract her?

She needed to let her thoughts settle before figuring out what to do next. Leaving her glass in the sink, she went upstairs and summarized what she'd learned from Hannah. That done, she took out a yellow legal pad and continued mapping. After linking Fox's name to "elderly mystery man," she drew a series of dashes between Fox and Rabbi Tannenbaum.

An hour into her work, the phone rang. It was Daniel, cashing in his rain check for the dinner they'd missed the night of her accident. She was still sore but not in enough pain to pass up an elegant meal. She limped upstairs to her bedroom and winced as she tried to pull a dress over her head. That wasn't going to work. Black pants and a button-up shirt would have to do.

With four hours to go before Daniel got home, she went into her office and returned to work on her cookbook.

Becks was at her desk, reading through a recipe for pineapple dump cake when the phone jangled. She picked up the receiver.

"What happened? I saw your name in the paper." It was Maya. "The article said you were run off the road. Who'd you piss off this time?"

Becks laughed. "I've got a few scrapes and bruises and a sprained wrist. I'll live. I'm pretty sure it was Fox. I was driving home from a meeting with him when an SUV rear-ended me. I've never been so frightened."

"I can imagine. Can you prove it's him?"

"I didn't get the car's plate or make and I couldn't see the driver in the dark."

"Too bad, but at least it'll convince your detective pal to look into the murder. Did you call him?"

"This morning. He said he'd look into Fox's background. But he thinks it was a case of road rage."

"No way."

"Before I could tell him what happened, he told me the crash occurred outside his jurisdiction. Then he repeated his mantra about Menny's death being an unfortunate accident."

"You've got a real fan club going there. So what's next?"

"I'm not sure. I've got a few other ideas. When I visited that Hasidic town in New York, I found out Rabbi Haziz, who runs the Chabad I visited in Miami Beach, lived there. He was forced to leave and no one's saying why. Menny lived there awhile too but I don't know if they met. Haziz knows Fox, also from the town. They all taught at the yeshiva around the time its administrators were indicted for conspiring to defraud the government."

"Sounds like a busy place. You think Fox is worried you'll expose his role in the conspiracy?"

"It's possible."

"Can you think of any other reasons he'd want to scare you?"

"He knows I suspect him of murdering Menny although I didn't mention it during our meeting."

"What makes you so sure Fox killed Menny?"

Becks pulled a pencil from the Mason jar on her desk and tapped it against her desk. Maya's questions often brought Becks up short. During their newspaper days, Maya had an exasperating, if practical, habit of making her slow down and think things through. It kept her from running in too many different directions.

"You want a list of reasons?"

"If you think it'll help. How about you write them down and call me back?"

Once off the phone, Becks grabbed a legal pad and scribbled Fox at the top. Below it, she wrote:

1. Fox threatens to hurt Gabe if Menny learns Fox is searching for him.
2. Menny frightened of Fox—kidnapping? drugs?
3. Dissidents contact Fox to kidnap Menny.
4. Fox deals drugs/uses Hasidic mules.
5. Menny's best friend a mule. Was Fox the dealer?
6. Fox in on Kleynshtot scheme?

Becks took a moment to piece her ideas together. Fox had several motives for wanting Menny dead. He may have feared Menny would go to the police with what he knew about the drug operation that landed Levi in prison. With the busts at the night club, he'd be particularly vulnerable if word of his criminal past got out. Becks couldn't link Fox to the Kleynshtot scam. But Menny might have done so. Fox may have killed Menny to prevent him from revealing what he knew.

Becks rubbed her eyes and stared at the list. She had plenty of theories. Problem was she couldn't prove a thing. She had to connect Fox to the murder scene, to find physical evidence that would point in the club owner's direction. Without police help though—even with it, probably—that might be impossible.

She called Maya and went over her evidence.

"It's pretty weak," Maya conceded. "I wish I could provide some guidance but I'm stumped. I don't know if this will help. I made a call while waiting for you—a friend of a friend of a friend. Someone with connections in the religious world. He said Fox has been supporting the Chabad for years. And I'm not talking spare change. Two thousand a month."

"That's generous."

"No kidding. And I don't think he's doing it out of the goodness of his heart."

Becks looked up as Mulligan jumped on her desk. He pushed his chin into her hand, demanding a rub. She gave him a quick scratch. "It doesn't link him to Menny, though."

"I know but, as they say, cherchez la money. Who knows where it'll lead? Could be Fox is paying the rabbi off."

"For what?"

"Your guess is as good as mine. Let's sleep on it." Maya chuckled. "Oh, wait, I'm seeing Guillermo tonight. I won't be getting much sleep."

"Very cute."

"That's what Guillermo says," Maya whispered in her sultriest voice. She resumed her normal tone. "We'll talk tomorrow."

51

It was almost worth putting up with the pain in her wrist and stiffness in her legs to dine at Taverna Rocco's, Becks thought as Daniel handed his keys to the parking attendant. She got out of the car, bracing her splinted arm against her body, and gazed at the restaurant's colorful entrance. The place resembled nothing so much as a New Orleans bordello. Its gas lamps spilled soft light across the sidewalk and its scalloped blue awning spanned a red brick patio with wrought iron furniture. The brothel theme continued inside where polished plank floors and wainscoted walls led through vaulted archways to intimate dining nooks.

A tall woman in a black sheath led Daniel and Becks to a quiet corner. After pulling a chair out for Becks, she handed her guests embossed leather menus. A soft murmur of conversation reached them from the main dining room.

"Is something wrong?" Becks whispered as Daniel took his seat. Mr. Rocco usually greeted them when they entered the restaurant.

Daniel shrugged. "I hope he isn't angry. I saw him at the office today."

Becks raised an eyebrow and her husband shook his head. She admired Daniel's discretion regarding patients and dropped the subject.

A wine steward came over and, after helping Daniel select a Chianti, left.

"I thought I'd wait until after dinner to bring this up but I've been worried all day," he said, settling back in his chair. "I'd like to know what you intend to do now?"

Becks looked up from her menu. "Order dinner?"

Daniel smiled. "Are you going to drop this investigation? After what happened last night, I'm convinced you're right. Menny *was* murdered. Whoever rammed your car is prepared to go to any length to hide that fact. I'm afraid of what he'll do next. Is there any way you can let it go, let someone else handle it now?"

Becks didn't have a ready answer. Daniel looked so worried, his crow's feet a network of lines around his damp eyes. He wanted to protect her, which was endearing. Still, his protectiveness rankled. She'd become more independent in their months apart, gaining confidence in her judgment as she made decisions she'd formerly discussed with him. He didn't seem to understand this choice was hers to make. Unwilling to start a fight, she held her tongue.

"The accident last night could have gone a lot worse and we wouldn't be sitting here drinking wine." He raised his glass. "Let the police take over now."

"The police?" Becks took a deep breath as she reined in her temper. "You've got to be kidding. I spoke with Detective Cole today."

Daniel tilted his head. "And?"

"He claims the accident in Hollywood was a case of road rage. That some nut job rear-ended me because I cut him off in traffic. You can forget about the police."

"What about that officer in Hollywood? Detective Fernandez."

The waiter arrived and Becks held her tongue as he filled their wine glasses with glossy red Chianti.

"She's an accident investigator," Becks said. She took a sip, then drained the rest of her glass. "I might call her but not yet. She hasn't been involved in this investigation and I'd like to look into a few more things before I contact her."

"Will you see Fox again?"

Becks shrugged.

Daniel set his glass down so hard that wine sloshed over the edge and onto the white tablecloth. "Are you crazy? I insist you stay away from that thug."

Becks' chin shot up. "You *insist*?"

"Please sweetheart, I'm a nervous wreck. You were almost killed last night."

"I'm fine," Becks snapped. "I don't need you telling me what I can and cannot do."

"Maybe not, but I'm getting sick of watching you put yourself in danger. And you're upsetting Gabe."

Becks stared at Daniel. "He said that?" Her voice rose.

"Not in so many words. Think about it, though. He lost a friend and your investigation isn't doing him any good."

"Since when does Gabe confide in you?"

Daniel glared at Becks and she scowled back. After a few tense moments, he rose and tossed his napkin on the table. "Jesus Christ, Becks. That man is prepared to kill you. Even if the police don't believe it, I do. If you won't consider my feelings, consider Josh and Gabe's. They want their mother alive."

He turned and almost collided with a waiter, who jumped back, just managing to balance the tray of plates teetering above his head. Skirting the man, Daniel stomped off.

Becks glanced around and blushed. Many of the diners followed Daniel's progress toward the door but a few eyed her curiously. She debated running after him and decided against it.

She'd let him cool off. The waiter, drawing on the discretion for which the restaurant was known, waited a few minutes before sliding a bread basket onto the table. The garlicky scent of freshly-baked rolls rose from beneath the white linen napkin. She'd have dinner and take a taxi to the house.

With any luck, Daniel would be sleeping when she got home.

Daniel's familiar scent of worn leather and freshly-starched cotton lingered in the bedroom when Becks got home, but he wasn't there. She tiptoed across the hall to Josh's room, then to Gabe's, where she found her husband in bed reading a dog-eared copy of *Catcher in the Rye*. The room was impeccably tidy, with books arranged by size in the shelves above the desk and Gabe's baseball card albums stacked edge to edge on his bureau. The only item Becks dared touch, other than to dust, was the "Star Wars" poster over his bed, which periodically went crooked. Despite her anger, Becks smiled at the sight of Daniel's toes emerging from beneath the blanket.

"Good book?"

He looked up and offered a tentative smile.

"I'm sorry." She sat on the edge of the bed. "I've been edgy since the accident and I took it out on you."

Daniel closed the book and adjusted his glasses. "I understand but—"

"Hold on a sec. I need to talk. I don't think you realize how much I changed during our separation. I got used to my independence, to making my own decisions. It rubbed me the wrong way when you insisted I avoid Fox. My reaction was what gives *you* the right to tell me what to do?"

"That's the big question isn't it?"

When she nodded, he continued. "I don't want to get in your way or tell you how to run your life. You need to remember we're a family. Whatever happens to you happens to the boys and me. I was so frightened driving to Hollywood after your accident, my hands shook."

"I'm sorry. I—"

"Let *me* finish. I'm grateful we're back together and don't want anything to happen to you." He took her hand and squeezed it.

"I appreciate that. I'm not an idiot, though. I know what I'm doing. I may take risks. But they're calculated risks."

He eyed her splint.

"All right. Things don't always work out as I wish they would. I always land on my feet, though."

"Yeah, you and Mulligan." He laughed and elbowed himself up from the pillow to kiss her nose.

"Try to be patient for a few more weeks," she said as he settled back into the pillows. "I'm getting close. I feel it. I don't see any reason to visit Fox. If I do I'll take precautions."

"Such as?"

"I'll take Maya or my dad. Or you?"

Daniel sighed and pushed back the covers. Becks rose.

"It's late. Let's get into our bed." He rose and walked to their bedroom.

Becks followed him and paused in the doorway. She was glad they'd talked things through. Something about their conversation didn't sit right, though. Did Daniel understand what she'd said? Sure, she'd be more careful. But that didn't mean she'd abandon the search for Menny's killer.

52

The next morning, Becks was loading the washing machine when faint tapping sounded at the front door. The visitor waited a minute and knocked again, softly, as though afraid to be heard. Becks went to the foyer and peered through the eyehole. It was Kiki, a green and purple scarf wrapped around her mop of red hair.

Becks opened the door. "What a nice surprise."

"I hope it's not too early." Kiki's hands fluttered to her chest. "I don't want to be a bother."

"Not at all." Becks led her into the kitchen. After pouring her neighbor a cup of coffee, she joined Kiki at the kitchen table. Mulligan had taken his rightful place at its center and purred rambunctiously as Kiki rubbed his ears. "What a pretty pussy," she said, sliding her fingers along the cat's back. Becks bit her lip, hoping the animal—who could be selective about who touched him— wouldn't claw her neighbor's hand.

"I hate to impose but since you seem interested in Chabad, I thought I'd invite you to go with me tonight. Ladies don't usually attend on Fridays. This week, though, they're having a special service at seven and women are welcome. I can't remember which holiday it's for."

When Becks hesitated, Kiki jumped in. "Oh, you don't need to worry about driving on the Sabbath. The rabbi understands that most members can't walk to Chabad."

Becks considered. The service would be deadly boring but it might give her a chance to learn more about Fox. The prospect of seeing him made her skin crawl. Still, she'd have a valid reason to be there.

"I'd love to go," she said. "What time should I come for you?"

When Becks pulled up to Kiki's house at six that evening, her neighbor was barely recognizable. Kiki wore a lacy white ankle-length dress and had paid a visit to the salon. Her hair was beautifully coiffed, each strand in place, and Becks marveled at the difference a trip to the beauty parlor made.

"Thank you for driving." Kiki fastened her seat belt. "I hope you'll get a chance to talk to the rabbi tonight. He's such a lovely man. He spent hours consoling me after Andrew died. I still call when I need spiritual guidance."

Kiki went on and on about the rabbi and Becks suspected she had a crush on the man.

The traffic on I-95 moved swiftly but the roads surrounding the Chabad were jammed with young people. Judging from the yells and hoots emerging from cars, most came to South Beach to drink and party. Becks had rented a Ford Focus while waiting to find out if the Mercedes could be fixed and even that wasn't small enough to cram into the rare on-street parking spot. After circling the neighborhood three times, she pulled into a lot a few blocks from the Chabad.

Leaving the car, they turned onto Washington Avenue and fell into step with the young men and women who filled the sidewalk. Scantily clad girls with tattoos and pastel hair streamed around Becks and Kiki like schools of fish, while men in slim black suits and tight jeans trolled behind like sharks chasing prey. The air felt thick with pheromones and Becks could almost smell the raw sexuality of young people on the make.

The crowd thinned once they reached a block with homes and apartments and the revulsion Becks felt for the South Beach crowd ebbed into an eerie sense of déjà vu as she reached the Chabad House. Young women in stylish, though modest, calf-length skirts and long-sleeved blouses stood on the front lawn and driveway pushing strollers and calling *Gut Shabbos* and *Shabbat Shalom* to arriving friends. Children ran about, giggling and tussling on the grass. Becks smiled as a mother called "*akt vi a dame*" to a curly-headed little girl. How many times had she heard those words—"act like a lady"—from her Yiddish-speaking grandmother?

When Kiki and Becks joined the women, many greeted Kiki with a hug and asked after her health. Becks was touched by their concern for her companion and eagerness to introduce themselves as they waited to enter the building.

"I can see why Gabe's interested in Chabad," Becks whispered to Kiki as they approached the entrance. "Everyone's so friendly."

As Becks and Kiki drew nearer the entrance to the temple, a low murmur of men's voices rose above the women's chatter. An ancient chant vibrated through the house in a prayerful yearning that seemed to harken back to a more primitive era. It grew louder and louder as the men repeated the prayer and culminated with the loud stomping of feet.

Glancing over the shoulder of the woman entering the house in front of her, Becks started as she recognized one of the Hasidic boys she'd seen at Club Shukran. She looked for Fox and couldn't find him. Once inside, she followed Kiki to the women's section and did her best to peer around the divider to the front of the sanctuary.

Rabbi Haziz, a blue and white prayer shawl draped over his head, stood before the congregation rocking back and forth, *davening*, as he chanted. After a few minutes, he left the pulpit to roam the front of the sanctuary where both the men and women could see him. When he returned to the table, or pulpit, at the center, he drew the shawl forward on his head and stepped back.

Becks gasped. As though by magic, the young rabbi was transformed into an elderly man. Under the harsh overhead light, the folds of his shawl produced shadows that hooded his eyes and hollowed his cheeks, creating the apparition of an ancient priest. For a fleeting moment, Becks felt as though she was hallucinating.

Fascinated, she watched as the rabbi stepped closer to the pulpit and transformed back into a young man. She brought a hand to her mouth, amazed at the difference the lighting made. It was uncanny. The rabbi had gone from elderly rebbe to vibrant young man in mere seconds.

Becks looked around to see if anyone else noticed. Most of the congregants were studying their prayer books. It was unreal. How had no one else seen?

Goosebumps rose along Becks' arms as she recalled her conversation with the butcher at Shapiro's. In the rush of waiting on customers, had Malcolm mistaken Rabbi Haziz for an older man? For Menny's father? It wasn't impossible. But why was the rabbi driving Fox's car that night? And what earthly reason did Menny have for leaving with the rabbi after promising he'd bring dinner home? She considered what Hannah said about Menny's time in upstate New York. If the boy met the rabbi before Haziz left Kleynshtot, Menny might have been comfortable leaving the market with him.

"Becks?" Kiki's voice broke into her ruminations. The service had ended. "Let's say hello and leave. It's a long drive."

Becks joined her neighbor in wishing Chabad members good Sabbath but the crowd around Rabbi Haziz was too thick to penetrate. Becks was anxious to pull him aside and ask point-blank if he'd been to the kosher market. This wasn't the right place or time.

Walking back to the car with Kiki, Becks considered her next step. First thing tomorrow, she'd run a photo of the rabbi by the butcher. She'd seen one on the Chabad's website and could print it out. She'd also ask Maya to look into the rabbi's past. Fox's interest in Menny was obvious; his drug operation was at stake and Menny might reveal his role in the scam. But what was the rabbi's link to the boy?

It was dark and Kiki fell asleep the minute Becks reached I-95. A light rain fell and the earthy smell of damp soil rose from the highway. A half-hour later, as they neared the Stirling Road exit, Kiki woke up.

"Sorry for passing out." She yawned and stretched her arms over her head. "It's too bad you didn't have a chance to talk to the rabbi. He's so kind. Once you get to know him, you will want to attend services there."

"Is that right?" Becks' gaze swept the road. She'd checked her rearview mirror every few minutes since getting on the highway to make sure no one was tailing her.

"I saw you talking to some of the women before we went inside. Those rumors aren't true, you know."

"What rumors?"

"The ones about Rabbi Haziz. People like to make trouble."

Becks accelerated as a set of headlights neared her bumper, then eased off when the car swerved into the right lane and passed. "What kind of trouble?"

Kiki darted a glance at Becks then folded her hands primly on her lap. "It's not important."

"Hold on there," Becks said, "that's not fair. Now I won't sleep, wondering about the rabbi."

Kiki reached in her purse and drew out a small gold compact. She flipped down the passenger-side makeup mirror and applied powder to her nose.

"About the rabbi?" Becks said.

Kiki dabbed her nose with a tissue. "All right. Rabbi Haziz is a wonderful man. One of the older members of the Chabad doesn't like him and claims he did sinful things when he lived up north. Then you know how gossip spreads."

"What did he say?" Becks gripped the wheel. This had to be related to the rabbi's expulsion from Kleynshtot. His story about accusing community leaders of fraud might be true. But she had a feeling his exile was brought on by something much worse.

Kiki pursed her lips. "I'd rather not talk about it without his permission."

"The rabbi's?"

"No. The man who told me."

Becks' heart raced. Was Fox behind the rumors? That would explain his evasive response to her questions about Rabbi Haziz.

"I'll call tomorrow and let you know. Is that okay?"

"NO," Becks wanted to scream. "I NEED TO KNOW NOW."

"Sure. Could you keep my name out of it? I used to be a reporter and people tend to shy away when they find out."

They rode in silence for the remainder of the trip and pulled in front of Kiki's home at ten-thirty.

"You'll make that call tomorrow?" Becks asked as her neighbor left the car.

"First thing."

Even if Rabbi Haziz wasn't involved and the sins were nothing more than rumors, they might have something to do with Menny's disappearance. And that might lead to more information about Menny's murder. Maybe evidence implicating Fox.

Something she could bring to the police.

Becks had doubts that Kiki would share what she'd heard about her beloved rabbi. But she knew she wouldn't sleep. The rabbi's "transformation" from young to old and back again and Kiki's allusions to his questionable past opened enough possibilities to keep Becks' mind racing all night.

53

Becks ran up to her bedroom the minute she got home to tell Daniel what she'd learned and froze at the fury in her husband's eyes. He sat at the foot of their bed, arms crossed and lips drawn into a tight frown.

"What . . . what happened? Is everything okay?"

"Oh everything's just fine and dandy," he said, reverting to the Brooklyn accent that emerged when he was angry. "One of your friends called a half-hour ago."

"One of my friends? Who?" Her stomach cramped.

"That's the problem, Becks. He wouldn't say." Daniel's voice dripped sarcasm. "All I heard were a few words and banging. Sounded like your friend was smashing his phone on the floor."

"Damn." Becks shivered. She'd left the Chabad an hour ago. Would the rabbi have called so fast? Most of the congregants were milling about when she left and she doubted the gathering had broken up so early. The rabbi would have had to race to his car and phone from there. The banging sounded like Fox, though. Had the rabbi contacted the night club owner to tell him about Becks' reaction that evening? She didn't think he'd noticed.

She was afraid to ask what the caller said. Daniel's sneer compelled her. "What was his message?"

He rose and shook his head. "Your friend said you'd

better mind your own *fucking* business. And that you'd *fucking* regret it if you didn't drop your *fucking* investigation."

Daniel's emphasis on the F word—he rarely used it—convinced her he was repeating the warning verbatim.

Her knees felt weak "And that's it?"

"Isn't it enough?"

"Why'd he call now?"

She'd intended it as a rhetorical question but Daniel stopped pacing between the closet and bed to glower at her. "For crying out loud, Becks. Isn't it obvious? You're onto something. Fox is afraid you're getting close."

"Did you recognize his voice?"

Daniel resumed pacing and shot her a "don't be stupid" glare. "The voice was muffled, as though someone was talking through a sock. I wouldn't have recognized it anyway."

Becks sat on the bed and stared at her hands. Warnings again? She'd been through this before with her investigation of the construction company. Nothing had come of it. This was different, though. Fox was a thug. And the stakes were much higher.

"I've already called Gabe," Daniel said.

Becks nodded, alarmed she hadn't thought of it.

"He'll stay in his room until I come for him tomorrow."

"Good. How about Josh?"

"He lives pretty far away so I warned him to keep his eyes open and avoid going out alone."

When she didn't respond, he stopped pacing and stood in front of her.

"So what happened at the Chabad?" His voice had lost some of its sting.

"I had a bit of an eye-opener," she patted the bed but Daniel ignored the invitation. "I told you the butcher at Shapiro's said Menny left the market with an old man. He thought it was Menny's father."

"And?"

"Tonight, I realized it could've been Rabbi Haziz. I caught him at an odd angle to the light and he looked ancient with the beard and thick glasses." She described the transformation she'd witnessed earlier. "The rabbi may have seen my reaction and interpreted it as suspicion. I thought Fox had a partner but it never occurred to me it was Rabbi Haziz. "

"You think the *rabbi* helped Fox?"

"I don't know what to think. Maybe Fox convinced him to pick up Menny. I have no idea why the rabbi agreed or if he knew of Fox's plan to murder the boy. Rabbi Haziz claims he was expelled from Kleynshtot for raising questions about that scheme to defraud the government. Why would he help Fox? It doesn't make sense."

"Nothing in this whole damned investigation makes sense. What are you going to do now?"

"I need to learn more about Rabbi Haziz. Kiki told me she heard rumors about his time up north and refuses to share them. Pauline, a woman I met in Kleynshtot, told me he was banished from the community and refused to explain why. I'll start with her. According to Menny's mother, Menny lived in the village at roughly the same time as the rabbi and Fox. Something may have happened then."

Becks drew in a breath and Daniel whipped around as the door to the bedroom creaked open. Mulligan, his tail at full mast and his face a mask of indignation, sauntered in.

"Idiot cat," Daniel said, his voice affectionate as the animal jumped on the bed and licked himself. "Hates to be left out."

He opened the door. "We're both tense. How about we go downstairs for a cup of tea?"

Abandoning Mulligan to his evening ablutions, Becks followed her husband to the kitchen and made chamomile tea. Not that she thought sleep likely.

"Are you going to call Pauline tonight?" Daniel spoke, a cloud of steam rising as he brought his mug to the table.

"It's worth a try. I'll try to get her phone number from Faigy, the lady who drove up to Kleynshtot with me." Becks checked her cell for Faigy's number and dialed. It was Shabbat and she doubted the woman would answer. After eight rings, an answering machine picked up.

Becks got as far as describing the warning she'd received that evening when Faigy broke in. "Becks. What's wrong?"

"I need to know why that rabbi Pauline mentioned was expelled from Kleynshtot. It may have something to do with Menny's death. Can you get me her phone number?"

"Certainly, though I don't know if she'll answer her phone. If it's an emergency, you can always call the *Shomrim* and request they go to her home."

"*Shomrim?*"

"The security force. Hold on. I'll get her number."

Becks waited, doodling on the yellow legal pad she kept by the phone. Daniel picked up the sports section, snapping the pages as he turned to the scores.

She'd finished drawing a cartoon of a fox with a kipa and goatee when Faigy came back on the line with Pauline's number. "Call me when this is over, please? I want to know what happened to Menachem," she said. "And you'll contact his parents?"

"Of course."

Pauline, as expected, did not answer her phone. Becks debated contacting the *Shomrim* but decided to wait until the next morning. Who knew how the elderly woman might react to a late-night knock on her door?

Daniel rose as she hung up the phone. "Any luck?"

"No. I'll call tomorrow."

He stepped behind Becks and gave her shoulder a quick rub. "Time to call it a day."

She followed her husband upstairs, put on a nightgown and slipped between the sheets. An hour later she was still awake, staring at the ceiling. The rabbi's eerie transformation spooled across her mind in an unending loop. Old man to young man. Young man to old. She knew it was crazy yet, in the darkness, she imagined the rabbi as an ancient golem, the ogre of Yiddish folklore, rising from the mud and altering his appearance to become a monster, then a man. What did she know about Rabbi Haziz after all? Little more than that Menny may have trusted him enough to enter his car. What happened after they left the kosher market? Was Fox hiding in the backseat?

Becks' head swam with questions. Menny must have known something Fox was desperate to conceal. Why hadn't the boy gone to the police? Or had he done so and been rebuffed like Becks. Did Menny keep silent about what he knew to protect a friend or his community? Pauline, a grown woman, refused to violate Rebbe Sadowsky's edict to keep silent about Rabbi Haziz's expulsion. Why wouldn't Menny do the same?

Giving up on sleep, Becks read a Faye Kellerman novel until her eyes grew weary. When she finally dozed off, her dreams were plagued by images of Menny floating face down in the canal as Fox and Rabbi Haziz stood on the bank laughing. She woke up gasping but fell back to sleep, to a dream of walking in a desert wilderness beneath black storm clouds that rained Torah scrolls.

54

It was still dark when Becks rose and went downstairs to make coffee the next morning. Daniel was asleep and she took pains to avoid clattering the carafe as she filled it with water and started the brew cycle. She'd removed her splint the night before and it was much easier to work in the kitchen. She looked at the clock on the oven as she sipped the hot liquid. Almost six-thirty. In an hour, the kosher market would open and she could show the butcher Rabbi Haziz's photo.

She poured a second cup and pressed the remote control for the small television on her kitchen counter. Damn. Cartoons! She'd forgotten it was Saturday and the kosher market would be closed. She'd have to wait a day to show the butcher her photo. Meanwhile, she'd continue trying to reach Pauline.

After washing her cup and wiping off the counter, Becks checked the clock. Six forty-five. Too tense to settle in with the newspaper, she got to work reorganizing her pantry. She was carrying a bag of expired canned goods to the garage when Daniel came downstairs.

"I heard you murmuring last night," he said, helping himself to coffee. "Are you okay?"

"I hardly slept. Too nervous." She glanced at the clock. A quarter to eight. "I'm going to call Pauline. She should be up by now." She dialed the number on her landline and let it ring eight, nine, then ten times. As she dropped the receiver into its cradle, her cell buzzed. Daniel grabbed it off the counter.

"Yes. This is her husband," he said after a brief wait. "She's here if you want to talk to her."

He was silent a moment. Then his eyes grew wide. "What do you mean, Gabe's missing?"

Becks' knees weakened as she drew closer to listen. She recognized the voice. Meredith, Gabe's residence advisor.

Daniel swallowed once, then again, his Adam's apple rising with each movement. He pressed the speakerphone button and placed the cell on the counter.

"When did you last check? Did you notify anyone?" he asked.

"I am so sorry, Dr. Ruchinsky. I saw him leave at noon yesterday. I thought he was going to the cafeteria for lunch. He keeps to himself so I didn't think about it until this morning."

"What happened this morning?" Becks asked.

"We had a hall meeting that Gabe didn't attend. That isn't unusual but I decided to check on him anyway. He was gone and his room was messier than usual. He's usually so neat and—"

"I'm aware of my son's behavior." Becks' voice was cold. "Did you call the Coral Gables police?"

"Not yet. The campus police said I should call you to see if he went home."

"Well, he didn't. We're driving down now. I'll call them from the car." She nodded toward Daniel, who headed up to the bedroom. "In the meantime, ask if anyone in the dorm saw him leave."

"I've already—"

Becks flung the phone on the counter and raced upstairs where Daniel was slamming doors and cursing as he pulled on pants and a shirt. She threw on the dirty tee shirt and jeans she'd tossed in the hamper the night before. In less than three minutes, they were in the car. Daniel backed out of the driveway so fast he barely missed a jogger and, a minute later, tires squealing, made a hard right onto Jog Road. Becks googled the Coral Gables Police Department on her cell and pressed call.

The dispatcher who answered sounded so kind and patient that, to Becks' horror, she broke down and sobbed. Her throat ached as she handed the phone to Daniel and felt intense gratitude as he explained what had happened. After describing Becks' investigation and Meredith's report of Gabe's disappearance, he turned to Becks.

"She's putting me through to a detective."

A moment later, a deep voice sounded on the line and Daniel repeated what he'd told the dispatcher along with the warning he'd received the night before.

"Yes. They already called? Good," Daniel said. After a series of yeses and nos, his voice grew louder. "Well, he didn't make it home. My son's been threatened before and his life may be in danger." He paused. "Sure, I can tell you. A Miami Beach night club owner. Sid Fox." He looked at Becks.

"Club Shukran. On Washington Avenue."

Daniel repeated her words. "The other is Rabbi Haziz from . . ."

"The Washington Avenue Chabad," Becks said.

He passed on the information.

"All right. We'll be there in a half-hour." He hung up and scowled. "The police are sending a team and will meet us at Gabe's dorm."

Becks struggled to control her panic, willing her heart

to stop beating so fast. After a few deep breaths, she felt calm enough to dial Faigy. The shopkeeper said she'd ask the Kleynshtot *Shomrim* to contact Pauline.

Ten minutes later, Becks' phone rang. It was Pauline. "I'm so sorry. Please forgive me. I thought the badt man had learned his lesson. I didn't want to anger our rebbe. I should have told."

"Tell me now," Becks snapped.

"The young rabbi, he did terrible things to the children. The parents, they were so upset, they went to the rabbi. It was awful. A *shanda,* a shame. The rebbe made him leave."

"He was molesting children?" Becks was horrified.

"Yes."

"Did Rabbi Sadowsky or any of the parents contact the police?"

"The police? Why the police?"

"To report the crime."

"That's a *mesira.*"

"A what?"

"Rebbe Sadowitz is the only one who can go to the police. Jews aren't allowed to turn in Jews. The man was gone. *Baruch Hashem.*" Becks recognized the expression—praise God. "I thought that was it."

"Do you know where he went?"

"No."

Becks opened her mouth and closed it. Unbelievable. The head rabbi—the religious and moral leader of Kleynshtot—had blithely sent a pedophile into the world, unconcerned he'd molest more children and ruin more lives. Angry and nauseated, she ended the call.

Becks forced herself to put the outrage aside and focus on what Pauline's revelation meant for Gabe. Had the rabbi abducted him? But why? To end Beck's investigation? Her hand trembled as she reached for a tissue in her purse. Hopefully, the police would soon find out.

While she considered, the expressway merged into Dixie Highway. Although Becks had driven the three-lane road hundreds of times, today it felt menacing. The Metrorail station to her right, with its mildewed walls and overgrown foliage, looked deserted and seedy, a perfect hideout for pedophiles. The thick branches that extended over the road felt like cadaverous arms reaching out to grasp drivers.

Pauline's account of Rabbi Haziz horrified Becks. As a reporter, she'd encountered the scum of the earth— parents who shook children to death and husbands who dismembered their wives. However nothing had prepared her for the horror she felt at Gabe's kidnapping. Her sweet helpless son was in the hands of a drug dealer or a pedophile who'd already murdered one boy. And she and Daniel were powerless to save him.

They were waiting for the light to change at Bird Road when Daniel's cell rang. It was Detective Gurerra, the officer with whom he'd spoken earlier. Becks put the phone on speaker.

"I just got off the phone with Fox," the officer said. "I caught him on Club Shukran's landline. He says he doesn't know anything about Gabe."

"You believe him?" Daniel asked.

"I'll need more than his word. He said he slept in his office last night. I've got someone checking it out."

"Did you reach the rabbi?"

"Not yet. We'll keep trying. I'll meet you at the dorm."

Becks hung up.

Daniel reached across the seat and squeezed her hand. "Gabe could be at the library."

"Sure."

"We'll find him, honey. He's a tough kid."

She nodded and wiped her nose. A tough kid who didn't have the sense to avoid strangers. Sure, he'd run from Fox. The man *looked* like a killer. Gabe admired rabbis, though, had spent years studying with the rabbi from their synagogue and would willingly go with Rabbi Haziz. Just like Menny. She choked down a sob and looked at Daniel. The set of his jaw suggested his thoughts mirrored hers.

Ten minutes after merging onto Dixie Highway, Daniel zipped into a handicapped parking spot behind Gabe's dorm. Becks was reaching for the door handle when her cell rang. The caller ID read "restricted." She answered.

"Mom." It was Gabe. His voice trembled.

"Sweetheart, where are you? We've been calling all over." Her heart beat against her chest.

Daniel, who was halfway out of the car, dropped back in his seat and leaned across the console. She held the phone between them.

"I cannot tell you." Gabe cleared his throat and the line went silent.

She heard a muffled voice in the background. "Gabe?" Then louder. "Gabe, can you hear me?"

He returned to the line. "I am with someone. He says to stay away from the police. He says he will kill me if you do not keep your mouth shut about me and … and Menny." His voice echoed as though in a tiled room or empty warehouse.

"Why? What's going on?" She was playing for time and feared being disingenuous might anger Gabe's captors.

"He will let me go in twenty-four hours if you promise to stop looking for me and give up the search for Menny's killer. Please do it, Mom. It would be a *mitzvah*."

She turned to Daniel and raised her eyebrows. "Okay honey. I promise. You can tell them my word is good. Will someone call and tell us where to find you?"

Becks heard a deep snarl, followed by a crash, and pictured Fox—or was it Haziz—ripping the phone from Gabe's hand and flinging it to the floor. "Gabe, Gabe!" She was drenched in sweat. "Honey. Answer me."

Then the phone clicked. And deafening silence. It was broken seconds later by the blare of a police siren as a cruiser, lights flashing, pulled into the spot next to Daniel's Volkswagen.

Becks stared at her husband. "We can lie. Tell them Gabe called and said he was fine."

"It won't work. They'll want to talk to Gabe. That son-of-a-bitch has no intention of letting Gabe go. We need the police to find him right away."

Becks' heart sank and she nodded. Daniel was right.

He got out of the car and waved from the sidewalk. "I'm Daniel Gitlin. You here about my son?"

The two policemen who emerged from the cruiser could've been brothers, their café au lait skin tone, bulldog physiques and shaved heads virtually identical. As they approached Daniel, a late-model Cadillac pulled to the far side of the VW. A capable-looking gray-haired man with a Fu Manchu mustache got out. He appeared to be in his early seventies but seemed in fighting shape, his back straight and his shoulders solid inside a blue blazer. There was something reassuring about his presence, as if an adult had arrived on the scene and would make things right. Becks joined the group on the sidewalk as a petite black woman in a white shirt with a university emblem rounded the corner. She introduced herself as Suki Fielder and explained she was with campus police.

Though shaken, Becks recounted her son's phone call and answered their questions about Menny's death and her suspicions regarding Rabbi Haziz and Fox. It felt strange to be standing on the sidewalk sharing what she knew with the officers. She'd been in similar situations before but as a reporter listening in while police questioned a victim's family. Now she and Daniel *were* the victim's family.

It didn't take long to learn the police knew about as much as she did. The older man, Detective Gurerra, reassured them an officer had spoken with Gabe's residence advisor and that students in her son's dorm were being questioned. A team was checking Gabe's room. Becks told him about the background noise she'd heard during Gabe's call.

"I'm sorry. The echo could've come from hundreds of places. We'll try to trace the call, though." Then, changing the subject, "Is Gabe a religious sort?"

"It comes and goes. He's been interested in Hasidism lately," Becks answered.

"He used the word, mitzvah, during your conversation. Could that be significant?"

Daniel and Becks looked at each other. "It means a good deed. Maybe he wanted us to know he was with someone Jewish." This from Daniel.

Detective Gurerra ran a finger to either side of his mustache. "He might be trying to tell you he's in a temple. You mentioned this Rabbi Haziz. I'll start there and send a cruiser to the Washington Avenue . . . Chabad?"

Becks nodded. "It's what they call their religious center."

"The university sent us your son's ID and we're circulating his photo to local police departments. We'll show it to members of the Chabad." Gurerra pulled a cell from the inside pocket of his jacket.

"Could you ask them to check other Chabad houses?" Becks said. "The Lubavitch—the Hasidic sect Rabbi Haziz belongs to—has a few in South Florida."

"Right." The detective punched in a few numbers and spoke softly into the phone. That done, he turned back to

Becks and Daniel. "Why don't you stick around? I'm sure the campus police will let you wait in your son's room after we've finished there."

The campus officer nodded her agreement. "You can get a cup of coffee and something to eat at the student union." She motioned toward a two-story modern glass building on the far side of the lake.

"Thanks," Becks said. She felt like she'd swallowed a brick. She couldn't eat and doubted Daniel had an appetite. "I'd like to go to Gabe's room now. We can wait in the hall until the police are through."

The uniformed policemen returned to their car and Becks and Daniel followed the detective and campus officer past the dorm cafeteria, now deserted. Reaching a columned patio, they passed a row of orange and teal rocking chairs that faced onto a field in front of the dorm. A group of ROTC students drilled on the grassy expanse, turning briskly left, then right. A tiny girl barked commands.

Becks felt like a goldfish in an aquarium as she walked through the lobby of Gabe's dorm. Most of the young people lounging on sleek gray industrial couches had the manners to hide their curiosity but a few, perhaps those who'd heard of Gabe's disappearance, openly stared. Becks wondered if any were Gabe's friends. She doubted it. More likely, they knew him as the weird kid who never spoke or made eye contact. She tried to push the disturbing thought aside. It wouldn't help her find Gabe.

After giving their cell phone numbers to the campus policewoman, who was coordinating the university's search from her office, Becks, Daniel and the detective took an elevator to the dorm's seventh floor and Gabe's room. Technicians filled the small space, photographing the desk, bed and chair and brushing fine powder on virtually every surface. A few nodded at the detective.

"Anything look off to you?" Gurerra, who waited with them in the hall, asked.

Becks studied the room. "Gabe made his bed as soon as he got up so that's strange." She gestured toward the unmade bed. "And the books." She nodded toward a pile on the floor near the desk. Her chest grew tight as she pictured Gabe knocking them off during a struggle with his abductor. "He never left them out of alignment."

"Was anything taken?"

Becks was silent as her gaze traveled from the bed to the chair and desk. The room was austere but hadn't seemed so barren the last time she visited. Something was missing. She narrowed her eyes and reexamined the space.

"Gabe's quotations! They're gone."

"Quotations?"

"Gabe copied his favorite quotes from the Torah, the Jewish bible, onto large sheets of paper and hung them along that wall." She pointed above the bed. "Who would want those?"

"Do you know what they said?"

Daniel shrugged apologetically. "Neither of us read Hebrew." He paused. "Gabe translated one for me though. I don't remember the exact words—something about defending the weak and fatherless."

"Does that have special meaning for your son?"

"I don't know about the fatherless part. I think he viewed his Asperger's as a weakness."

Gurerra waited a moment but Daniel had nothing to add.

"Let me know if you think of anything else." Gurerra handed them each a business card. "I'll get in touch when I learn something. Please do the same."

"What if Gabe or the kidnapper call again?" Becks asked.

"Say you'll agree to drop your investigation, and that their request to keep the police out of it came too late. Tell them all we care about is getting Gabe back. They won't be arrested."

"Is that the truth?"

The detective shrugged. "As far as you're concerned."

He turned and strode toward the stairwell, his gait confident. Becks dreaded the prospect of dealing with Gabe's kidnapper without him. How soon before she heard from the detective? Would his news be good?

Once the technicians packed their gear and left, Daniel and Becks let themselves into the room. Daniel dropped heavily into his son's chair and picked up the *tefillin* Gabe had left on his desk. Tired and emotionally drained, Becks slid into Gabe's bed and pulled his fleece blanket up to her chin. Breathing in the familiar musky odor of his body, she yearned to sink into a coma until Gabe returned. After a few minutes, she heard sobbing and turned to find Daniel at the desk, his shoulders heaving.

"Honey, it'll be okay." She reached for his arm. He jerked it away.

"You think so?" He glared at her through narrowed eyes. "How do you plan to make that happen? You going to call the bastards and tell them you'll undo all the damage you've done. And just like that"—he snapped his fingers—"Gabe will be back?"

Heat traveled up Becks' neck like warm oil under her skin. His words shocked but didn't entirely surprise her. Of course, he blamed her for Gabe's kidnapping. Why shouldn't he? She'd nosed around without considering the consequences. Daniel was right. Gabe *was* paying the price for her bull-headed pursuit of Menny's killer. She felt sick.

Swallowing the thickness in her throat, Becks rose and smoothed the wrinkles from her tee shirt. "Arguing won't get us anywhere. I'm not going to sit here waiting. We need to search this room. See if the police missed anything."

"Great idea, Becks. Let's do the police department's job for them. You're so good at that."

Becks glared at her husband and walked to the foot of Gabe's bed. His arms crossed, Daniel watched as she picked up the books the police had left on the floor. *English Composition, Economics, Biology.* She leafed through the pages, then dangled the texts by their spines. Nothing there. Returning them to the bookcase, she noticed a book that seemed older and more worn than the others. *Religious Practice for Observant Jews.* She pulled it from the shelf and turned to the table of contents. "Morning Prayers." "Sabbath Rituals." "Female Modesty." That sounded interesting. She turned to the chapter. A line drawing of an ancient mikvah—a ritual purification bath—filled half the page. It depicted a simple chair next to a set of stone steps that led down to a small, tiled pool.

"Mikvah," Becks said. Her fingers tingled and she repeated the word, louder. "Mikvah?"

Daniel's head shot up and his mouth opened. "Oh my God. Mitzvah. Mikvah. *That's* what he was trying to tell us."

Becks' hands trembled and her breath came in quick gasps as she closed the book. "He knew we'd remember how he used to confuse mikvah with mitzvah." She smiled grimly. "Bar mikvah. That's it. He's being held in a mikvah. All we have to do is . . ." She brought a hand to her lips. How many mikvahs would they have to visit before they found him—if their hunch was even correct?

She grabbed Daniel's arm. "I'm going to go online and search for mikvahs. You see if Detective Gurerra's still around and tell him what we suspect. Then find the university's rabbi and see if he has any suggestions about where to look."

Daniel took off.

As Becks picked up her cell to search for mikvahs in the area, she noticed a missed call from her father. In the rush of leaving the house, she'd turned the sound off and missed the ring.

She dialed his number and spoke the instant he picked up. "I can't talk, Dad. Gabe's missing and we're at the university with the police. I think he's being held in a mikvah."

"What are you talking about?"

"I'll tell you later. I've got to look for him."

"Okay, Doll. I'm here if you need me." He sounded worried but hung up.

Becks googled mikvahs in Miami and Miami Beach and was surprised to find only six. She started with the closest one, located a few miles south of the university, and called two on Miami Beach. It was, she realized early on, a pointless exercise. It was the Sabbath and none were open.

She was debating whether to contact another mikvah when her cell rang. It was Tootsie.

"Hi, Doll. I remembered something that might be helpful. My mother used to go to a mikvah in South Beach, back when the area was still Jewish. It had to be around 1950. Daughters of something. I doubt it's still in use but—who knows—it might be worth a look."

"Do you have the address?"

"No. It's near that old synagogue on Washington they turned into a museum. Come get me and I'll find it for you."

Becks reviewed the list of mikvahs on her phone. It would take twenty minutes to pick up Tootsie and another ten to cross the bay to Miami Beach. If Gabe wasn't there, she'd have to repeat the trip. That would take a big chunk of the twenty-four hours she had left to find him. Still,

Tootsie's mikvah sounded promising. An abandoned building would be a perfect hiding place.

"Can you be ready in twenty minutes?"

"I'm ready now."

She called Daniel, who was still with the university rabbi, to share her plan.

"Wait for me and we'll go together."

"I can't. I'm picking up my dad."

"Are you sure that's a good . . ."

"I need to get going." She hung up.

Jostling aside two young women loitering outside Gabe's room, Becks raced downstairs, through the lobby and around the back of the dorm to Daniel's Volkswagen. The day, which had started sunny and bright, had clouded over and the wind had risen, forcing the young palms bordering the campus to bend with each gust. Leaving campus, Becks headed up Dixie Highway and onto I-95. Despite the blustery weather, she drove fast, determined to pick up Tootsie and reach the mikvah before the storm broke and before Gabe's captors . . . she drove the thought from her mind.

55

When she pulled up to her father's building, Tootsie was waiting outside in a yellow slicker patched with duct tape. He ran to the car and opened the door. "I can't believe that bastard took Gabe. Head across the MacArthur and I'll tell you how to go from there."

He remained quiet, eyes ahead, fists clasped to his thighs, as Becks filled him in on Gabe's abduction. Her father smiled when she explained how Gabe's childhood misuse of the terms "mitzvah" and "mikvah" led to her suspicion he was being held in a ritual bath.

"The kid is sharp," he said. "He never forgets a thing."

Becks nodded. Gabe's impressive memory—thought to be an Asperger trait—was a mixed blessing. If she made a promise, she *had* to keep it.

Following Tootsie's directions, Becks crossed Biscayne Bay and took the Fifth Street exit to Washington Avenue. Her father directed her to slow down as they approached a yellow and white stucco building topped by a copper dome. Stained glass windows flanked the double-door entrance and a sign identifying the structure as "The Jewish Museum of Florida" spanned the soaring archway. Next door, linked by a glassed atrium, stood a more modest stucco structure with a triple-arched entry.

"Park there." He pointed to an empty spot near the smaller building. "The mikvah's around the back."

Becks didn't know if it was the weather or the Sabbath, but the only signs of life on the tree-lined boulevard were a pair of skeletal dogs loping down the deserted sidewalk. Gazing at the sky, now a mass of angry black thunderheads, she shut the engine. She was reaching for her door handle when a clap of thunder splintered the afternoon silence. Raindrops heavy as pebbles clattered against the roof of her car.

She turned to her father. "You want to wait in the car while I have a look?"

He scowled and zipped his slicker before getting out of the VW. The raincoat barely reached his knees and Becks felt a wave of gratitude toward her father. She grabbed an umbrella from the back seat and raced to catch up as he entered the alley to the left of the building. By the time they reached a small concrete porch at the back of the structure, her jeans were soaked to the knees. Shivering with cold, Becks followed her dad up four rain-slicked stairs to a small porch. A rusted mezuzah hung on the door frame.

"This is it." Tootsie's hand shook as he pointed to the bronze Star of David. His voice was unsteady, whether from excitement at finding the place or the emotion of rediscovering his mother's mikvah, she couldn't tell.

The brass doorknob had blackened over time but responded to Tootsie's grasp. Goosebumps rose along Becks' arms as she fought to keep her hopes from rising. She reminded herself that this was one of many mikvahs in South Florida.

The wooden door opened with a loud rasp and Becks winced but charged in after her father. Entering what appeared to be a reception area, she brought a hand to her nose at the stench of decayed fabric and rodent droppings. Pale light from the overcast sky filtered in through filthy windows to reveal a rattan desk and wicker chairs layered with dust.

Motioning her father to remain where he was, Becks stuck her head through a narrow opening in the sliding doors behind the desk. A small dressing room held a single chair and an old-fashioned floor-model hair dryer, its elastic hose in shreds. Waving at Tootsie to join her, she entered the room. The open doors to either side revealed generous white-tiled rooms with toilets and stall showers. The small doors at the far ends of those rooms were shut.

Becks approached the door to her left and froze. Footprints in the dust. Were Gabe's abductors in the mikvah? Looking at Tootsie, she put a finger to her lips and pulled her cell from her purse. It was time to contact Detective Gurerra.

She was about to dial when a faint groan sounded from behind the door. Hands shaking, she dropped the phone in her purse and tried the knob. It was locked. She struggled to open it, shoving her shoulder against the door.

"Stand back," Tootsie hissed after a moment.

Startled by his voice, Becks whipped around. Her jaw dropped at the sight of a gun in his hand. He took her arm and shunted her aside. A second later, the room exploded. The knob shattered and the door flew open.

Becks grabbed the weapon from Tootsie and slid it into her purse as she raced into a large white-tiled room. She was halfway across a landing to a set of descending steps when a groan rose from below.

Abandoning all thoughts of safety, she ran down the stairs and found Gabe tied to a chair in a corner of the six-by-six foot bath. His face was ashen. Sobbing, she knelt and tugged at the ropes that bound his feet and hands. "Sweetheart." Her voice broke. "Thank God we found you." She pulled the tape off his mouth, apologizing as he winced. Tootsie pulled a knife from his pocket and got to work on the ropes.

"What happened?" Becks said. "Who did this?"

"Don't talk so loud," Gabe whispered. "He'll be back soon."

"Who?" Tootsie said. He continued slicing the rope that bound his grandson's wrists.

"That rabbi Mom forced me to see. At the Chabad."

"I forced . . ." She caught herself. "How did he convince you to go with him?"

"He came to my dorm and said he had a message from you. That you'd sent him to bring me home. So I let him in."

"You what?"

Gabe glared at her. "He is a rabbi. Rabbis do not lie."

"I see." Becks kept her voice even. "What happened after that?"

"I went with him. I didn't know anything was wrong until he brought me here and tied me up. He had a *gun*." Gabe's eyes grew wide at the word.

Tootsie grunted as his knife split the rope. Gabe kneaded his wrists and his grandfather started on the rope that bound his ankles. Becks wanted to scream at her father to speed it up but knew Tootsie was sawing his fastest.

"Did he hurt you? Or say anything about why he kidnapped you."

"I told you on the phone, he wanted you to swear you would not look for Menny's murderer. He said I could go home after you promised."

Becks bit her lip. Gabe had no clue the rabbi intended

to kill him. She was grateful he'd been spared that fearful knowledge.

"Did he admit to murdering Menny?"

"What do you mean?"

"Did he mention Menny?" Becks controlled her impatience.

"The rabbi said Menny was even nosier than you are but that he had learned to keep his mouth shut." Gabe tilted his head. A moment later he scowled.

Becks waited for the realization to sink in.

"You do not think . . ." He stared at her, mouth half open.

"I'm sorry, honey."

Gabe flapped his hands and blinked for a few moments. When he spoke, his voice was high pitched and his words came fast. "The rabbi yelled a lot and said it was Menny's fault that he kidnapped me. He said Menny stuck his nose where it did not belong." Gabe looked confused.

"When is the rabbi coming back?"

"Soon, I think. He has been gone a long time."

Her stomach lurched. The minutes were racing by as Tootsie struggled with Gabe's bindings. She was desperate to get out before Rabbi Haziz returned.

Becks was pulling her phone out of her purse to alert Detective Gurerra when she heard the distant sound of a door opening. "Hurry," she whispered, returning the cell to her purse. "Someone's coming."

His forehead beaded with sweat, Tootsie worked at the rope. The sound of footsteps drew nearer and Gabe's eyes grew wide. Becks kept a hand on the gun in her purse. A minute later, the rope split and Gabe jumped from the chair.

Becks cursed as she realized it was too late. Rabbi Haziz stood at the top of the stairs, his teeth bared, his eyes glassy with rage. A pistol trembled in his hand.

Becks let the cool steel slide back in her purse. Even if she fired before the rabbi, a bullet might ricochet off a tile and kill Gabe or Tootsie. It was one of the few things she remembered from the firearms training she'd taken when she was threatened after her article on government corruption."

"What the hell to do you think you're doing?" the rabbi roared, his peyos flying as he sprinted down the steps. His scraggly beard dripped with spittle and the strings of his tzitzit hung knotted and filthy below his shirt.

Tootsie grabbed the rabbi's arm, then jerked back as Haziz aimed his pistol at the older man.

"You two. Sit." The rabbi pointed his gun toward a corner of the pool. Tootsie and Becks complied.

Then to Gabe. "Back in the chair." The boy returned to his seat.

The rabbi smiled contemptuously as he pulled a cell from his front pocket and dialed. It was a clumsy maneuver that involved holding the cell and gun in one hand while punching numbers with the other.

"Shalom," he said, his tone ironic.

The conversation continued in Hebrew and Becks, recognizing a few words, struggled to hide her panic.

She heard only Rabbi Haziz's end of the exchange but recognized the term "shual"—Hebrew for fox—and knew he was talking to the night club owner. After arguing for a few minutes, Haziz screamed, "It's your problem too."

Had the rabbi admitted to abducting Gabe? Or killing Menny?

"Son-of-a-bitch," Haziz said, abandoning Hebrew. "Get here now or I'll call the cops about your yeshiva boys." After a few moments, the rabbi gave a short harsh laugh. "Tell whoever you want. I'm not going back to the Chabad. You'll have to find them somewhere else."

Becks drew in a quick breath. Now she understood. The rabbi didn't care if the police knew he was a pedophile. He was leaving town. What's more, he'd allowed Fox to recruit drug carriers from the Chabad—if she was hearing things right—in exchange for Fox's silence about his pedophilia. It was outrageous yet made perfect sense. Each was trapped in the other's snare.

There was no question in her mind now that the rabbi had abducted Gabe and killed Menny.

A minute later, Rabbi Haziz held the phone in front of his face and yelled: "Well, fuck you, too." As he dropped the cell to his side, Becks noticed its case was chipped and remembered the banging Daniel had heard over the phone. Had last night's warning come from Rabbi Haziz? Was his conscience operating from some deep recess of his disturbed psyche, forcing him to alert Becks and Daniel to his kidnapping scheme? The memory of Haziz's transformation from young rabbi to ancient holy man, and now murderer, scared her. The man was in constant flux, perhaps on his way to a breakdown.

Becks considered her options as the rabbi leveled the pistol at Gabe. Haziz's right eye twitched as his gaze darted from her to Tootsie and back to Gabe. He was about to cross a line.

She swallowed as an idea came to her. It was a long shot but all she had. She eyed Tootsie, who was watching her, and shifted her elbow ever so slightly toward the rabbi. Her father's nod was so subtle she wasn't sure she saw it. If Tootsie picked up on her plan to attack the rabbi, they might take him. Haziz might get off a shot. She was confident, though, that he'd focus on her, leaving Tootsie and Gabe safe.

Her muscles tensed as she prepared to attack. She bent forward ready to spring when Tootsie lunged at the rabbi. A deafening blast rang out and her father stumbled back, a blood-soaked hand to his stomach. Catching Haziz off balance, Becks sprang into action, grabbing him by the neck and shoving him to the floor. His head made a loud crack as it hit the tile and his gun slid across the floor to Gabe's chair. Cursing, the rabbi rolled to his knees and crawled toward the weapon as Becks and Tootsie grabbed at his legs, his arms, his belt—anything to restrain the more powerful man.

"Come on Gabe, pick up the gun," Becks yelled. "It's under your chair."

Gabe sat motionless, staring ahead, the only reality the one in his head.

Emitting a loud grunt, the rabbi pulled free and snatched the weapon. He rose and grabbed Gabe's arm. "That was stupid." He nodded toward the corner. "Both of you. On the floor."

Tootsie and Becks obeyed as Haziz yanked Gabe out of his chair. When the boy resisted, the rabbi held the gun to his head.

"Forget about following us," the rabbi said. "If you want to see your kid again, wait ten minutes before leaving the building. If I see you outside, he's dead."

Haziz jerked Gabe up the steps. The boy flinched. "You got that?"

Becks opened her mouth to answer. No sound came out.

Tootsie nodded. "Ten minutes."

Once the rabbi and Gabe were out of the room, Becks turned to her father. "Are you hurt?"

"A bullet grazed me." He raised his left elbow, now crusted with blood. "I wiped it on my shirt so the bastard would think I was injured." He stood and headed for the stairs.

"Please Dad." She jumped to her feet and grabbed her father's arm. "He'll kill Gabe if we follow."

"Don't be an idiot. He'll kill him if we don't."

She released her father's arm.

"You have the gun?" he asked.

Becks drew the weapon from her purse but put it back before Tootsie could grab it. "I'll keep it."

"Okay. Be careful."

Becks led her father outside, then through the alley to the front of the building. Flattening herself against the wall, she peered around the corner and felt her legs tremble at the sight of the rabbi and Gabe fighting. As she drew nearer, she realized Gabe was resisting the man's effort to force him into the car.

She pulled the gun from her purse. "Let him go," she yelled, taking the stance the gun instructor had taught her.

Ignoring her, the rabbi struck the side of Gabe's head with his fist.

Becks' arm jerked as she pulled the trigger; she'd forgotten to brace herself for the recoil. The rabbi whipped around, eyes wide, and Gabe leaped away from the car. She'd missed. Still, the gun had done its job. Haziz raced to the driver's side and sped off.

Becks ran to her son and threw her arms around his neck. "Are you all right?"

"I am fine, Mom." He jerked out of her embrace. "We have to go after him."

"I'll call the police. They'll find the rabbi."

"No," Gabe yelled. Becks and Tootsie stared at the boy. "He killed Menny. We cannot let him get away." He raced to the car, Becks and Tootsie close behind. "I heard him on the phone last night. He is leaving for Israel."

"The boy's right. We don't want to lose him," Tootsie said. "I'll call the police while you drive." He climbed into the back seat. Becks slid behind the wheel and Gabe jumped in on the passenger side.

Becks started the engine and pulled a sharp U-turn, tires screeching as the tread grabbed the tarmac. I-95—the most direct route to Miami International Airport—was five minutes away. Once the rabbi hit the expressway, the odds of catching him seemed slim.

Gabe leaned forward, both hands on the dash. "Faster."

In the back seat, Tootsie yelled into his cell. "Miami Beach police? This is an emergency. We're on Washington headed toward Fifth, chasing the fucker who kidnapped my grandson."

"You do not have to yell," Gabe said, glaring at his grandfather.

"Yeah, kidnapped," Tootsie continued, "from the University of Miami." He spelled out Gabe's name. "Check with . . ." He caught Becks' eye in the mirror.

"Detective Gurerra. Coral Gables police."

He repeated her words. "We just turned onto Fifth, heading for the causeway. A Buick LaCrosse. Black. He's a block ahead of us, heading west."

Pushing the VW to seventy, Becks raced through a yellow light and caught up with the Buick. The road was crowded and, in short order, both cars were stuck in traffic. Staring at the rear of the Buick, Becks remembered her panic at being trapped in the SUV's headlights. The driver that night had been the rabbi or someone he knew. Narrowing her eyes, she tapped the Buick's fender. Haziz shot an angry glance over his shoulder.

"Mom!" Gabe drew out the word.

"Watch it, Doll." Tootsie said.

Ignoring them, Becks backed up a few feet and hit

the Buick harder, this time setting off a crunch of metal. Haziz turned and glared at her, jaw clenched. She smirked and waved.

A minute later, Haziz got out of the car.

"Son of a bitch," Tootsie hissed. "Give me the gun."

Becks cut the engine and reached in her purse. "I've got this."

She sprinted out of the car, onto the road and took a stance. "Don't you dare move a muscle," she yelled.

Rabbi Haziz, his black hat gone and his hair a greasy tangle of knots, reached inside his coat.

But Becks was faster.

The rabbi jerked back as the bullet bit into his thigh. He stared at her, mouth ajar, and dropped his gun.

56

Sitting in the back of the police cruiser, Becks shivered. She couldn't tell if it was from shock or the cold front that had arrived in the wake of the storm. Her hands trembled as she recounted the afternoon's events to Detective Gurerra. Outside, headlights flickered in the late dusk as drivers slowed to stare at the line of police cars.

After firing the gun, Becks had frozen in place as the enormity of what she'd done sank in. She'd shot a man! She'd felt detached from her body as the rabbi fell to the ground. Seconds later, she was sobbing and shaking so violently her father and Gabe were forced to walk her to the car. When a uniformed Miami Beach officer came over, she couldn't finish her sentences without crying. Tootsie stepped in, explaining about Gabe's kidnapping and their pursuit of the rabbi. He put the officer in touch with Detective Gurerra, who was on the scene in minutes.

"Your husband reached me this morning with your hunch about the mikvah," Gurerra said. They'd been talking for almost an hour. "It would have been a lot smarter to wait for the police. We sent a cruiser to South Beach but couldn't find you."

"I wasn't taking any chances. I . . . I didn't know how much time we had. The call this morning . . . it could've been a tactic to give the rabbi time to . . . kill Gabe and escape."

Becks knew the detective was upset with her and didn't care. Gabe was safe and they'd found Menny's killer.

"What'll happen to the rabbi and Fox?" she asked. She'd told Detective Gurerra what the rabbi said about killing Menny and letting Fox recruit couriers from the Chabad.

"I don't think there's any question about the rabbi. He'll face kidnapping and murder charges. I'm not sure about Fox. We need to find out why his car was used in Menachem's kidnapping. As for the information about mules, I'll pass what you've told me to Miami's drug unit."

Becks nodded. The rabbi and Fox weren't her problem now. She hoped the night club owner went to jail. The rabbi could rot in hell.

"I called your husband from the car. He's on his way." The detective said as he peered into Becks' face. "Are you all right?"

"I'm fine." She tried not to sound petulant. She felt frail, on the edge and knew she'd break into tears at the least provocation.

"I'd like you to come down to the station tomorrow to answer questions and sign some papers. The Miami Beach police may want you to come in as well. I'll try to convince them to hold off until tomorrow."

"Thanks." She strained to see in the dark. Daniel wasn't there yet. They'd have to drive her father to his apartment before returning home. She was amazed by how calm Gabe had seemed after the shooting. She'd have to watch him for a while, though.

Despite her relief at recovering Gabe, a small voice at the back of Becks' mind sounded a warning. Would her son hold her responsible for his kidnapping as Daniel had done? It was an alarming prospect and she'd have to deal with it at some point. All she wanted now was to go home and sleep. It had been a horrible day—for Gabe, most of all.

Watching her son emerge from the cruiser in front of hers, Becks' thoughts turned to Menny. She tried to picture his face and could only remember the confused expressions that played across his features as he struggled to do things that were second nature to most people. Lighting an oven. Turning on the television. Making a bed. Her throat caught.

The poor kid. He'd been in the wrong place at the wrong time. His death wasn't a matter of fate, or *bashert,* as his father would have it. If he hadn't left Crown Heights. If he hadn't moved to Kleynshtot. If he hadn't learned of Rabbi Haziz's pedophilia.

A frisson of anger filled her chest. Menny's death, Gabe's abduction, none of this had to happen. It was all due to that primitive religious code. What had Pauline called it? *Mesira*? Menny would be alive now if Rabbi Sadowsky had reported Haziz to the civil authorities

Gazing at the lights along Fifth Avenue, Becks considered the paradoxical nature of the South Beach she'd become acquainted with in recent weeks. How had this verdant scrap of land at the foot of Miami Beach become a center for religious Jews while, steps away, prostitutes and drug dealers plied their nefarious trades?

And both worlds, the sacred and the profane, collided in Rabbi Haziz, who'd taken advantage of his position to betray those too trusting to perceive his evil.

Hugging herself against the cold, Becks remembered the icy morning she'd emerged from a subway station into the wind-blown streets of Crown Heights. She'd been curious to find out if the ultra-religious Jews there would *feel* like her people. She'd known nothing then of the community's ugly secrets or the kindness of its members.

Now they didn't feel so foreign. She appreciated the sense of religion, spirituality and belonging that drew people to Hasidism. At the same time, she deplored the reality that many people, like those in Kleynshtot, willingly abandoned their freedom and moral compass to an irresponsible leader.

"Mom."

Becks looked up. Gabe's shoulders slumped as he leaned into the cruiser but he seemed fine. "Dad's here. He wants to go home."

Becks slid across the seat to where her son stood. Daniel and Tootsie waited behind him.

"What do you say, honey?" her husband asked, helping her out of the cruiser and enveloping her in a hug. "Ready to call it a night?"

She turned to Detective Gurerra, who nodded.

"Okay then, let's go home."

57

A major storm struck New York the day before Chanukah and the snow had turned to ice, leaving the sidewalk along Kingston Avenue dangerously slick. Becks leaped back as a car passed, sending waves of slush onto the sidewalk where she, Gabe and Maya were walking. Gabe scowled as she grabbed his arm. Becks held tight. Behind them, Maya cursed under her breath as she struggled to keep up in high-heeled boots.

"Two more blocks," Becks called over her shoulder as they passed Faigy's shop, now shuttered and dark.

It had been three weeks since Rabbi Haziz's arrest and Becks was touched by Hannah's invitation to spend the holiday with the Tannenbaums. Daniel couldn't get away. He said his practice was too busy. Becks didn't believe him. He was still angry about the danger to which she'd exposed herself and Gabe. They'd been arguing for weeks and had hours of discussion to look forward to before they resolved their differences. *If* they resolved them. She'd decided to give it a few more months. See if Daniel could come to terms with her independence. And if she could deal with the over-protectiveness she'd once considered endearing and now found oppressive. If not, well, she'd lived alone before.

The night they returned from the mikvah, Gabe told her he'd torn up his Torah quotations out of hatred for the "bad Jews" who killed Menny. Becks was sad he'd given up what seemed to be a growing faith but relieved he hadn't become Hasidic. It was so foreign to the Judaism she knew. She was upset when he admitted he blamed her for his kidnapping. Thank goodness he'd forgiven her.

Becks paused before climbing the steps to the Tannenbaum's porch. Mud patches still bordered the concrete walkway and the rail was damp and grimy. Even the child's pail, left to erode in the winter weather, remained where she'd spotted it months earlier. But the house looked different. It took Becks a moment and she smiled when she noticed the change. The front door had been painted a cheerful white. She hoped it signaled that the worst of the Tannenbaum's grief had passed.

As Becks mounted the stairs, the front door opened and Hannah stepped outside. "Come in, come in." Her rich chestnut hair, worn in a tight bun during their previous meetings, flowed across her shoulders and pearl earrings complimented her creamy complexion. She ushered everyone inside, hugging Maya and nodding at Gabe as Becks introduced them. The sound of children's laughter drifted down the hall, growing louder as they entered the kitchen.

Schmulie and Asher, their curls topped by kipas, kneeled on the floor spinning dreidels and giggling. The teenage boy reading on the couch near them looked up and nodded politely. Hannah's eldest, Rachel, was too engrossed in frying latkes to notice the newcomers but her sisters smiled shyly. Hannah's puffy eyes seemed the only sign of the family's grief. Becks sensed that the others were more successful at hiding their pain

Turning at the plod of heavy footsteps, Becks felt an unexpected dread as Rabbi Tannenbaum approached from the hall. He greeted the women warmly and shook Gabe's hand. "And you, you must be a friend of Menachem, may his memory be a blessing." He nodded gently, his eyes damp. "For your friendship toward him, I am thankful."

Gabe blushed and avoided the rabbi's gaze. Their host had the good grace to pretend not to notice.

"So come, sit." Tannenbaum waved them to the wooden table where Becks had joined Hannah and Faigy for tea weeks earlier. "Faigy will be here for dessert."

Dinner was traditional and delicious—chicken soup with matzo balls, brisket and potato pancakes with applesauce. The rabbi kept conversation light, asking Gabe about his classes and beaming as his sons recited the Hanukkah blessings. "I wish you could've heard Menachem sing *Rock of Ages*," he said, catching Hannah's eye. "Such a beautiful voice."

His wife's lips quivered as she attempted a smile.

Hannah was bringing out dreidel-shaped cookies when Faigy arrived, and the older woman received hugs all around. Becks hadn't spoken to Faigy since the morning of Gabe's kidnapping and knew Hannah had kept the elderly shopkeeper informed.

Once dessert was over, Hannah shooed the children off to their rooms. Only then did she let down her guard, removing a tissue from her sleeve and dabbing at her eyes.

Becks took her hand. "I'm so sorry, Hannah. It isn't much comfort but the rabbi will be punished."

"What about that night club owner?" Hannah said after a moment. She left the table and returned with a flowered teapot. "I thought you suspected him."

Becks looked at Maya before returning her gaze to Hannah.

"I was certain he'd abducted Menachem after your son left the market in Mr. Fox's car. But the police found out the rabbi borrowed it, claiming his was in the shop. He may have been trying to set up Fox."

Turning to Gabe, she explained, "make it look as though Fox killed Menny.

"The police also found a Star of David charm on the bank of the canal where Menachem was found," Becks continued. "It resembled a belt buckle Fox wears. The police believe that was planted. They don't think Fox was involved in Menny's death. He may face drug trafficking charges though. He kept the rabbi's pedophilia secret in exchange for being given free rein to recruit drug couriers from the Chabad."

"Do the police know why Mr. Fox was looking for Menny?"

Becks caught Rabbi Tannenbaum's gaze and looked away. "No. At least they didn't mention it."

"And Rabbi Haziz?" Hannah asked. "He'll go to jail?"

"I'm sure he will." Maya spoke up. She'd become Becks' liaison to the Boca Raton police. She turned to Becks. "Have you heard anything more about child molestation charges?"

"It doesn't look like he'll face any. No one's come forward."

The rabbi's face darkened. "It's a terrible problem in these isolated villages. Town leaders insist the children are lying and refuse to punish the monsters who abuse them."

They chatted a few more minutes before Becks rose. "We'd better go. It's a long ride to Manhattan."

Hannah leaned forward and took Becks' hand. "I still don't understand why the rabbi murdered Menachem." Tears glistened at the corners of her eyes.

Becks had explained what little she knew to Hannah. "I'm sorry. I haven't heard anything more. The police suspect your son saw the rabbi molest a child in Kleynshtot. Menachem may have told Rabbi Sadowsky, who expelled Haziz but refused to report him to the police.

Rabbi Sadowsky still refuses to confirm what happened. When Haziz spotted Menachem at the university, he may have been afraid that your son would tell Chabad members about his perversion."

Pulling a fresh tissue from her sleeve, Hannah blew her nose. "Thank you," she said. "We're grateful for everything you've done. And please know it wasn't your fault. Because of you, the police have Menny's killer. *Baruch Hashem*, he'll be punished."

Rocking sleepily with the subway's motion, Becks considered Hannah's words. The woman had offered them in a spirit of forgiveness to absolve Becks of responsibility for Menny's death. She stared ahead catching her reflection in the glass windows. The heavy girders and dim lights of the underground tunnel rushed past. Hannah was right. Becks was not responsible for Menny's death. Still, *she* had driven him away with her anger. Anger she should've had enough compassion to control. For that alone, it would take some time to forgive herself.

If you enjoyed
The Hasidic Rebbe's Son
your review in Amazon, Goodreads and
other social media would be appreciated.

Thank you
www.joanlipinskycochran.com

Acknowledgements

The concept for *The Hasidic Rebbe's Son* came to me at a dinner party where I met a young man from London who was doing a semester abroad at Massachusetts Institute of Technology. He grew up in a Hasidic Yiddish-speaking enclave, the son of an eminent rabbi, and left his community at the age of seventeen with a smattering of English and little secular education. By the time I met him, he was in his early twenties and had taught himself to speak, read and write English, obtained a secular education and was a student at Cambridge University. As with Menachem, he overcame remarkable obstacles in both the secular and religious realms to live the life he wanted.

I would like to acknowledge the support I received from my critique group—Prudy Taylor Board, Joe Fraracci, Buck Buchanan, Maria Amsbach and Mary Yuhas. Leah Handwerger directed my research throughout the preparation of the novel, referring me to indispensable books, knowledgeable people and answering questions about the religious community of which she is a part. My friends, the award-winning author Dr. Deborah Shlian and Eileen O'Brien, provided encouragement and editorial advice while Susan Lebrun, Roz Strauss, Linda Weiss and Joyce Davell are among those who read and reread the novel, redirecting me when I went wrong. Thanks also to

Fort Lauderdale Police Chief Richard Sievers for his help with the fire scene. Finally, much gratitude to my husband, Michael, for his patience and editorial advice as I wrote and rewrote *The Hasidic Rebbe's Son.*

I'd also like to applaud Footsteps, a New York-based organization (Footstepsorg.org) that helps individuals leaving the ultra- orthodox world adjust to mainstream society. Several books, television shows and documentaries have referenced this organization's outstanding work in helping individuals deal with an often-excruciating break with their communities.

And last but not least, many thanks to my readers, those special individuals for whom I spend my life creating worlds, characters and stories.

Made in the USA
Monee, IL
03 April 2021